Elizabeth's Field

by

Barbara M. Lockhart

For Sadie, my extraordinary granddaughter

ACKNOWLEDGMENTS

This work began when John Creighton, our tireless local historian, shed light on the richness of our history through his workshops. I thank him and Carol Smith for their reading of the novel in its infancy, and Chris Noel, my mentor at Vermont College, who guided me through the first of several revisions, with, as always, a great deal of patience. To Kathryn Lang, my former editor at Southern Methodist University Press, I send appreciation for her warm encouragement and wise insight. With love and gratitude, I acknowledge my daughter, Lynne Lockhart, for the use of her painting for the cover, and her husband, Kirk McBride, for his technical advice and cover design.

To Mary Taylor, wherever she may be, I send this message: Thank you for so willingly telling me your story. I'm passin' it on.

PROLOGUE

TWENTY-TWO ACRES, MORE OR LESS

———•—•———

*I*n the forty years I've lived on this small farm on Maryland's Eastern Shore, I had largely ignored the land that was rented to the neighboring incorporated agribusiness. But after being challenged about the number of acres I owned, I researched the deeds and found the original dimensions had remained intact since 1849: twenty-two acres, more or less. One deed, in particular, written in 1857, caught my attention. Elizabeth Burton, recorded as a *free Negress,* owned the land from 1852 until 1857. My curiosity was whetted. The fact that Elizabeth was able to acquire ownership at all was startling and to lose the land before the Civil War told a significant segment of Maryland's history when it was a border state and people of the Eastern Shore were largely of Southern sentiment.

What happened on these twenty-two acres is only hinted at by the sequence of names on the deeds and wills of the time. It is a scant record to be sure, a time that easily lends itself to the imagination, a time fueled by oral histories passed on by an isolated race. What was not recorded invites fictionalization based on the merest of facts. It is a liberty I take humbly, and it is based on the assumption of the desire for freedom, for ownership, for inalienable rights. It encompasses the immense struggle to survive in a time of the greatest peril for any single group of Americans, the so-called free Negro of antebellum days.

Through the exploration of long forgotten stories told in local workshops regarding the history of Harriet Tubman and others, the tale of the preacher, Samuel Green, who served as an agent of the Underground Railroad, emerged. The church he ministered is down the road from what was Elizabeth's farm. He was imprisoned for owning a copy of *Uncle Tom's Cabin*, an event that received national attention in the 1850s. It reflected the atmosphere in which runaway slaves, white planters, and free blacks coped in a political climate struggling with the same moral conflicts as the rest of the nation. It was during this era and here in Dorchester county that Harriet Tubman was born and whose legacy is celebrated.

Long ago, in this quiet agricultural landscape, some land was likely cleared by the Indians, but much of it was cleared by slaves and free blacks, for the shipbuilding industry was prominent in this part of the world and white oak needed for that purpose. The stump-riddled land was good for planting tobacco which didn't have to be planted in neat rows. However, the growing of tobacco was labor intensive, and planters and landholders depended on enslaved and free blacks for its production.

When the tobacco crop had spent the land, the tree stumps were cleared for growing wheat, then corn, and more recently, the truck crops: asparagus, cantaloupes, tomatoes, soybeans, string beans, and potatoes. It was in the time of wheat when Elizabeth lived, in a time when a Maryland farmer could get a thousand dollars for a slave if he was having a bad year and needed to pay his debts, a time when Georgia traders walked the streets of Cambridge, Maryland, with $20,000 in their pockets, ready to buy enslaved men, women, and children to pick cotton in the South. The others, the free black population, had to be kidnapped if profits were to be made. It was the free Negro whose life often hung in limbo, whose freedom was not acknowledged, who pricked white society's sense of righteousness and conscience, who challenged simply by his existence the anomaly of the idea of black freedom, and who had to be suppressed with a violence only frightened men can muster.

From the time of its clearing, the land was tainted by the existence of slavery. The silence of the fields began to hide visions of cruelties in its soil like a bad dream, fluid, ephemeral, and unsubstantiated, for the black man's history was largely unrecorded, erased as easily as the newly plowed field erases all evidence of last year's crop. It was a long time ago, and the fields know no time, only the rhythm of the seasons.

In the future, those who will look back on the present will have an overwhelming record of detailed statistics to refer to regarding yields, government subsidies, fertilizer, herbicide and insecticide costs, types of runoff, surveys, and aerial photographs, all in the complicated network of food production. Now, massive irrigation systems spread over the fields, insuring yields despite drought. Huge machines, driven by men encapsulated in air-conditioned cabs, prepare the soil and harvest crops. With the great strides in food production, there is more than enough to feed the nation. It is easy to forget on whose backs the initial profits were made.

And for this reason, I include the present day story of Mary Taylor, my neighbor, who worked Elizabeth's field and the fields in the surrounding countryside one hundred and fifty years after Elizabeth's time. Her oral history lends credibility to the larger picture of our national struggle with civil rights.

Who is buried in these fields? What tears, hopes, and fears were lived here in the long hours of labor? Nothing we can hold in our hands, no artifact, no piecing together of a civilization, a passing culture. Nothing but a silence only the wind might remember, reminding us that in the end the fields are only loaned to us. The definition of ownership began with the land, and we've used it to measure ourselves by deed and status, yet how worthy are the people who worked the fields and had little to show for it.

MATTIE, 2000

———— · · ————

I passed. I knew I would, those last days. But what I didn't know was there'd be more. I was Mattie Thomas and I'm not now, bein' part of somethin' bigger. I was scared at first, at the thought there might be more, though I didn't waste a lot of time thinkin' about it, figurin' it was for the churchgoers to figure out. The faithful. And I ain't never been faithful. Another operation, they say, stickin' needles in my arm already black and blue under the brown. Another tumor, they figured. And then I knew. And it was soon after that, two days before my eighty-second birthday. I never thought *pass* was the right word, but it is.

The amazin' thing is what I thought about in life is true, even though I only been lookin' out at these Maryland fields for fifty years. All that time it was like seein' a house with one dark window and one wide open. When I passed, I could see everythin'. A light shined on all the long ago times I'd only guessed at and pieced together from what my mama and papa told, and from my grandmother and my friend Gordy. A lot of it nobody wanted to talk about. Even Grandma wouldn't talk about much from slave days. "Them days is best forgotten," she'd say. "Over and done with." But in the stories we told and passed down, that's where true history is. It goes from mouth to mouth. It's not in no books.

Not much was written down 'bout us anyhow, a will, a deed, a list of who-ever a farmer owned put down right next to his cattle. That was it. Lots of times there'd be no last names, no lastin' names to tell how they connected, nothin' but

4

silence, the flat fields holdin' everthin' in the wind till the day we pass. Like that field 'cross from my place. I call it Elizabeth's field since she the one what owned it before the Civil War. Nobody heard tell of a black woman ownin' anythin'. But my friend, Gordy, knew from stories passed down. He the one what tol' me about Elizabeth and how she got her field. For generations, they'd plow it, plant it, harvest it, plow it again, and everythin' would get covered up till there was no memory of any one year at all. Yet ever one who lived around here knew how the cold would come and the heat, and how it would look in each of those times, but who married who, and how they did, and what they thought, and who stayed with who, how the kids got raised and what they loved—all of that weren't written down because we in our brown skin just didn't matter that much. So I used to wonder 'bout Elizabeth, what her life was like, thinkin' her spirit still hung over that field. I did a lotta guessin'. I don't have to guess no more.

Sittin' under my peach tree them last days, chewin' tobacco, and watchin' the rows of corn 'cross the road, I had time to study how the leaves looked when they were stirred by a soft breeze on a summer mornin' and how they flashed in the sun. There'd be so much light my eyes would sting. I'd be squintin' and at the same time tryin' to block out the roar of that diesel engine sittin' 'cross the road not twenty foot from my door. It drove the irrigation system 'cross Elizabeth's field. Still does. When rain was promised, they'd shut it off and I'd hope to get a good night's sleep.

I learned to pay it no mind though. Most of the time, I'd be wanderin' around in my own thoughts, caught in a veil of rememberin' that would come over me with all the colors and smells and feelin's of a lifetime. I could pass between 'em and the shade of the peach tree without tellin' 'em apart, because it seem like everthin's connected in one long thread. Maybe I was so old it was my last sightin' of home come to haunt me. I could be standin' before the clapboards of Mama's house in Georgia and my house in Maryland with its 'sbestos shingles and padlock swingin' from the door latch and think they was the same. Maybe the work of a lifetime is to make a home like the one you left.

I'd watch the corn leaves shine and the streams of water sprayin' from the irrigation pipeline, the wheels turnin' slow as time itself. I'd always look for a rainbow. It was company to have tractors and trucks go by and people wave. Webster's white pickup would pass, and I'd think he'd kill himself with hurry and worry. He both owned and rented a lotta fields around here. He tilled 'bout 3,000 acres, I heard. He'd wave a finger as he rushed by. If I called out to him, "Hey!" in a voice I hoped was louder than the diesel engine, seem like he still wouldn't hear and go on.

Sometime he'd stop on his way back, though. If I was out of chewin' tobacco, that Redman, he'd pick me up some, since I had no way to get to town. That old Thunderbird sat in the yard all peelin' paint and rust, dead as a stone. One time I painted the vinyl top white, but soon after that the engine froze, like it'd been through the worst—a roof painted with a brush.

My house sat on the edge of a wide field of potato plants bloomin' pretty by June. All that food growin' under the ground, enough for the potato chip plant down the road and plenty for me to set by for winter after the harvester gone through. First the potatoes, then string beans, then sweet corn, then tomatoes and cucumbers, then cantaloupes and watermelons and field corn. And at the last, the soybeans. Everythin' in its time, year after year. In so much plenty, white peoples didn't mind if you walked on their land and took some. "Go ahead, Mattie," they'd say, "Take what you want." I did, and give some back to 'em washed, shucked, cut, peeled—everythin' ready for the kitchen. Maybe it was my religion, if I had any. I just hated to see food wasted.

I'd sit under the peach tree thinkin', fritterin' away the time without a care about what would come. What couldn't help but come. Lookin' the other way. Watchin' the family I worked for grow, raisin' up the babies and nursin' the old, sittin' on the edge of their field watchin' their tractors, their plantin's, listenin' to their irrigation diesel outside my door, waitin' for the harvester to come through so I could go out in the field with my bucket and pick up what was left. There was always plenty. Too much, most times. To see potatoes roll offin the truck and never picked up, string beans layin' by the side of the road, corn seed spilled along the ditches, and combines come that could do the work of a whole congregation, water from the pipes spillin' over the road on days when even the peach tree was parched. There's always plenty for the takin'. It weren't like the old ways I was used to.

But now, I'm not sure it weren't all a dream. We don't pay no mind to death because the onliest thing we know is the fight to survive. Yet, when you pass, you see all of it. All the layers. All the feet that walked through the dust on these big fields. My friend, Gordy, used to tell me stories 'bout Dorchester County, 'bout what happened to the people who lived on the fields, and 'bout Elizabeth. If Gordy was right, I used to think, then that Elizabeth was near about the onliest one of my peoples around here who owned land. Then when I passed, I understood. I saw her and all that happened, and it weren't much different from what I seen all my life. I saw how her time was cut short, and how the best of dreams make you be wantin', and then wantin' more, it all tastin' so good you want it forever. I saw how that story would end like all the others, how the owners of everythin' get to own more.

Lotta peoples don't know nothin' 'bout livin' hard, 'bout makin' it day to day with your life on the line—not some line drawn in the sand, but somethin' like a skunk smell. A thing you knew was there and would one day jump out of the bushes at you. Elizabeth stay in my heart a long time, she wantin' so much and expectin' it because she was free. You only hope that much when you see a way and the way come to you dropped right there in your lap. Her hope was big. It was probably the brightest thing about her. I had a time like that in my life, too, when I went to New York up from Georgia on the train with money in my pocket from my aunt and my papa, and they tol' me to find my peoples in New York and stay with them. I had a fine time in New York.

I had to go. I stabbed my husband. After that, nothin' was ever the same. But sometime, our worst times bring us somethin' good.

Ol' Gordy was right. That's one good thing about sittin' 'round on a summer night and tellin' stories. There's stories you'll never forget, and I'm findin' out most everythin' he say was true. I want to tell ol' Gordy there's much more than we ever knowed. Bet he can see that for himself by now.

Gordy and me was just friends. I been married twice. Came to Dorchester when I was thirty and already I was finished with men. Had some hard times with 'em, and I figured there was no way I'd be bamboozled into that again. When I met 'im, Gordy was married, livin' over there next to Elizabeth's field. Lived in a cabin with no electric. His wife, Margerite, did ironin' for peoples and Gordy worked the field. I remember when they got electric and Margerite got a new iron, he'd run outside and watch that ol' meter spin 'round and he'd get plenty ticked off. Started yellin' at her to heat the ol' iron on the cook stove. "Never mind this modern stuff," he say. The summer Margerite died, me and Gordy been workin' the fields and I guess he got real lonely. No way was I gonna get hitched up with him, the way he hollered at Margerite. But when the crops come in, we'd work together all day pickin'. When we got done, he say, "Come on down for a beer, Mattie." So I did. That's when the stories started.

I wasn't from Dorchester County, Maryland so I didn't hear them kinda stories before. I was born in Blakely, Georgia, and I had my own stories. But I only lived there till I was nine, and then Mama died. After that I was havin' my stories laid out for me, and I got caught up in my own hard times. Before that, it seem like the stories were mostly good, or at least that's what I remember.

One thing about Gordy, he didn't just talk, he'd listen, too. So when I started tellin' my stories, I felt like he was enjoyin' himself. He said it brought him back to the way things used to be. So I tol' him just 'bout all of it, even little things like when we were chilren there in Blakely, my younger brother, Bo Pete, and I played in the yard all day and I took care of Bo Pete while my mama and papa went to another farm, different from the farm we were living on, and went to hoe for different peoples. They called me "Pete" then because I was a tomboy and was always climbin' trees. I called my youngest brother little Bo Pete but his real name was John. My older brother, Willie, was Tater, and my oldest sister, Lizzie, was Sister. Next come Alace, who we called Baby. There were five of us, and the older three worked in the fields hoein' with my mother and father.

"Think I'll call you Pete," Gordy say, his face all wrinkled up like last summer's squash. "Sound like you got no use for a woman name no more." I knowed what he was gettin' at, but I wasn't goin' for it. Once I got started on the stories,

I was on a roll and that was all that mattered. Now I'm goin' through it all again, seein' it in this here afterlife. We stayed friends, Gordy and me, and it lasted longer than any man I got hitched to.

One way our stories were the same. My folks didn't hardly get enough to live on, and neither did his. The white peoples took it all and charged them for everythin' they could think of. By the time my folks were paid, there was nothin' much left so they went and hoed for other farmers, too. White peoples paid to hoe by the acre. Two dollars an acre. Five of them hoein' could hoe two acres in a half a day and make four dollars.

One fall, we was pickin' cotton. I hated it. The thorns would get up under my fingernails, make 'em bleed and come off. I was six year old and didn't know how to do it right. Mama took my hands in hers and wiped them on her sack. She say, "Mattie, you go on home and take little John with you. Stay with him in the yard. You don't have to pick no more, but you have to take care of John." He stuck a marble up his nose once, and I had to get it out. I knew if I didn't, Mama'd take care of me when she got home. I got whipped more'n anybody in that house. Mostly for pickin' on little Bo Pete. But me and him played in the yard and stayed there till the others got home. We had chores to do. We had to get the kindlin' and clean the lampshades. My parents were strict. We couldn't act wild like some do now. When company come, all Mama had to do was point that finger toward the door and we got to get out of there or we was give the backhand whip. Oh Lord, we was give a backhand whip.

When I was sittin' under that peach tree and watchin' the school bus go by with the kids all actin' wild, I used to think 'bout Mama and her backhand whip. Some o' those kids coulda used it. My parents taught us a lot—how to act, get along in the world, have a garden, and feed ourselves.

We always had enough to eat because we raised our own. When she come home from work, Mama would kill a chicken. Didn't take her long to pluck 'im out, boil 'im, or fry 'im up. The chicken that was raised on the farm was better'n any chicken you get now. They weren't filled with all them chemicals.

And turkeys—we'd be so glad when that old gobbler hen would come up in the yard with those turkey babies. Once, one came up there with twelve little turkeys. "Don't you go back in the woods," Mama say. "Stay right here!" We had hogs and we even had a cow so we could have milk.

The trouble was you farmed but you never got nothin'. We worked hard to get the crops in and the white man got the money and said you owed him this, and that cost that, and this cost this. Thanksgiving come by, then Christmas, and we'd pick the last ball of cotton and Papa would have just enough left over to get a whole bolt of cloth. Mama made all our clothes. She'd sew up shirts for the boys and dresses for the girls on her ol' treadle machine. It still workin'. My sister, Alace, still usin' it. Some years, there'd even be enough for Papa to buy us some shoes, and when the soles went off, he had extra leather and put the soles on himself.

Now in this aftertime, I see us in church, Mama holdin' my hand, all of us in clothes she made, the girls in white dresses with big bows in the back, the boys in shirts too big but made to last for a long while, all of us sittin' in the long pew with Papa at the other end. I hadn't been to church since Mama died, but back then there weren't no choice. You had to go and pray and sing your heart out. But it never made any difference as far as I could see, and I still don't see anythin' in it. It helps peoples, I know. I see peoples need God to keep 'em in line. But it only work for some.

Best part of church was Christmas. In our house, there would always be a Christmas. You could count on it. Mama cooked up a whole lot of potato pies because Papa dug a hole down in the ground and put in sweet potatoes and he'd put pine shavin's down there and dirt on top. Mama made sweet potato pies and sweet potato bread and cakes and sweetened them with honey. You could go out in the woods and get all the honey you wanted in those woods. Bees made their honey in the trees and Papa smudged them out and got the honey. He'd get a rag and burn it for the smudge. The comb was our chewin' gum. I've chewed many a bees' honeycomb.

A lot of white peoples had electric, but we didn't have none. We used kerosene lamps. We had a fireplace for heat in the winter, and we had a Home Comfort stove. Some white peoples moved away and give us that old stove. It had a place on the side to heat up water for baths. We used the tub we washed clothes in to take a bath. We had to wash our feet every night though.

I need to tell you how it was, because everythin' so different now. Talk 'bout bein' on our own. We had no insurance, no hospitals. Dentist? Papa pulled our teeth. We did have an ol' doctor, Dr. Jack. He had a buggy and a horse and he'd come around and leave Mama a quart bottle of castor oil for us. He tol' her to give us a table-spoon of that every night so we wouldn't get colds or nothin', and she did. We were pretty healthy. Dr. Jack cared for colored folks. He wouldn't doctor on nobody but the colored. He was white, but he helped the colored. He come from the North and he did a good thing. Most peoples couldn't pay him money, but they paid him with ham or middlin's or potatoes or peach preserves. He loved Mama's preserves. He'd take whatever she give him, and he was glad to get it. Mama always say, "You feed your own, but there's always extra. You supposed to spread it around. It always come back to you one way or another. Same as bad. Bad come back to you, too."

All the places I been, I lived in Maryland the longest. Didn't like Texas much, even though the cotton was so tall it was like pickin' it off trees and a lot easier. Much as I loved open sky, it was too big out there, and I felt lost and worried each night before I fell asleep thinkin' I might never see my home again. The one with Mama in it. That was the only real one. I still see the tin lunch pail I took to school with a sweet potato left over from dinner. Maybe a bit of pork or whatever she had left. A mama makes a whole world, with good rules and warm biscuits. The rightness of everythin' is in that world. Papa say since we be goin' to school for only a little while we should learn to read some, but the most important thing was arithmetic so we could tell if we was paid right. He made us go, but Mama sent us with lunch and paid the school-mistress in ham or chitlins or whatever she had. Mama made things happen.

I never got no further than fourth grade. I had to go to work then. My papa couldn't afford to buy no books. White children went to school and got the books for free, but Papa had to buy the books we used. Papa loved arithmetic, but he helped us with readin', too. If he found a piece of paper in town with a bit of writin' on it, he'd fold it up and put it in his pocket. When he come home, he took it out and tried to figure it out. It would take him a time, but he'd get it and read it to us. He taught us how to read the Lord's Prayer from the Bible. He'd say it and point to the words and then we'd do it. That's how we learned to read. I could read good, but sometime the big words took me a while to figure out.

Maybe if those chilren on the school bus had to walk to school, they wouldn't have as much fight in 'em by the time they got there. We walked two and a half miles to school. The wind hollered through them old school windows, no glass, just wood shutters, and there were cracks in the walls so big you could see right through to the outside. So cold our hands froze. I see the teacher settin' a bucket by the fire when we come in the mornin', and we'd hold our hands in the warm water so we could write. Whoever got there first made the fire. Usually, it was the teacher, Miz Wall. So old she had snow-white hair. She couldn't do nothin' 'bout the books from the white school, though. They was torn with pages missin'. "What's left, read that!" she say, and we did, if it made sense or not.

Once we had a man teacher. Good Lord, that man was rough. He was the only man teacher we ever had, and he'd whip us with a razor strap. Hold your hand out and he'd hit it one, two, three. After that he'd send us to the corner and make us stand on one foot.

But Miz Wall was nice. One time she got some pencils and cut 'em in inch-and-a-half pieces so each chile could have one.

Papa wrote down much as he could in the Bible, but he could only write what he knew. The first name in there was Leola, Mama's mama, but there was nothin' wrote before her name, like she come outta nowhere. She was a slave 'til she was thirteen. Mama say her mama tol' her that her own papa, my great-grandfather, was a freeman in Maryland, way back before the Civil War, but once they got a holt on him, they shackled him and brung him down to Georgia to pick cotton. I didn't know more till now.

Papa never wrote the date Mama was born, only the day she died. I'd had the Bible since Papa died, and I give it to my daughter, Juanita, when my time was close. Papa's name was first,

John Henry Thomas, bone December 30, 1878

Each year a baby came, he wrote:

Willie Henry Thomas, bone December 31, 1910
Elizabeth Mary Thomas, bone July 3, 1912
Alace Ann Thomas, bone September 10, 1914
Mattie Louise Thomas, bone January 3, 1918
John James Thomas, bone May 16, 1920

Then farther on down the page is Mama.

Emmie Elizabeth Thomas, died August 9, 1926.

When Mama passed, it seem like my chilehood was rolled up like a carpet and set out in the rain. I don't know what Mama died of. Her heart wore out, or maybe it was the cancer. Her skin and hair got gray at the same time. The doctor didn't know what to do, so Papa carried us to Dania, Florida, where Aunt Lizzie lived. Even though Lizzie took good care of her, Mama didn't get better. She just got weaker all the time and the pain spread to all her body. Then one day, she called me to her bed and axed me to lie down with her. "Here," she said so soft I could barely hear, and patted the pillow. "You be a good girl, Mattie, hear?" Then I heard Mama's breath leave her like a deep sigh and I started to cry. When I thought about it all through the years, I still cried. The look of Mama's quiet face used to come and sit with me on a summer evenin'. I was glad to think about how her arms were filled with nobody but me when she left this earth. Leavin' the earth—my own turn's come and gone. I was with my family when it happened, and I was holdin' Juanita close in my arms, she in her sixties and hair all gray by then. Despite all what happened, it weren't too much to ax.

When Mama died, Grandma Pattyroll come on the train and saw to everthin'. She patted our butts all the time, so we called her Pattyroll, but it weren't until another lifetime, another day, we found out a pattyroller was somethin' bad in slave times, somethin' to be afraid of, a white man comin' in the middle of the night to check your papers or arrest you if you wasn't where you belonged or scoop you up for the holdin' pen in Macon. Grandma Pattyroll dressed Mama in her church clothes and laid her out on a coolin' board. We had to take turns wipin' Mama's lips with turpentine. There was no embalmin'—no money for anythin' like that—and no casket, just a wooden box the undertaker made.

We watched over her for two nights and one whole day in the August heat, takin' turns at her side till I thought I couldn't stand it one more minute. Friends came and looked and brought sweet potato biscuits. We were told to be quiet, so we tiptoed. What I hated most was the hole they put Mama in. The darkness of it. Mama always loved sunshine.

Papa made the cross himself out of scrap wood and carved Mama's name on it with his knife. He was sad he couldn't take her back to Blakely, but he had no way. She was buried there in Quincy. All of us, even Bo Pete, went along the edges of the fields and picked Queen Anne's lace and strawflower, tiger lilies and butterfly weed. We picked so many the whole grave was covered with flowers like a blanket for Mama. It was 1926.

After Mama died, Papa went back to Georgia alone and tended the boiler for the icehouse in town. Grandma Pattyroll took Bo Pete with her to White Springs, and me and my two sisters went to my Aunt Mary who didn't have chilren. She was glad to have us help clear some land. Meantime, back home in Georgia, our yard stood weedy and lonesome. Then the roof on our cabin sank in and the porch rotted. The last time I went, there wasn't nothin' but vines. It makes me sad, but I don't know why. Everythin' changes. I can see now how my way of livin' is disappearin'. Has to be. *When somebody dies, a whole world dies with 'em*, somebody once say, but I don't remember where I heard it. Not that I pined for remembrance for myself or livin' in heaven like the church promised. No, not that. Just a story or two to tell the ones comin' up. Just rememberin' passed on. Most of 'em weren't bothered 'bout the past. In a way, I couldn't blame 'em. They need to look ahead.

We ate good. That is, until Mama died. Seem like Papa gave up after that. He was left with five chilren, some only half grown. He couldn't make it without a wife to keep the home, work beside him in the field, and preserve the food. Mama died from workin' too hard. She was small, Mama was. Not much bigger'n when she first got stole at fifteen. I had a picture of her as a young girl holdin' her first born, Willie. She had on a short white dress and her knobby knees stuck out from the hem. A chile. No more ripe than a green tomato. That's what she must've looked like when Papa crossed the bridge over the Chattahoochie River to the Alabama side and took her right outen the field and brought her to Blakely, Georgia. She woulda been easy to steal, slight as she was. Her family was mad, but they didn't stay that way because Papa was a good husband and gave Mama a good home although she the one what made it so. Women are the current; men are slack tide without 'em.

I been through a lot, and I could get through anythin' because my parents *raised* us. They really *raised* us. That's why we survived. All but Willie. He gone off to the war and come back in a box. "You don't know what's in that box," Papa said. "Could be rocks." We never knew what happened to Willie. What was left, we buried next to Mama in Florida. It was August then, too, and the flies were bad. I didn't need to see that time again, but ever so often it come back to me. But the good part is, I can see Willie now, an' I know what was in that box weren't rocks. Now he stay 'round me sometime mumblin' nonsense about castor oil. That's how I know it's him. He hated it.

When I passed, I went straight home to Blakely, but there was nothin' to see, nothin' left 'cept a chain dug up from the field, a piece of broken pottery, a shoe lyin' on top of the soil like somethin' that should never have been brought to light. I often wondered what would be left of my place—my shack in Dorchester with the padlock on the door, the three rooms, the freezer outside the door, the car seat restin' on cinder blocks, the chickens, and the pump with the sink standin' on a choppin' stump to catch the water, the strain of geraniums I grew from cuttin's every fall and put out in the spring. *There'd be nothin' left*, I thought, and I was right. They pushed over the house with a bulldozer soon as I left and filled the space with more potato plants. I knew there'd be nothin' left of me, 'cept maybe a river of words.

Papa say, "If you have a garden, you can always eat. It's the most important thing there is. You plant yourself a garden, you'll not only survive but have plenty to share. You give some of yours and the other person gives you some of his and both have enough and more. It goes against all the hate in the world, puts its back right up against it."

In my own garden, I kept that hoe leanin' against my tree and an empty bucket by the rows to collect whatever I had plenty of. Any time of day, I'd be tendin' the garden. None of the irrigation water ever reached my plants, so I'd fill the bucket at the pump and pour little splashes along the beets and string beans. But it was when I started hoein', row after row, scratchin' the earth, worryin' it, that the sound of the hoe would be like an old hymn and would bring back the time I worked in the fields with my brothers and sisters, when it seemed like Mama hoed with me and Bo Pete and Alace along with the older two, Lizzie and Willie. How many miles I hoed? 'Nough to bring me 'cross the nation, I guess.

I always had plenty to share. I loved it when Fran, the mail girl, come by. I'd wave and yell, "Hey!" and the mail truck would slow down. "I got somethin' for ya," I'd say, and she'd lower the window and lean out. I'd wave some lettuce at her, or a bunch of beets. I'd tell her, "I'll loan you the bucket, but you bring it back, heah?" while she'd linger and look into my door, maybe catchin' sight of bushel baskets standin' in the kitchen. White peoples don't have bushel baskets in their kitchens, I guess. Then she'd look back at me with those muddy brown eyes, the wrinkles under and around her eyes stirrin' like ripples on a pond. White women dry up quick.

"Need anythin' from town, Mattie?"

"The strawberries come on yet?" I could count on her to bring me some. She not been livin' here long compared to my livin' by that diesel for fifty years. From Georgia to Florida to New York to Texas to Maryland, that's where all I been. I come to Maryland because they was payin' fifty cent an hour to pick cantaloupe. This was the cantaloupe capital of the world, they say. Was a little railroad station in town where we used to pack the crates onto the cars. I loved the smell of cantaloupe. Couldn't wait for 'em to come on. Nothin' better with a little bit of that Breyer's vanilla.

So Fran brought me strawberries, and sometime she bring me a fish or some crabs. Her husband was a waterman. She was good to me. Her eyes could look gray sometimes. Maybe they used to be brown. They were a mix—some yellow in there, too. I wondered 'bout the strange potful of ancestors that bring a mix like that. I'd never thought of that before. White was just white. Anyway, she was my friend. She'd stop by and read my mail for me if I couldn't.

Ever year, I looked forward to when the first of the sweet corn was ready. I'd pull the fattest ears from the stalks and put 'em in a bushel basket, pushin' the basket along with my feet. I'd feel rich, then, and safe, with food for all winter. At the end of the row I planted beets—my favorite—leaves with big red veins. The greens were ever bit as good as the root, and I'd cook 'em at night when the heat lifted. I'd bring the basket of corn to my seat under the peach tree, find my brush—the one with soft bristles, shaped like a U—to get the corn ready for the freezer while I waited for somebody to pass by. There I sat, on a spit of land I never owned, watchin' the crops come on, takin' what was left with my own hands, not from some modern-day tractor where a man drives in an air-conditioned cab with the radio on. No, my feet were in the soil, my hands on ever ear of corn. I'd brush away the last of the silk as if it was a ceremony. I always shared some and filled the freezer too, thinkin' how I'd have some summer in the middle of January.

I worked crops all my life. Few now know what it was like, 'specially gettin' in the tomatoes, which were no longer grown in the Dorchester fields of Maryland when I left. I missed 'em. There was plenty of work in the fields, pickin' 'em, and at the cannery, peelin'. In the morning, the five-eighths bushel baskets stood waitin' at the beginning of the rows, and we'd pick all day to fill 'em. When we brought the baskets to the end of the rows, the crew leader'd keep a tally and we'd get paid. When the baskets were loaded onto the trucks, they were stacked in pyramids, bottom edges standin' on top edges. The driver had to go slow over the ruts. There were only dirt roads back then. Most covered with oyster shells.

Ever tomato that got put in a can was peeled by hand. We worked in the fields all day and then worked until eleven o'clock at night, peelin'. We peeled till the last tomato got done. The smell of tomatoes was all around, from field to town, like one big tomato soup. On Friday night, there'd be the beer gardens in town. We'd be ridin' the bus, singin', money in our pockets. But too soon, all the strong, young ones were gone. They disappeared when the machines came through, even though machines left too many tomatoes wastin' in the field. Nothin' was as good as human hands on a tomato, careful and respectful. Gone with the tomatoes was Gordy, the storyteller, and my card-playin' friends, Tizzie, and BeBop, Carlisle, and Henry O.

Forgive me for stayin' in my life a little longer. Some things I ain't done with yet, I guess. I think the way this aftertime goes is you start as close to the present as you can and work backwards to the times before. Why is our own time so precious? Is it because we hate to give it up, hate sayin' good-bye to everthin'?

Toward dusk, the irrigation was most times turned off, and the world was quiet. My ears would ring for a while, gettin' used to it. Sometime my friends from town would beep at me while I was sittin', but I'd pull my cane in front of me and lean on it as if to say I'm stayin' put. I loved company when they did stop. "Here, set yourself a minute," I'd say, and reach for the old kitchen chair I kept under the peach tree for visitors. The cat curled up on it all the time, so I'd have to tilt the chair and make the cat scramble down. There was always extra room on the turned over buckets. We'd slide into conversation beginnin' with the heat and me sayin' no heat like Georgia heat, or Florida, too, for that matter. There's a gossip bench in town for the white farmers to get together in the evenin' and tell the news of the day. But we had our own gossip bench under the peach tree.

"You know who went to the migrant camp for a little night visit?" We'd guess a few names, sniggerin' after each one.

"You know them white ladies what play bridge on Tuesdays? Well, the ambulance had to come get one of 'em today. Probly laughin' too hard."

It weren't long before we'd be sayin' 'bout the trouble in Cambridge when the National Guard had to come in. And the blacks burned down the elementary school because it weren't fittin' for chilren to be in, and the fire department refused to put the fire out. And Gloria Richardson—nothin' feared that woman—tellin' it like it was right there on the streets of Cambridge. Yeah, we be talkin' into the night, tellin' favorite parts over 'n over. I loved those times. When they started slappin' mosquitoes, the visit was over. I guess it was the chewin' tobacco, but they never bothered me. It'd be with a sinkin' feelin' I'd watch 'em pull away in the night. I never could stifle the need for company, for the give and take of those ol' stories.

One thing. They never forgot 'bout the Ku Klux Klan. Some thought it still around. It set me to thinkin' how Mama'd push us back from the window and we'd be peekin' 'round her, lookin' anyway—how they dragged that man down the road and killed him—I don't know why—and all the time Mama was tryin' to keep us from lookin'. They had the sheets on in broad daylight. Didn't even wait for the night. And burnin' crosses, I saw that. But you know, my papa—we'd be sittin' around the fireplace and it'd be cold—and he'd say, "If they come after me, I'm goin' to take some of 'em down before I go. I'll go down fightin'." He kept a couple boxes of shells for the shotgun in the closet, but white men never would bother him 'cause he never bothered them. He say, 'If you see white chilren on the road, leave and go 'cross to the woods, go all the way around.' We were taught to do that for safety from little on up. It didn't make us angry or nothin'. We knew our daddy was right. If we went next to those whites, they'd call us names or throw somethin' at us, and they'd go home and tell a lie about how we started it, so we did as he told us. Our parents taught us a lot.

It was better in Florida. Not so prejudiced. You didn't see no Klan down there where we were. After Mama died, we stayed down there, and me and my sister Alace worked to clear a field for my aunt and uncle. Well, we cleared five acres of bracken but never did get no money off that field. The Depression started, you see, and Hoover was in the seat. You couldn't sell a thing. We had some pretty cotton but couldn't get nothin' for it and had to plow it under. We didn't plow the peanuts under because the hogs could eat the peanuts and fatten up. Then we'd have meat. Didn't get nothin' out of those crops, though.

Everbody was in the same boat. White and black folks both came to my aunt's door for a bowl of beans or cornbread, and she always fed them. They was all lookin' for work. They'd come down from the North to Miami. Alace got tired of it all and hauled it, just took off and wound up with a job in Lake City, Florida, takin' care of chilren.

Boy, the peoples were glad when Roosevelt got the seat from that Hoover man. When Roosevelt came in, peoples were hongry. Roosevelt saved the nation. God knows that man weren't in there two weeks before he was puttin' out relief. Givin' peoples food. Peoples started comin' up again. He knew just what to do. That Hoover man wouldn't do nothin' to help.

Oh, I had plenty of stories to tell, but there were too many blank spaces. What I wanted to know was why my grandma wouldn't talk about slave days. What happened before that? Who came before her? What were their stories? There was only mystery behind my Grandma Pattyroll, as if it was her own shame she'd been a slave.

Many times, when I'd sit at the close of day, I'd watch the sunset and wonder, *who lived here? Who walked these fields? Who watched the sunset from this very spot at the edge of the field?* I was the last of 'em to walk the field, and maybe that's good. Not even the migrants come through anymore 'cept for watermelon pickin' time. The men sing while they throw the watermelons to the next one in line, all the way from the field to the truck. I looked for 'em comin'. I miss 'em. Strong young bodies made me think of the ol' days. Yeah. Well. At least babies weren't lyin' at the edge of the fields in parked cars anymore, doors open wide to catch a breeze that might come along, flies all over 'em while the mamas picked tomatoes. I hated to see that.

Never mind. It weren't no harder than anythin' else I seen. I figured I could get through anythin'. Kids comin' up have no idea. What if everthin' stopped, electric, gas, clean water? Who'd survive? Who'd know what to do? The further man come along, the more a prisoner he is; the more he depend on somethin', the more helpless he get. And the worst of it is there ain't much he can do about it. Things are on a roll. I see it all now.

And then, bless God, comin' between the thinkin' about the whole world, there'd be Mama again in her housedress, pullin' Spanish moss off the trees and bendin' over her cannin' pot, scaldin' the moss and stirrin'. We'd all help to hang the long strands up in the yard and when they was dry, we'd help lay 'em along with chicken feathers inside a sack of tickin' for our beds. There weren't nothin' Mama couldn't make or do. And more'd come to me about her, one thing on top of another, more so at the end of the day when I be tired. But at the bottom of it all, I knew somethin' drew me to the Eastern Shore of Maryland, somethin' deeper'n I could figure. Right off, it had the feel of home to it and always had, ever since I first stepped down from the crew leader's truck at the age of thirty-two. Or was it that my story was only part of one big story, where everthin' was linked together in a chain, where one time of trouble could tell the story of us all? Anyhow, now I know. And for one last moment, I can still remember the taste of strawberry on my tongue, how I'd leave the whole berry there before bitin' into it, how I'd bend my head to the quart basket of berries, takin' in their smell, the sight of 'em so red even in twilight, and the taste—the sweet-sour juice—take it in together and all at once, which always pulled me away from loneliness. A friend's gift could do that.

And it could take me away from my wantin' to know, too. I'd sit there so satisfied I thought I knew what heaven'd be like if there was one. But it ain't like that. This ain't no heaven 'less you could say knowin' somethin' for sure was it. Truth could be a kind of heaven, where all the questions you ever had would be answered. It lonely watchin' years unroll like on that big movie screen in Hurlock, where I seen Elvis Presley once. People move 'round so real you think you can touch 'em, but you only get to watch. On the other hand, you get to see it all without anythin' to distract you like somebody's opinion, or decidin' if it true or not. Nothin' you can do about any of it now anyhow. It just happens, a story you're swept up in and you go along for the ride.

None of this was ever wrote down. I wish I'd a done it. There never seem to be time because for me just writin' my name took a while. Little did I know I'd see it all again in this here afterlife. I can tell you my spirit still stays by my

Blakely home. I cain't leave it yet. But the rest of the story has to begin some-time. I get started on home, and I get so's I cain't stop. Somethin' in me wants to stay there and never grow up.

But James Spry is waitin'. And his story is the beginnin' of everthin' I never could figure out. Here, time is rollin' backwards, faster'n you can think, much faster than time moves forward, and Lord knows that was always plenty fast. In between all that rememberin', time bunches up and never stops surprisin' you. All of a sudden, you're old.

THE BURTON HOUSEHOLD, 1844

---

*J*ames Spry, sawyer, returning from the woods of St. Michael's, stood on
the schooner's deck and watched the water skim by. He turned away from
the brilliant sun to see the sails full and straining in a stiff wind that was warm
for November. But as soon as they left the wide waters of the Chesapeake and
rounded the peninsula into the mouth of the Choptank River, eerie gray-white
clouds lay close to the eastern horizon. All at once, as if they were entering a
tunnel, the wind dropped and the heavy canvases collapsed. Mist moved about
them in its slow, subtle way, barely noticeable at first, but steadily, determinedly
bringing dampness enough to moisten the deck.

As they drifted in the current, James watched the hazy edges of the opposite shore, where grassy marshes lined the tidewater between woods and creeks,
mysterious places that would welcome a man on the run. The edge of the land
always called to him in this way, the plans he made in idle moments teasing him
as if there would always be that possibility. He had to think there would be, if
worse came to worst. He wondered how the bonds of his life could have pulled
him so deeply inland to the thickest woods when it was the river that drew him.

Silently, moving with the tide and hardly stirring the water, they approached
the wharf. The air felt expectant, full of unnamed ghosts as voices echoed across
the water. In the harbor, oyster boats lay side by side in a maze of rumpled sails,
their apparent disorder made orderly by masts in precise and uniform angle.
The schooner slipped close to the landing now, and James helped with the ropes

that would secure its berth. He'd paid for his passage himself, like any free man, his life's station depending so weightily on the thin paper in his pocket that he patted now and then. Earlier, he'd wrapped the manumission certificate in oiled parchment. It was the only thing of value he owned besides his own two hands.

The trees he'd cut in his lifetime had numbered in the thousands or tens of thousands. The specific amount eluded him, and he wished he'd kept track until he understood the numbers. He was never sure of the years: when he began, when he was sent from his home, and when he'd been set free, when the old master, whom he remembered only vaguely except for his boots, had died. But he knew the present year and that it was the sixth day of November. He revered the certainty of the calendar.

He'd been hired out as long as he could remember. He thought he was around thirty now. So say he'd been a sawyer for twenty years. He'd been strong enough as a child. Been born big, his mother often said. He pictured himself standing knee-high to his papa with his hands reaching for the saw, but he could never picture his father, who disappeared early from his life. A few years ago, he'd been camping in the woods with a work crew for several weeks, and when he returned to the big farm, he couldn't find his mother anywhere. Some said she'd wandered off. Some said she'd been spotted in the woods. But there were those who said Master had turned her out because she was lame. He looked for her a long time, scared of what he'd find, and then gave up, hoping beyond any real hope that she had run.

Before he'd left home that last time, he'd told the story to Addy, who listened while she quilted in the evenings, her round face and high forehead shining in the light of the pitch pine lamp. She held the needle and thread high above her belly that was just beginning to show. There might be a baby by now, along with Libby, who was just five. It would be sweet to see them again, feel the peace in the cabin that belonged to Elizabeth and Perry Burton where they stayed while he saved enough to buy some land. He'd marry Addy this time. He owed his children that. She still lived in the house she was raised in, and their child darted in and out of Elizabeth's door. His children should be rolling around in *his* home, but it was only a wish, not a practicality, only something that gnawed at his pride. Perry had been generous, and Elizabeth, too. They'd taken him in like family. They'd raised Addy like their own as well as James's and Addy's daughter, Libby. Then there were two other children who stayed with them, Daniel Johnson and Eziah Fleming, whose mothers had fled. When James returned, there would be eight of them under one roof.

The men on board called to one another in the still, gray hush, which produced a strange cacophony of voices that appeared to come from far away and near at the same time. With the boat tied up at the dock, he helped carry trunks and bags down the ramp, and on each return, he carried barrels of molasses and flour, lumber, bales of shingles, vats of oysters, and muskrats. The Negroes talked in low voices, gesturing and averting their eyes, exchanging news. When their tasks were done, they walked down the ramp together.

"Where you goin'?" said one of them, a man they called Emery, also free, who glanced at him sideways, furtively, each of them aware that any collusion would be suspect, white folks being nervous like they were. He nodded upriver toward the east and wished he was still on board heading toward the mouth of the river again and north to Baltimore. There, a man could disappear among the crowds and head farther north by foot or train to Pennsylvania, an idea that was ever on his mind, the Way. Some days, the men talked of little else—who along the line of "safe" places they could trust. On the land side, though, it was only through swamps and creeks and forests and farms that a man could run. Some did. Always just ahead of the dogs, and always dependent on others to take him in. *It took a lot of trusting*, he thought, and he was short on that. No, the sea was the Way.

There shouldn't be a need to prove he was free if the paper could be trusted. Yet it was a flimsy defense, vulnerable to whatever devilment a patroller could conjure. And anyway, with family ties, his choices had narrowed. But being on the water did things to him, made him long for a severance of all bonds. He wondered what it would be like to be on the ocean with the land out of sight. He could imagine himself truly free then.

"Near Crotcher's Ferry," he answered Emory, although the truth was the place was far away from anything he could name. All he knew was it was nearly all forest with a few cleared places, somewhere near the Marshyhope River.

"The worst place from what I hear."

"We're three miles from there. Don't go down to Crotcher's."

"Take your life in your hands if you do."

The tavern at Crotcher's Ferry was notorious for keeping alive the legacy of Patty Cannon, who'd lived down the road on the Delaware border and who'd made a living kidnapping, free or slave, didn't matter. She'd been dead for fifteen years, yet her spirit still lived at the tavern, a place no black man would enter, a place so devilishly close to the route north it tempted him. He'd never have chosen to live nearby if it weren't for Addy. He'd met her when they were both hired out to the same farm that one summer, and it was the serious, shy way she had about her that he found himself answering to.

He was back, then, following woman and wood. For most of his life, he was like the marsh grass blowing this way and that, wherever there was work. But for now, with new shipyards at Jamaica Point and Crotcher's Ferry, a new sawmill at Cabin Creek, there'd be plenty of work. Word passed quickly along the farms and waterways. Men looking for jobs could always find them. He liked his work. The sound of a falling tree excited him, the crash and thunder a signal that he'd had power over something big even if it was a kind of pillage. But it was the white man's pillage, not his. He, James Spry, sawyer, had a skill. He was better than a field hand, which he'd been a long time ago, too far away to remember and didn't want to remember anyhow.

Once more, as he set foot onto the road in the fog, he thought about the cabin that stood by itself on the old Indian trail, where he would be home with his Addy—seventeen miles or thereabouts. And he thought as he walked, how grateful he was for a place to go, for a woman and a fire and a child, or maybe two, and friends. He knew he was vulnerable despite the money and paper in his pocket—or maybe because of it—with only his feet to carry him, his watchful eye and listening ear his only defense. *Still he was free*, he told himself, repeating the word again and again as though it would bring him luck.

At the first sighting of marsh grass, he turned off the main road and headed into the woods to follow the creek to its end, a safeguard into which, if need be, he could wade at the sound of dogs. It was a precaution taken from old habit.

And now, in the deep woods, anxiety seized him, a feeling he should have been finished with. Then it occurred to him that his love of felling trees might have been the start of it all, that one who spent his life clearing them was forever clearing away the forest he feared. He stopped and listened to the night, to the settled-down cloud muffling and mystifying the sounds around him. The air was still warmer now. Where the ground turned to marsh mud at the creek's close, he took off his shoes to save them and walked on. Where the earth was firm, he stopped, cleaned his feet with wet leaves, and put on his shoes again. He imagined nothing for it would only feed his fear, but he listened with as keen a sense as a blind man. And he began to think that because of his fear, he would never be free even with the paper in his pocket. He knew he shouldn't be more than ten miles from his home; the patrollers weren't just to catch runaways. Yet, to have money in his pocket was enough, wasn't it? *Ought* to be enough to prove he was a freeman earning his keep. Even if it was stolen from him, whoever did the stealing would know he could earn his way. *Too much thinking*, he said to himself, *could make a man crazy.*

Six miles to go, he judged, glad the leaves under his feet were wet and soundless, glad he would be there by first light.

Addy looked to Elizabeth. She had no other way. From the day her mother died, she had stayed with this woman. Even after James came with his big, gentle hands that knew just what to do, she stayed with Elizabeth. Even after Libby was born. And now there was a baby boy who looked just like his father. She studied the baby's face as he lay beside her on the straw-lined bed. It had been an easier birth than the last although she was soaked with sweat in the chilly damp. It was but a short time before she heard the baby cry. She hadn't called out even once. Blood poured out of her still, though. She lay quiet while Elizabeth began to pack her with rags soaked in bloodroot, wild indigo, and vinegar to stop the flow. The baby, too, was quiet. His fat, round cheeks gave her comfort as she traced them with her finger. Another child born free because she was free. It made her proud. It was the best part of giving birth. They were all free, all but Perry. Elizabeth was free, and so was she, Addy, because her mother had been free. And now her children were free. She was family with Elizabeth and Perry, who took in children like they were their own. And if the bleeding didn't stop, Addy knew they would take Libby and the baby, too.

She thought of all this as she lay there, not believing what was happening, worried about the dull pain she still felt, glad of the empty place inside her, the fire that Elizabeth had just stoked, and the weight of the child on her arm. Surely the Lord would not take her. She began to will it so and stroked the baby's face again. James, Jr. from James, Sr. He couldn't deny it. The child would have his father's name if it was the last thing she did. James Spry, Jr.

Elizabeth opened the door and turned to pick up the pan. In the gray light, her deep-set eyes dominated her narrow, dark face. Addy couldn't tell if she was worried or not. Like iron, her face didn't change. Her unlined cheeks remained vaguely hollow; her thin lips were held constant, registering neither surprise nor horror nor joy. Addy was glad for it now. She didn't want to know, she thought, as she watched the beautiful straight hair that was Elizabeth's, the thick black braid down her back, go out the door as she retreated with the pan in her hands, the contents of which she would bury. It must mean that she, Addy, would live, or Elizabeth would have waited and buried everything together.

Libby skipped across the floor. "Mama?" She was tall for her age. Her round face held a pleading, anxious look that belied her forced smile while her forefinger twisted the side of her smock, round and round. "Mama?" she said again with a tremor that caused Addy to say, "You stop that worry now 'fore I get the switch and give you somethin' to worry you." Of course, she never did, and Libby would run away, giggling, but not today. From the first moments of labor, the look had stayed on Libby's face. All Addy could manage was, "Love your new brother, Libby baby. Ain't he somethin'?" as she sank into sleep. *Just sleep*, she said to herself. *Hear me, Lord? Please hear me. I got these chilren to raise.*

There were no hills in the countryside, no rolling landscape to awaken the eye, not so much as a wrinkle in the flat terrain, so it was surprising that the new church stood on a grassy knoll as if it was in some way exalted, an oracle from God. And praise Him, too, they didn't need a white sentinel at the services—the only Negro church in the county to be so honored—so trusted was Samuel Green, the preacher farmer who gathered his flock in the small wood-framed building just outside of town. He worked among the white farmers, poor and not so poor, but none with huge plats of land that contained whole villages with hundreds of slaves to run things. None of that here. Just a quiet struggle in the northern part of the county away from the auction blocks of city and town and the slave traders in both, apart from the moneyed and the professionals. Just a quiet reach of land between rivers.

He worked his farm as hard as or harder than the best of them, and all the while, he was careful to subdue passions when problems arose. *He knew his place*, said the white farmers around him, and for that he'd won the favor of being left alone. It was a strange dance he did, he decided, but a necessary one. His strength was the land he worked, two spreads of thirty acres each, and his freedom, granted to him when he was thirty-five by his master, Henry Nichols, through his will. Nichols had managed to reach into a future in which he would not be present, having written words that would have power over Green for five years after his master's death. That's how it was. Words had power. As an enslaved farmhand, he'd learned how to do, but the words taught him how to be. Slowly, painstakingly, he'd learned to read them and now the Word was his. He'd saved his money and bought his freedom four years earlier than Nichols had intended. Armed with both his freedom and the Word, when the woman of mixed blood, Sarah Young, gave a few acres to the community of seven free black men in the hope of establishing a church, he was ready. Sarah had been Nichols's slave as well, and she was favored. About that, Green had nothing to say except that it hadn't been Sarah's choice, of that he was sure. To be fair, Nichols had given freedom in his will to many of them, and Green would always be grateful for the leniency. A speck of good luck had come his way. And because of it, he felt he'd been chosen for the Lord's mission. He would act obsequiously and with stubborn dignity in the white community so the parish for enslaved and free alike could flourish. There was a great need for a black sanctuary.

With his profits from farming, he was able to buy Kitty, his wife, two years ago. He was still astonished by having to do so especially when he listened to the white farmers complain about the lack of rain or a broken axle. A hundred dollars for a wife. He'd manumitted Kitty the same day he'd bought her, too, and this was more meaningful than the wedding vows made under slavery. This was his gift to her, one of her right and power, not acquisition. But children born while the mother was enslaved had to remain enslaved, no matter if the mother's status changed. He and Kitty were allowed to raise the children, but at sixteen and thirteen, Sam, Jr. and Sarah, slaves for life, had been taken from them. That his children were not free pained him and cut through any rapport he might have fostered with the white men whose farms surrounded his. Even though he did what they did, and they were all subject to the same winds and rains, he could never be as free as they, nor could his progeny. True, his son, Sam, Jr., was trained in blacksmithing now, but that he should be owned and beaten was an injustice that tested even the most devout man of God. So when he told his congregation they must be strong and loving, that kindness would be met with kindness, that they should be good servants in their life's work as well as to the Lord, he wondered at his own words that were crowded out by the image of Sarah's sweet, round face broken into weeping and screams the day she was taken from him and Kitty. He did not know how or when or even if his people could claim all that white men took for granted, but surely the way to begin was by being respectful, trustworthy, hardworking, and quietly determined, while appearing to be one of them. The Lord would provide. He'd seen it hundreds of times. But why the Lord had allowed one man to own another, he did not know. That was another question. And maybe God was not in control of everything either. But He did make opportunities, allowed hard times so a man would be tested and would grow in his faith. He, Preacher Green, would watch for the Way that would surely open as only those trusting in the Lord could do.

He rode down the back road from his farm to the church and paused at a narrow stream to let the mule drink. From here, the stream widened to creek, to inlet, to river, to bay, and finally to the ocean. He thought of his church in this way, too. It was only a small stream, gathering momentum. Hadn't his people dug canals for the shipment of logs for the white man's profit? Didn't the harvest of wheat and corn and whatever else depend on *them?* Any people who could build a civilization and not receive any profit or comfort for their labor owned a mighty strength. They endured, and they still had the capacity to love.

The mule waited while Green pondered. It was Sunday. As always he asked the question, *Where to begin the song, Lord?* Once he got started, the pitch and roll of his own voice showed the way. Was it the Lord's voice coming through him? He only began the calling, then waited for the answers. The great sweep of earnestness from his flock, the *Yes, Lord*s from believing lips, always swept him to greater heights. The Lord did the rest. *Tell me, Lord, where to begin*, he prayed to the mule's ears, for he believed God resided even in the most humble of beasts. In the distance, the sight of the wooden steeple rising above the peak of the main roof, its cross poised toward heaven like an arrow, filled him with gratitude. *Yes, Lord. Thank you, Lord.* His eyes filled with tears.

A figure on the road before him appeared out of the trees. The man stumbled, went on, and then turned as though looking for someone. It was too early for his parishioners, Green decided, but he raised his arm in a wave anyway. The man waved back. He knew him, or at least the swagger that belonged to James Spry, sawyer and father. He was a mountain of a man, powerful in chest and shoulders, with long arms that almost reached down to his knees. Now his hands fluttered at his sides, too large, restless, dangling, but, my God, could they work the wood. When James had raised timber as he had seen him do at the church site, all Preacher Green could think of was an old oak, limbs as huge around as a man's chest. But now James looked worn, his shoulders hunched. As he approached, he said, "Preacher?"

"James! Addy's been expectin' you."

"Just home. Got to Cambridge late yesterday. Been walkin' ever since."

"You know better than to walk alone in the open."

James's head jerked to the side. "Then I can see what's comin." When he looked back, there was a question on his face, and the words came slowly as though wasted breath would cost him. "Preacher, will you marry us, me and Addy?"

"James, from the looks of things, you already are. You have two children."

"Two?" His grin lit the day.

"By now, surely. She was ready last Sunday from the looks of her. If you're lookin' to give that baby your name and Libby, too, then I'm ready to marry you soon as Addy can stand."

James shook his head. "Well, now, that's all right," he said slowly, the words parting from his lips like a sigh. "All right," he repeated as he turned down the back trail to Perry's cabin with only two miles to go.

Elizabeth watched the figures on the bed of straw. The baby lay beside the mother. When he stirred, his mother woke instantly. Elizabeth breathed easier. She'd seen women sent to the field right after giving birth, babies brought out to mothers to be nursed in the hot sun, babies left in troughs while the mother, still bleeding, picked or raked or hoed. Addy would have surely died. But harvest was in and with early dark, they were in slow time. There was mostly the spinning, weaving, and sewing now.

"Addy?" she whispered. "Don't move, chile. I'll fit a pillow under your head and put the baby in your arms. Be still."

Still. The word hung in the air and with it all the painful silences she'd had to bear each time she'd had a child. Baby after baby, seven in all, appeared to be perfect but had died within a few hours. She would stare down at them, cradling them, singing to their brief lives to keep their spirit flowing until the terrible stillness descended and the tiny ears and soft body could neither feel her warmth nor hear her welcome. She hated her own expectations and false hopes. What had she done or neglected to do? Was she being punished? How could the Christian God be so cruel?

She carefully raised Addy's head and laid the baby in the crook of her arm. Funny how an arm bent at just the right place for a baby's head to turn toward a mother's breast, how some things just could not be better. In the larger scheme of things, she'd had several children come into her life, she told herself. Still, to have given Perry a child such as this one would have been grand. Many things in her life had turned out well, her husband, Perry, their slow, easy fitting together in the night, the weight of the baby within her, the hopeful births. How, amid such perfection, could there be such a vacancy and denial of life? Looking down into the quiet baby faces, she stopped fearing her own death. It was nothing but a great stillness. Hadn't she died a little more with each one? Hadn't she known death so intimately that it was forever part of her, all of her willed to prepare for its eventuality even now with Addy, the child she'd raised, and again with Addy's children?

Yet she was fortunate. It was given to her to borrow other people's children. Who knew what fate had been brought down on the fugitive mothers who hadn't returned to claim their offspring, who had died in their effort to flee or who'd wound up in some southern cotton field. Poor souls. The not knowing frightened her and frightened them all. Made them stay in one place, making the best of it.

She looked under the quilt to see if there was fresh blood and turned to Libby who stood as close to her mother as she could get, pulling at her own thick, cropped hair and shivering in Elizabeth's shawl, waiting. Elizabeth would make some star grass tea for Addy out of the last she had, but she had nothing to ease the child's frightened look, save, "Libby, come here, chile. It'll be all right, don't you know?" She pulled the child to her lap to rock her, crooning softly. But she didn't know. She didn't know anything, not even if there was a God who listened or if all was purely accident. When Libby fell asleep, she lay her down on the pallet and turned to her sewing. She'd wait for Perry, wait for him to open the door and call her name.

Perry was owned; he was Gaines's asset, listed on Gaines's property tax assessment along with horses, cows, and hogs. It was true that within bondage lay a certain amount of protection, a fact with which he tried to placate himself and be without rancor, for if he were kidnapped, somebody would be out looking for him and offering a reward for his return. Now that he was older, what he'd worried about all through the years, separation from Elizabeth, was unlikely. In his prime, he was probably worth as much as a thousand dollars, he guessed, but now he realized that was no longer the case. Gaines, who Perry knew was in debt, might be glad to receive a fair price for him, might even be very glad for an offer from Perry himself. The hope maddened him, and he realized that he harbored a quiet rage at the idea of a man having to buy himself.

The years had been hard with the crops poor and wheat prices down. Not a farmer in the region prospered, and Gaines was among them. He and others like him borrowed and begged among themselves, owning either one or two or five slaves whom they hired out or freed, depending on finances. Or religion. But most of the time, as far as Perry could see, money came first, then religion. White men meant to free the enslaved in their wills only after their own deaths and some, a long time after, but making things all right with the Lord in the end, saving their souls.

Gaines hired Perry out and collected his wages. Sometimes he let Perry keep a portion, but it was never enough. With the fields in poor shape and the weather a ghastly procession of heavy rains all that summer and fall, Perry began to think Gaines might appreciate a lump sum. Besides their field wages, with extra coming in from Elizabeth's sewing and spinning, he and Elizabeth had saved a small sum. It was a good time for him to ask for his freedom.

When he wanted to be glad about something and stave off worry, he'd imagine the chain of events that would bring him his freedom, from the slow realization on Gaines's face about the money, to the trip to the county seat in the oxcart. Elizabeth would buy Perry and then she would manumit him like Preacher Green did when he bought his wife, Kitty. As he trudged toward Gaines's cabin in the November dusk, Perry was grateful for a good woman to turn to, one with Indian ways who blended in quietly with what there was and made no fuss about it, one from a long line of survivors in the wilderness, one who knew the land and creeks like her own hand, one whose lineage no longer appeared on the census as Indian but was lumped together with the rest of his people. There was one major difference. She was listed under *free black* on the census, his dear Elizabeth, who was his Betsy in the warmth of their cabin and through the comfort of their nights.

J. R. Gaines owned a few acres toward the Delaware line. Unfortunately, much of the area was lower than the surrounding land and when the rains came, half the crops were under water. Across the road from Gaines's land on which the Burtons' cabin stood, lay twenty-two acres, mostly wooded, some cleared, bordered by the Indian path to town. One time, Gaines said he wished he'd gotten a chance to buy it, but he was lucky to have what he had, the better part of which had been Marietta's dowry. Work seemed to loosen Gaines's tongue as he and Perry labored side by side. Although his land was low and only partly cleared, Gaines said, "It came with you, Perry Burton, and I thought I'd made a fair bargain. It was a dry year when I'd married Marietta. She was right plump and fair with milk-white skin, and you, Perry, were known to be a helluva good worker. Still are."

Another time, Gaines said he liked being off the main road where the only sound was that of windsong in the pines. In the old days, there'd be an occasional wagon on the old Indian trail road, but for the most part, he and Marietta were cut off from the world, particularly when it rained, which had happened often in the last few years when the road sank into a stream of its own. Gaines would complain, and then, as if Perry's skin was as white as his own, he said, "There's a law that says free blacks got to donate their time digging ditches to make the roads drain off, but they're not made to do it. In fact, they get away with too much." Perry nodded. There was nothing else to do. Was the message that Gaines's hatred of free blacks was an attempt to make Perry's position seem enviable and to squelch any hope of manumission? At such times, despite Preacher Green's teachings, Perry hated Gaines, and he hated as well the need to keep his thoughts hidden.

Over the years, despite the mud in spring, and summer's powdery dust, the path was widened and hardened until it became a proper road down to the river. Traffic to Crotcher's Ferry was substantial, a place said to be unsafe on Saturday night if you wanted to keep both ears and all your fingers. It was a deadly place for a black man, a hub for the white men who traded liquor, lumber, grain, coffee, sugar, stories, bruises, and cuts. On occasion, Gaines was known to dip on down when the weather was good, especially in the spring and fall. Sometimes there was music, which he was as fond of as the whiskey. When the harvest moon was huge and orange, he'd hitch up his horse and ride toward the ferry landing, toward the camaraderie of men guffawing boisterously despite the bleakness of their days. Gaines rarely missed a Saturday night down at Crotcher's, but Marietta sometimes sent Perry to fetch him home when he didn't appear in Sunday's early hours.

No matter what Gaines said to him, Perry suspected the rough talk at Crotcher's would inspire Gaines to complain. Gaines didn't hide the fact that Perry had a wife who took in children, a whole cabin full, even though Perry and Elizabeth had none of their own. Sometimes there were four children staying and through the years, several more, some until they were fully grown, Addy for one, and now her man and her two children, all of them free except Perry. "Too many free blacks together in a small space make me nervous even if they are good workers," he'd tell anyone who'd listen. And then he'd add that he didn't know why he allowed it. He guessed he had a soft heart. But the truth was Perry's hired out wages brought a bit of income.

Despite all the talk whirling around them, it was Elizabeth who convinced Perry to ask for his freedom. And Perry surprised himself. He went to Gaines, and with a sudden show of confidence he didn't own, he said, "Me an' 'Lizabeth been savin' an' I think it be time for me bein' free." Gaines didn't say, *no*. He didn't say anything, like he hadn't heard Perry. But Perry knew the man long enough to see that by his hesitation, he was tempted. Yet all Perry could think about were the reasons why not. He was fifty-six this year and by law, too old to be manumitted. The age limit was forty-five, the supposition being that age brought with it an inability to be self-sufficient. And then there was Marietta. She would need Perry to take care of everything in the event of Gaines's death, and she'd need the income Perry brought in as a hired out. Then again, Gaines had stopped planting long ago, discouraged with drowned fields. Pigs were perfectly happy in the mud. There was little labor in pig raising except for the slaughtering. Perry thought he could still handle everything alone if he stayed close by.

So when November came, after he and Gaines shot the first of the pigs and hung four of them on the sugar maple to bleed out, as they stood in the sharp cold rubbing their hands together by the fire, Perry said, "Sir, I'd like my freedom, sir. I've got a hundred eighty dollars saved."

Gaines stopped in his tracks and stared at him. Perry couldn't ever remember Gaines looking him square in the face as he did now.

The water in the trough was hot enough to scald the bristles off the hide of the first carcass so it could be scraped, and Perry thought, as they hoisted it, how often they'd done the same thing together, how in all his time on this land, he'd made money for another man and neither one had much to show for it. Especially him. With the sale, Gaines could pay off some of his mounting debts. As Perry saw it, Gaines couldn't lose. He could collect rent for the cabin they stayed in, and he wouldn't have to think about feeding them.

And then, surprisingly, Gaines said, "Yeah, I guess it'd be time, Perry." The two men looked at each other eye to eye. Perry noticed the sagging skin under Gaines's eyes and was surprised to see that the man had a wen on the side of his neck. He knew full well that except for the wen and the color of skin, it was like peering into a looking glass. He and Gaines had grown old together.

"I'll sell you to Elizabeth, then, although what the difference is being owned by a man or a woman, you'll have to figure out," Gaines was saying, smiling as he said it.

Perry said, "Can I stay in the cabin till I get my own? Pay you rent?"

Gaines sighed. "Lord a Jesus, there'll be no end to what you'll be needin', Perry. I can see it now. You do these hogs, get in my firewood, plant the garden in the spring, and harvest like we've been doin'—only in your *free* time now—and I'll let you stay one year more." The word *free* came out a mockery. Gaines went on, "But no trouble, hear? Don't want patrollers to have to come around snooping, disturbing my nights, you and your house full of strays."

With that, Gaines promised to talk to John Prouse about the piece across the road. "Twenty-two acres is more than a colored man needs," he said, "but keeping you close by is part of the deal."

Not long after, Marietta found her husband face down in the mud. She'd fallen into a deep sleep the night before, unaware that he hadn't come home. *He could be sleeping off a Saturday night drunk somewhere between the farm and Crotcher's*, she thought, but when she heard the horse whinnying in the stall and had gone out with her shawl around her head, she saw the saddle still on the horse's back. Thinking Gaines had been distracted by a sound or something he needed to investigate, she went out back to the pig slab and that was where she found him. Bending down and attempting to roll him over, she saw instantly that she would be alone forevermore. There was no one, no children, no family, no connection to the outside world she could claim. She could do nothing about anything. As the body of her husband, with its own insistent unwillingness, rolled face down in the mud again, the shock of her new helplessness made her shudder. She broke into a run, and as she ran, she began to scream, "Perry, Perry, Per—ry!"

He heard her, knowing in that instant that Gaines was either gone or hurt enough to be gone. With her shriek, he saw how his fate was unendingly tied to hers.

"Miss Mari?" he said. Already running toward the pig sty, he caught sight of her through the trees along the well-worn path between her house and his cabin.

When he stood before her, she glared at him and her breath came in gasps. Her eyes were dry. "You're all I have now, Perry," she said, not pleading like a woman would, but her words breathed out in anger as if she'd been told of the agreement and would have none of it. Or hadn't heard of the agreement and nothing, absolutely nothing, would change.

He did what he could. He brought his master up to the big house, washed him, removed his clothes so Miss Mari could launder them, made the coffin, and set it in the parlor for the waiting time. On the day of the funeral, he brought Miss Mari and the coffin to the cemetery at the white man's church. He stood by with his hat in his hand like he was supposed to, Elizabeth at his side, his heart in turmoil and worry as his master was buried, for while Perry had accepted his position, he bore no love for the man and woman who'd kept him in it. He never showed or spoke about any of it to Elizabeth, and he pondered, as he stood staring down at the deep, rectangular hole in the earth and listened to the Word by the white minister, how he had come so close and missed his chance.

In time, after the funeral, after the will had been read and the debts recorded, after thinking and praying about it, after returning one night when the stars promised to be spectacular with the descending light of a cloudless sunset, after he came in from feeding the pigs and had watched the trees silhouetted against a yellow-orange sky, Perry approached her house and knocked gently on the door. She was unsmiling as she let him in, and he talked softly beneath the iron will of her, that will he so feared, the one with the long-ago claim and dowry. He watched her eyes. When he told her about the agreement between Gaines and him, there was a slight tick of her eyebrow, a quick shift of her focus. She knew of it, he was sure.

He offered the money. He promised his service to her till the end. He'd always taken care of her and he always would, but Gaines and he had agreed it was time. One hundred eighty dollars, he told her, reminding her she could pay off Gaines's debts. No need to sell off her goods and acreage.

"But you're hired out for the year. I can't break it," she said. Then, to his surprise, went on to say, "Wait. 'Less you pay rent for the cabin out of your earnings, much as I would have gotten for you hired out—then I would, long as you will do around here what you always did."

He stared at her. It didn't matter if he was free or not. It would always be the same. He'd never be free of her. Yet he nodded, not used to making decisions about his own fate. He bowed his head. He didn't know where the words came from, erupting from another self, from a desperate longing he rarely acknowledged. "Could you write it down, Miss Mari? Could you make it right with the law?"

She nodded. "In my will, you mean? You waitin' for my death out here in these woods? Is that what you think I ought to do?" She sighed. Her face had changed and her chin had grown tremulous in the dusky light. She shook her head slightly and when she looked at him it was without malice, far as he could tell. He took heart.

"You're my shadow, Perry. You've always been here. I don't know what will happen to you when I pass, 'less you pass first, and I dread to think what would become of me then. Let me think on it."

"Hirin' me out will only bring you forty dollars."

"This year. Then there's next year and the next."

The sun was setting. A beam of light through the window shone on them both, so that her skin and his had the same hue, nearly the same bronzed color, everything bathed in the deep golden light for one blazing instant. He tried once more. "One hundred eighty, Miss Mari, and I'll run the pigs like always."

The movement of her head was slight but it had the resemblance of a nod, a quick jerk and blink of eye, was all. She'd agreed. She was quite alone and he understood the bond.

From her pallet, Addy watched Elizabeth leave, her arms filled with the quilt she'd finished the night before. Two of the boys Elizabeth took care of, Daniel and Eziah, trailed behind. Then Addy heard Elizabeth's laugh, and a "Shhh!" With the baby at her breast, Addy shifted her weight on the straw bed just as the figure that was none other than James Spry filled the cabin doorway. Her relief was immediate. She wouldn't have to fend for herself entirely, or depend on Elizabeth for food and shelter. "James, why you been so long?" was all she could manage, accusation already on her lips before she could check it.

"Aw, now, Addy. You *know*. What you got there?"

"James Spry, Jr., free and hongry." She lay next to the fire for warmth. James's heavy footsteps scuffled on the dirt floor—and there wasn't a thing else in the room but him. Not her, or the baby, or the pot hanging in the fireplace, or the bed with its quilt that Elizabeth had made. Nothing but him. He filled the space. She could smell the woods on him, the marsh mud and his sweat worked up from walking the long way. He threw himself on the floor beside her, right there on the packed dirt, and looked across at her.

"You all right?" he said.

She nodded. "But I got to keep still, Elizabeth say."

He stared at her for a while and the baby, too, and waited. When the baby had stopped sucking, James reached over and took him from her. "I'm stayin' this time, Addy," he said, his voice sounding like it wasn't even his.

"Heard that before, James."

So he took the fifty dollars he'd earned and laid the bills on the quilt. "I mean it," he said, looking directly into her eyes. "I already axed the preacher to marry us. He said soon as you can stand."

She closed her eyes. "And if I cain't?"

"Then he'll have to do it while you're layin' down."

"That's good, James. That's good." In her fever and with the child in his father's hands, she drifted off, the prayer about sleep once more on her lips.

By way of celebration, there was only the kettle of winter greens, cornbread, and some rye whiskey Perry had saved from the last wheat harvest when the cheapest grade had been passed around. He'd been hired out and had gone off to five farms for the season but saw very little of the pay. It would be different from now on, he told himself, glad that James Spry had shown up, glad of the marriage, glad of help although he never said any of it out loud. The child, Libby, stood close to him, her arms around one of his legs. He couldn't take a step without her hanging on. "Come away, Libby. Let the man walk," Elizabeth said, but Perry answered, "Pay her no mind." He laid his hand on top of Libby's head and pressed it to his side.

Addy was still confined to the bed. With the baby in her arms, her hair platted behind her ears, and a new shift, she greeted Preacher Green, who stood at the foot of the bed with the cold still on him from his ride down the road. James held her hand. She couldn't wait, she'd told him, because "I want the children to have a name, a righteous name in this world, James, and I want them protected because they'll be taken, the both of them, to Orphan's Court if no mother and no father are around. You know it. It shouldn't be left to Elizabeth."

So it was done, and afterward, Green said to Perry, "You start by rentin' the land. Tell Prouse while he harvests the timber, you'd like to rent. Later he'll probably not want to clear it himself and fight with the stumps. Maybe he'll let you buy it."

It was unusual for manumission to be granted to a man as old as Perry, but Miss Mari had testified about her husband's wishes for the sale and the assumption that it would mean freedom for the slave of her dowry. Elizabeth was ecstatic. "I am Elizabeth Burton," she heard herself say at the courthouse and said it again after she'd listened to the strange, complicated words read to her: "Be it known that I, Elizabeth Burton of Dorchester County in the State of Maryland, for diverse good causes and considerations, have released from slavery, liberated, manumitted, and set free my husband, Perry Burton, being the age of fifty-six, able to work and gain a sufficient livelihood, whom I this day purchase from the estate of James Gaines as witnessed by Dr. Edwards."

There was more but she didn't hear it. There was only Perry, standing taller it seemed, hair softly graying at his temples, his mouth working and his nostrils flaring as if he were both tasting and smelling his good fortune. His eyes were wide as a child's when she stooped to make her mark on his behalf. Oh, they laughed on the way home, the papers in his pocket, the sun warm on their backs, the cart rumbling over the ruts. When they stopped at Preacher Green's house, the preacher came out to greet them saying, "Praise the Lord," over and over. He knew better than anyone what it was like. He told them they'd have to be more careful than ever, but they already knew that. Before they went crazy with freedom, he warned Perry always to carry the papers, and if he or Elizabeth or any of theirs ever felt in danger, they were to come to the church. While Elizabeth figured he just wanted them to keep in the circle of the faithful, she also sensed a necessary secrecy about him. Not that the white planters suspected anything, she didn't think, but the more secrets there were, the greater the danger. Preacher Green was the cover for all of them. Just how much he knew he never let on. She believed he was tuned in to everything greater than they: to God, to the spirit world, to the society of white men, and to the biblical knowledge that would save them. He knew where the Way out was, who could be trusted, and who couldn't. And underneath what he allowed the world to see, there was that stubborn hopefulness that hung on in the worst of circumstances. Whatever Perry and Elizabeth hoped for that day of manumission, they knew Preacher Green would help them see it through.

He was right. They'd have to get land if they were going to make it. It was the next step on the ladder where the space between the rungs was greater the higher you got. Elizabeth worked in the fields in summer and during harvest, in the slaughtering of the pigs and sausage making, meat salting and smoking, but in the quiet of every night, as long as there was pitch for the lamp, she wove and sewed. Then, too, she would be called on at a moment's notice for the Prouse families, the Lees, Miss Mari, the Websters, the Wallaces, and whoever else. She gathered flax and wove cloth for them, and when she finished sewing, she used the scraps to make quilts and rugs. All the while, she kept the children close. She'd heard that some were kidnapped, one boy taken right out of the yard. Parents died, were stolen, or on the run all the time, which meant there would be children with no one to care for them. She took them in. Addy was the first, but there were others who came. Sometimes people came back for their own after they settled up North, but most of the time the children stayed. She never thought anything of it till Preacher's wife, Kitty, had her children taken right out of their home and returned to their owner. In her sorrow, Kitty took in children, too. She'd say, "We're in the path for a good reason. We know how to raise them, Betsy, you and I. Don't it bring you comfort? Ain't it the Lord's way to be there for the chilren? Otherwise, they take 'em. Any chile under twenty-one, they take, the devils. Free or not, they steal 'em, make 'em indentured or sell 'em to the Georgia traders. I thank God mine are close, though they're still owned. No one pays mind to *free* anyhow."

On the trip home from the courthouse, Perry began a great hope. It was all he could think about. It burst out of his heart and branched along his bones. It made him young again, and quick, which he'd never been. It steadied him while Elizabeth sat up all night sewing. He was often gone from her for days, traveling fourteen miles each day, working wherever he was needed. He found work with John Prouse, hauling timber while James sawed. They both dug ditches along the roads on days off without pay. And while James grumbled at this, Perry accepted it as a sign of his freedom. As soon as he'd struck a deal with John Prouse that the land would be his after the last payment of money held back out of his wages, he began eyeing trees and saving scraps. He was able to collect wood not fit to ship and shingles poorly hewn to build a cabin he'd one day put on his land, on the twenty-two acres. The cabin would be larger than the slave house if he could manage it, with a wood floor—not packed dirt. Eventually, with enough lumber, a stairs would go up to a loft for the children. No matter that the sale wouldn't be complete until the timber was harvested. No matter that the land would have to be cleared. No matter. This was his faith: that the land would someday be his. All he had to do was live long enough.

With the coming of first light, James Spry was walking again, this time toward the mill belonging to Eben Prouse. A few weeks before he'd found work at John Prouse's, Eben's brother, but John was heavily in debt and there'd been no pay. If he, James Spry, was going to own land he would have to find additional work at one of the nearby mills. He walked swiftly along the old Indian trail that led to the creek. His overalls were soiled but not his white shirt with its full sleeves gathered at the wrist, freshly laundered by Elizabeth, nor the vest she'd made him. The day was warm for late November. Magenta, almost black, star-shaped leaves still clung to the gum trees. The trail was slightly wider than a deer path. Under the carpet of leaves from the oaks and sweet gums, there were years of needles fallen from the pines that cushioned his steps. The air was not yet so cold he couldn't smell the decay that was peculiar to autumn. Addy was on his mind. He couldn't understand why she was slow to get well after the baby, why the bleeding began each time she tried to rise from the pallet. He was thinking so hard about it he missed the single sound that might have saved him, the step of a boot from behind. He only felt an explosion in his head, a sudden brightness and then nothing. Nothing at all.

Later, when James did not return, Perry searched along the trail he must have taken. There was nothing save the places where deer had scraped their hooves on the ground, clearing a place that would be saturated by their musk. But one bare spot looked as though it had been scraped by a man's boot. There was a young sapling nearby that tilted toward the small sunlit opening, its bark scraped at the base, a place too low for a deer to rub its antlers against, a wound that could have been made by a heavy boot or horse hoof, or by a man falling into it, a man with enough weight on him to bend the young tree to the ground, but he wasn't sure until he found the small tear from James's overalls, part of his pocket maybe, the one that had held his paper. James. He would not have been missed at work. To white men, he was just another free colored roaming around. James, a skilled sawyer, now just another hand for the cotton harvest, bound, as Perry well knew, for Georgia by way of Crotcher's Ferry, down river to the bay, to some holding pen and auction in Virginia, and to the coffle. *Kidnapped, sold,* were the words on Perry's lips, the words he could not say to Addy when he returned, but which he whispered to Betsy, who'd kept a corn cake for him, her hand flying to her mouth when she heard him whisper, *I think he been stole.*

They had a hard time with Addy. Turning gray, she lay on her pallet and cried the days away until Elizabeth finally gave her some laudanum to calm her, for fear the bleeding would begin again. Addy's grief now poured into the faith that Sam Green would find her James. In the night, Elizabeth tried to imagine it—James not able to fight. If he could, he would have fought hard and well. No one man could take James. There must have been two or three together, their hearts pure evil. Everyone in the Negro community knew where the slave traders from Georgia congregated. They were interested in the young—children, teenagers and young adults, and women who could be "breeders" as well as men fit to work in the cotton fields. Someone must have been watching long enough to know James would be back for the birth of the baby and knew he'd fetch a high price.

Preacher Green said these times and the evil were sent to test them. Make them stronger. "It won't do any good to report it, Elizabeth," he said wearily at church Sunday, "but I will anyway. The law is for white people. For us, there's only the sheriff, and he makes his own laws. Nothing will be done because James is free. If he'd been owned, they'd be out offering a reward, you can be sure of that. Man strong as he. Another one was taken, too, but he's not free. There's a reward out for him. He's gone to the ship by this morning, that's sure. They'll get more for him on the block than they will with a reward."

She didn't know if Preacher ever did tell the sheriff. He was always careful not to stir the pot. White people trusted him, but Elizabeth wondered if the price for that trust was too high. He was playing the whites all the while. He did what he could and the rest he had to let go, like water through fingers.

Free. She spat the word on the ground. They couldn't testify in court, give evidence of wrongdoing. Couldn't vote. Lost their children to bondage. And here a grown man who had his paper in his pocket was taken while the family lay in the aftermath like broken crockery.

She watched Preacher Green that Sunday morning with huge doubt in her heart, anger that held an enormous hatred. She knew she mustn't. She knew she had to make herself ready so that when the preacher raised his arms and called on the Lord to listen, she could let herself be caught up in it. Her body shook with longing for some purpose, some deliverance, something bigger than all of them who scrapped and scraped on the fields. If they didn't matter, then all they had was to endure and survive, reach into a better day with the children, raise them up and send them on. That's all they had.

But despite Preacher Green's desire to smooth it all out, the word spread everywhere in the community, one mouth to another like a ribbon threading them together. *James taken.* The words hissed by some, received by others only with a nod. They prayed for a long time that Sunday so the Lord would hear. They sent their voices straight up to the heavens and named their anguish. When it was over, they went back to their cabins grieving, but in an attitude of peacefulness and strength, just like Preacher Green said they would. Elizabeth kept the children close. They were never out of sight since the traders were about. Not Libby, nor the baby, James, Jr., nor Eziah, who was just nine, nor Daniel, who was twelve, whose mothers had never come back to put their arms around them.

Then came winter and while the earth lay somber, Elizabeth spun cloth and sewed quilts, wove baskets and made brooms to sell in town. Miss Mari said they no longer were entitled to get staples since Perry had been freed, and they should be glad enough to be allowed to stay in the cabin. But, in the end, she gave them scraps from the hogs, the head and the feet, some fat back and bacon, and they made do with that.

Out of the still morning with the first snow drifting down in flakes as big as gumballs, a white man came on his oxcart, bareheaded, his hair thick with snow, his cheeks red. Elizabeth thought she'd never seen such red skin. On her way to the woodpile, she watched him approach, old suspicions quieted by the fact that he was alone. Then she recognized him. Of course. John Prouse.

She first saw him at the church camp meeting, where he'd announced he didn't believe in a man owning another, that he took God's Word seriously, that his soul was made clean by the Lord's forgiveness. "God said for a man to enter the Gates of Heaven, he had to give up his ownership so the names he kept as assets could be entered on the page of the free. It's wrong to own people. This much I know. And I say it again before all of you. Amen!"

He was a well-meaning but hapless figure, one who gave the impression he didn't try as hard as he said, one given to outbreaks of blushing enthusiasms but not a man who drew confidence in people. It was as if his power was undergoing a rift, a doubt that peppered his mind like gunshot. The Prouses were kind for the most part, but Mr. John's father hadn't hesitated to send Elizabeth's half brother, Jez, to the auction block three years before instead of freeing him. She understood that sometimes the need for money got in the way of a man's morality, but she'd never forgiven him. Now his son rubbed his hands in the cold and expected more of them. He spoke gently enough, almost pleading, saying that he'd heard there'd been a baby born.

"Yes," she said quietly, and because she'd worked in his field during harvest many a year and in those of his two brothers and because she knew him as a gentle soul, she felt safe motioning him to follow her inside the cabin. He ducked his head and entered. Casting his eyes quickly around, he spotted Addy, and without asking her, said to Elizabeth, "I need to bring her up to the house right now. The wife's poorly and can't feed the baby."

"Addy's poorly herself," said Elizabeth.

As if he hadn't heard, he went on, "She can bring her own with her. She won't have to do anything but nurse the baby. I'll wait outside till she's ready."

"Mr. Prouse, I don't mean no disrespect. But you remember James Spry who worked for you?"

His eyes looked vacant. He could be either daydreaming or searching for a right way to answer. Hesitantly, as though he wasn't sure of his recollecting, he said, "I figured my sawyer man disappeared. Just didn't show up for work one morning. Someone told me he was looking for millwork so I didn't pay it any mind, thinking he just went off because I couldn't pay him directly."

"Well, sir, he's gone. About two weeks now."

"He was a bit of a wanderer."

"Only to find work, sir. We think he been stole." The last word came out in a whisper. It was all she could manage.

John Prouse's thick eyebrows went up and down and his face flushed even redder. He searched her face. She couldn't tell whether or not he had known. How could he not know? All he said was, "Has the sheriff been told?"

Elizabeth's eyes filled with tears.

"I'll make it known, Elizabeth," he said softly, "although I wish I had known when it happened." He turned to Addy. It was clear he fully expected her to rise and go with him. Out of a mix of gratitude and old obedience, she picked up James, Jr. and followed him out the door.

Elizabeth watched them go. Addy carried the baby who was wrapped in one of Elizabeth's quilts. She told Addy if the bleeding started again, she was to tell them. "Tell them you got to get home. Bein' free, you can do that. Don't be afraid to say it."

They disappeared into the snow. Prouse was taking Addy in the best time, the time when the baby was at the breast. How she loved to see that, how it was almost as good as having a baby at her own. She was crying, although for what she didn't know because the money would help, and Prouse was a good man. Besides, she had the other two children plus Libby. It was just hard, when they all felt like open sores with James gone. The baby gave them comfort as he lay plump and warm in their arms. Addy was on the mend. There was the peaceful snow, the harvest done, and planting time a long way off. She turned to go back in the cabin that was dark now, no bright place where the baby lay sweet. How quickly everything changed. James here and gone. Addy, so resigned as she climbed onto Prouse's gig, never turned her head. Elizabeth felt Libby watching her with her eyes wide.

"No," she told her. "You not goin' nowhere. You my girl now," and she smiled. Libby was six but still eager to crawl into her lap. She was large for her age and muscular. She would be a strong woman, with a solidity and concern that Elizabeth already loved. She wished she could save Libby for something better, but as far down the road as she could see, there was nothing but more of the same. Fire burned in her heart for Libby's father, walking south, feet chained, she was sure. She held the child's head, her fingers lost in the short, wild tangle of hair, and soon began to plait it. Her hands, kept busy, eased her heart.

Sitting next to Mr. Prouse on the wagon seat, Addy held the baby close and covered his face with the shawl. The infant anchored her. She would fly off the face of the earth without him. She watched Mr. Prouse's hands as they held the reins. The skin along his knuckles was split, showing rivulets of dried blood. She vaguely wondered why he didn't have gloves. Clutching the baby tighter, she heard him cry out and she loosened her grip. She did not want to nurse a white child, did not want the pale skin that close to her, taking nourishment. If the situation was reversed, would the white woman nurse her child? She did not want to be alive. What was she saying? It was terrible to be filled with such poisonous thoughts. Tears streamed down her face.

Suddenly there was James, sitting backward on the horse before her, facing her with his great hands hanging at his sides, his balance perfect. Silent as the snow and veiled by it too, he sat staring at her. She could not look away. Would it be enough to know he was alive? Or was any absence a death, any final leaving the same as the grave? How could Prouse see to drive the wagon in the thick snow? In a while, or a second, she didn't know which, James was covered in white. He was nothing but a ghost now, his eyes shining through the veil, not blinking, not sparkling, not alive. She knew she'd never again see him on this earth, and when he disappeared from her sight altogether, hope and worry, like twin angels, left her to sit on a wagon that moved swiftly through the gray-white world, horses' hooves muffled, Mr. Prouse's voice sounding slightly echoed as he said, "You warm enough, Addy?"

Preacher Green minded his own business. He offered no opinions, reported no misdemeanors, and tattled no evidences of ill treatment. Rebellion was not his way. As he saw it, thoughts of insurgency had to be smoothed over, ground down to polished stone, for the good of all.

"Accept your fate," he told his people. "Love the good within it and transcend the evil." The part he never spoke out loud, but believed with all his heart, he would have put into words if he could: *At least for a while. Till you can make a choice, to flee or help others to do so. Be listenin', and be ready. Meantime, silence, like a mask— house to house, the darkened path that disappears into the incoming tide, the tall grasses, the waiting skiff.* For that purpose, he kept an open door, a lighted room, and Delaware train schedules by the lamp.

As for his white neighbors, he knew who his friends were and fostered his relationships with them. If he could have said to one of them, *Look, this happened to one of ours. Can you ask the sheriff? Can you speak for us? Say that a freeman of our community was struck down and kidnapped and brought to Crotcher's?* But in truth, there was none he could ask, none he could trust, no risk he could take in light of his larger purpose. Although it grieved him that his own two children were still enslaved and taken from him and Kitty, it did not cause him to raise his voice against the way things were. It would do no good. Far better to go the way things flowed and, like a stone, let the waters flow over him, but not forgetting. No, never forgetting.

The kidnappings were too large to contend with, as were the auctions in town. The lesser evils, the payment of taxes for the sheriff's salary, and schools only for white children, the requirement of papers, the threat of search and seizure by the patrollers or citizen's committee (otherwise known as the "committee of gentlemen,") arose from the white community's fear. He believed his people would someday rebel, but the thought filled him with grief, too, because the taking of freedom would be violent. It was only a matter of time. If he had a task larger than those of a farmer and lay minister, it was to practice and preach restraint while following the undercurrent, keeping alive the secret network. For that, he did all he could.

His only book was the Bible and from that he had taught his son and daughter to read. On Sundays after church, he began to teach a few of the young the printed words of the Lord's Prayer that they knew by heart. They pointed to the words and said them aloud. Miraculously, they began to remember which word said what. And they would carefully copy the letters down in the dust of the cellar floor. Some only managed their own name, but he was satisfied.

To the larger world, he was seen only as a Negro man with a mule and a plow. He tilled and harvested alone unless Kitty was beside him, sometimes with the children they took in. He kept one cow and a small herd of sheep that grazed peacefully within the fence he'd built. His thirty-acre piece was neatly squared off into small, tidy fields where he raised wheat and corn. If a man needed work, he hired him more out of kindness than out of a need for help. He watched every penny he made, thinking he would one day buy his children. That he had to buy them after he'd begot them was one of the things he had difficulty understanding unless he said to himself, "It is the will of the Lord." He wasn't entirely sure he believed that.

Meanwhile, there was the Underground Railroad—conductors, station-masters, stations—a secret way through the labyrinth of briars that was man's infernal inhumanity. And with it, there was the whispered word, not of the Bible, but of a secret practicality he so loved. *The Way northward—from safe house to dirt path to marsh to water passage to a Delaware road.* He never spoke of it anywhere except to tell the runaway of the next house and the next. But he felt his congregation knew, somehow, that the words he himself never spoke were so powerful they could travel along the ground through the vibrations of running feet.

The disappearance of James Spry grieved him. He could do nothing. He wanted to be invisible, an empty vessel, a calm man just growing his wheat, driving his mule, but this disappearance angered him, and he prayed to the Lord his anger would not show. He wanted only to be seen as a simple, peaceful man. Which is why, God forgive him, when the sheriff approached him this December day in the time of Advent and asked him about rumors he'd heard of a Negro who'd been roaming the area looking for trouble and found it, about which some in the community were stirred up, he said with a shake of his head, "Don't know. Haven't heard tell of it, Sheriff. They were in church on Sunday loving the Lord like always."

He learned some Negroes had been brought to town a few days before and sold to a trader. It was said they were freemen and the kidnappers had been arrested, one in town and the other in the county seat, seventeen miles away. James Spry was not one of the kidnapped, but encouraged by the news that justice would come down on the kidnappers, Preacher Green had driven to town with the intention of speaking to the sheriff about James.

Main Street was eerily quiet that day as though people were either preparing for an ambush or concealing a conspiracy. From last year's harvest of oysters, pearly white and steel gray shells lined the road. The only sound was that of the shells crunching under the wheels of his wagon. He had driven the mule slowly, thinking how best to phrase his concern and not name his anger. The bare trees laced the sky. Suddenly, the door of the tavern burst open and a crowd of men emerged into the cold, shoving one another and shouting, "Hear! Hear! Bail him out! He's done us a favor!"

A hat was passed and its contents were brought to the jail. Minutes later, the kidnapper was free. Green was astonished to see two men loosen a wide railing from one of the fences that they carried now toward the former prisoner who was hoisted onto it and who now sat triumphantly raising his arms in a gesture that encouraged adulation from the unruly crowd. Watching from a safe distance and infuriated by the injustice of freeing a man who'd been caught kidnapping, he turned the wagon around and headed home.

He could help the ones in bondage, but the ones who were free walked a far more precarious line. They were not much more than bait as far as he could see, and their freedom was as fragile as the papers they carried. The difference between him and the other freemen whose numbers were increasing year after year was the thirty acres he tilled. But the land was not his, and even though the Lord provided as he labored, all, all was tenuous.

As his eyes fluttered open, blinding sunlight came to James in star bursts. He shut his eyes against the harshness, felt the ropes on his hands and feet, slowly aware now of his helplessness. The voices that surrounded him were those of white men. Water slapped the hull, and he felt his head roll with the pitch of the ship. Seagulls laughed. He was in a pen made of oak strips through which the ribbon of sky shone a stark and empty blue. The door opened.

"Get up!" he heard, and felt the swift nudge of a boot, not quite a kick. Again and again. "Get up!"

He just made it to his knees when he reentered the darkness. When he awoke, it was night. The stars told him the ship was sailing westward. He watched them as though he was trying to see through a caul. He might be moving southward now. What he'd always dreamed about—was it happening? Freedom from everything he ever knew? The Way by water, his salvation? Floating by trouble, land ties, fear—was he finding release at last? He could not raise his head and so rolled to his side. Lying in a pool of his own blood, he was aware that he was alone as he'd never been. And nothing mattered.

Day followed and during another night, he still lay on his back, not caring, when someone brought him water and freed his hands so he could drink. The ship slipped through quiet waters and the air was brisk, clear as November nights can often be. He was distressed that he didn't know what day it was, or the date, or even the year, but it was November, of that he was sure. Or was it December already?

When they pulled into port, more of them were let into the pen. Ten more. He counted. And he was number eleven. He did not know more than that. Someone tried to raise him, and James clung to the man as though it was his long lost father come to save him.

There were three more days of sailing. And some corn mush. And slowly, slowly, out of the mist, it occurred to him that this was the opposite of what he'd thought. The men around him were silent and bereft. They were heading south. How could he have thought otherwise?

In some port or other, the pen was emptied of men, and they were brought to the auction block. Townspeople gathered and watched. Looking over the crowd, James saw that everything behind him would be erased like a newly plowed field. There were no children, no wife, no friends, no private world where he could think and breathe and live out his own thoughts. *Maybe my mind been set free*, he thought, *free to live away from my body forever*. When he tried to speak, words came in a jumble. So he gave up talking and silence was where he stayed. Astonished, he felt as though he was looking back on himself while he watched the men in front of him making bids for his flesh. The man on the platform with him said he was dull, but strong and in good health. For a long while, it was all he could remember, and even of that he was unsure.

In the months that followed, the cutting of timber drew teams of oxen and a small gang of men to the twenty-two acres Perry Burton had already thought of as his despite the few remaining payments to be made. The deed wasn't to be signed until all the trees had been cut. Meanwhile, Perry worked at timbering and drove the oxen that hauled the loaded sledges to the mill at Crotcher's Ferry, three miles down the road. Sometimes he had to help lay logs on the road when it disappeared into mud. The days the road was frozen were the best, as the logs would mysteriously rise above the ground again, making the going easy. Since the standing trees belonged to Prouse, Perry didn't ask for any, but seeing his need, Prouse offered him a small stand. It was a kindness Perry wasn't used to, and he wondered what he'd owe Prouse in return. He made no connection to Addy feeding the Prouse baby until Elizabeth reminded him.

"He a true Christian man, Perry," she said, nodding and tucking her thin lips in like she did when she was pleased. His Betsy smiled with her eyes, rarely with her mouth, for she was a solemn woman, holding back grief, it seemed to him.

The Prouse sons had always been fair. Perry remembered old man Prouse in a different light, and when memory went back that far, it was easy to understand the backlash that caused men either to follow their forebears or rebel against them. Prouse, Sr. did well farming since he had his sons to help and several slaves besides, but he was a hard man who'd sold his slaves instead of freeing them in a county where free blacks outnumbered the enslaved, in a region between two attitudes, southern and northern, where side by side existed a strange mix of doubt, righteousness, and empathy that, like water and oil, never blended. For the elder Prouse, it was all about profit. Perry never had to wait to be paid. When the old man died, the land was divided among his sons and acreage scattered throughout the northern part of the county was assigned. Thomas, the oldest, and John, ten years younger, had inherited land that was thick with white oak, while Eben, the middle brother, held three plots at Cabin Creek, one of which was close to a good-sized grist and saw mill. On one lot he'd built a house with a steep-pitched roof and wide veranda that was the envy for miles around. A carpenter by trade, Eben farmed for subsistence, but wood was his passion. His house had the finest split-shingled roof and clapboard exterior a man could desire.

The three brothers worked alongside the help as did their wives and children. They looked out for free blacks as if to make up for their father's cold heart. Eben Prouse, the man Perry most respected, was never in debt, but the shadow of the almshouse was a constant threat to John Prouse. It was John Prouse's debt, though, that made it possible for Perry to buy a bit of land. John was easy going and likeable, but he had a way of shrugging things off, not paying attention. For the ordinary farming man who fought drought, torrential rains, blight, and meager profits, not to pay close attention spelled disaster. Perry worked for each of the Prouse families for many years, and they had, in fact, passed Perry between them as the need arose, that is, when Gaines decided to let him go. Perry had worked with them all through drought and flood. He felt like an integral part of their community, although that would never be put into words on either side. Still, there was a mutual trust, born of years of getting the work done together.

In the spring, when the land lay stump-ridden and briar-ensnared, Perry approached John Prouse, hat in hand, reminding him about the issuance of a deed. Prouse had good intentions but being long on promises and short on action, signing the deed did not happen right away. Perry was patient. Anyway, there were still two payments to be made. He wouldn't say anything more until harvest. He bought bricks for the fireplace and a single piece of glass which stood against the outside wall of the cabin, its preciousness noted with daily warnings to the children.

There was a change in Perry. He'd never taken anything before, but now that he was a freeman he needed things of his own—an ax, an adze, and a maul. He'd always used Gaines's tools, of course, and now that Gaines was gone and there was just Miss Mari, Perry borrowed the tools. He put them back when he was through, but he hated to ask if he could have them. Yet the time came when, because he used them so often, he neglected to put them back. He acquired them, telling himself, *what would Miss Mari do with them anyhow?* It was a small point, but it was the way things were now. He had a need to own and the act of owning went beyond need to the satisfaction of desire. He kept the tools sharpened and hung them inside Gaines's cabin door. They were the marks of his new independence. Before he snuffed out the lamp each night, his last image of the day was that of the smooth oak handles and iron heads of his means.

Before sunup and after feeding the pigs, he and Elizabeth took turns hacking at the stumps with the adze and the maul and then set the wood to burning so that there was always smoke rising out of the ground as though the roots of the trees reached down to hell itself. They often cooked over the heat of the stumps, the children glad to be out of the cabin where Elizabeth made them stay during the day if she was gone. She cautioned them about climbing over the smoldering stumps or getting too near, but Libby's shift got caught on a stump that burned low to the ground. Perry sprang to her and tore the burning cloth from her body, crying, "Lord, Lord, Libby!" over the child's screams. He doubted then. He doubted he could clear the land, the years doubling up in that moment, his age greater than it really was, the task too much. It was a feeling that stayed with him all through the winter as he listened to Libby's cries whenever Elizabeth cleaned and dressed the wound where flames had scorched her from foot to knee, the healing wound discolored and rippled into shreds of pale and rosy flesh. He wondered if burns healed any different on a white person, if underneath, everyone was the same color.

The cutting of timber was accomplished quicker than the removal of stumps. He figured it would take a year to clear two acres. He and Elizabeth kept at it. There was nothing else to do. He planted a few acres of tobacco between the stumps even though only a few farmers now grew tobacco, and then built a drying shed for the leaves. He built it before he started their cabin. They'd all have to help with the harvest. He'd have to borrow Prouse's hogshead to bring the tobacco leaves to market come fall. Elizabeth and Addy would help and even Libby, Eziah, and Daniel were old enough to count on.

Meanwhile, on the rest of the land, the stumps smoldered all spring. When the blackened wood was doused with rain, they had to wait for them to dry again and be rekindled. Elizabeth watched over them like a witch over her cauldrons, the look on her face mean as the stubborn stumps, her eyes narrowed against the smoke, the smell permeating her hair. Perry wanted the land cleared well enough to use a plow, but Elizabeth remembered the old Indian way where the land was never entirely cleared, just enough to allow the sun to reach the crops. Stick farming, like her grandmother had done, was easily accomplished in the sandy soil. That would be enough. With each cleared space, her hope brightened until one day, in one small patch, she pushed some dried peas and corn into the soil and established her garden. Watching the helter-skelter places for the plants to appear, she was pleased to see early dandelions and wild strawberry, new shoots of milkweed and blackberry just beginning, seeds blown by the wind or dropped by birds, some in the ground all that time waiting for light.

She hadn't forgotten the old ways, how her Indian grandmother farmed and foraged while her grandfather hunted. What was different was the ownership. Where there had once been a mutual sharing of the land, there was now ownership. Her mother's people roamed the land and left cleared places fallow for the plenty that would appear on its own. Their cabin sites were the only lands held constant and only for five years at that. Once the white man appeared, he claimed huge tracts and established himself in a brick home. He became busy with managing and owning. Meanwhile, Indian blood joined Negro blood under the label free black, and although none of it ever meant land ownership, they were the working backbone of the land. Ownership was a new idea to Elizabeth, a possibility she'd never before considered.

Their cleared land would feed them through April, May, and June until her garden came on. She would never give up her roaming, collecting nuts and seeds from the woods in the old way, digging the roots of the sassafras and the bark of the sweet gum for tea. In the spring, before the new crops began, she waded along the sweetwater marshes of the Marshyhope for tuckahoe and the new green shoots of cattails. The fallow land would offer a variety of plants she had not foraged for a long time. She watched over the sun-drenched places with great hope. Somehow it was easier to trust the earth, something she could see and believe in, its rhythms dependable, than a Lord God who appeared to favor some and cared nothing about others. Her doubt would never leave her lips, not even to Perry, who would merely say, *The Lord helps those who help themselves.*

In the spring, they began the cabin. There were four stumps, one at each corner of an approximate twenty foot square and that's where Perry laid the first logs. The house would be built up out of the mud with a true floor. In the center, he dug a good-sized food bin, and the thought crossed his mind that it was large enough to hide two people if the need arose. Safe houses for fugitives were increasing all over the shore. Aloud, he said to Betsy with pride in his voice, "This is for our store, for all we'll harvest from our own land." Some of the men from the parish came to help with the laying of logs, and in three Sundays, they were notched and set for the walls. Inside, Perry stood on the new floor, turning slowly, surveying the room. They would cook, eat, work, sleep, and die here in all likelihood. There was a narrow stair that led up to the loft for the children. A window faced the afternoon sun, and it was here that Perry, having framed the glass in wood, attached it with hinges made out of leather. It was their one luxury and Elizabeth was pleased. When they'd gathered enough scrap wood, they would cover the logs with clapboard. Meanwhile, Elizabeth chinked the logs with cement. One batten door faced east. The other faced the morning sun and Gaines's old slave cabin. Perry could look across the road and think that although he hadn't really come very far, Gaines's cabin was a world away. It was a good time, the best of all the times he could remember. He was still bound to the same labor, but now he would own field and house. At dusk, he looked toward the setting sun, knowing what a good thing had come to him, that between him and the final rays of sun lay his own land marked out and waiting for him.

James Spry, in a Georgia field, barefoot, the bend of his body perpetual as he leaned over the cotton plants, filled his burlap sack hour after hour, day after day. To pass the time, he tried to remember his journey south, guessing at some of it. At first, the only thing he could recall with certainty was that his head hurt as they walked for hours in the hot sun with little water, the whole coffle of them moving slower and slower as the days wore on. Some of the time they rode in wagons, and he'd watched the land flatten in fields like those in Dorchester and rise into rolling mountains such as he'd never imagined. Colors softened and seemed to yellow in the humid air. He remembered wondering about the names of the places they'd passed through. He'd forgotten about the calendar; the names of the days and numbers were still a mystery to him, which made him feel disconnected from his own existence. His sweaty body, roaming through time, held no clue. The unknown terrain confused him. Fear rose in his throat that he couldn't swallow away. Mostly, he'd kept his eyes down at his feet. His shoes eventually disintegrated and he'd thrown them aside on some dusty road.

His knowledge returned slowly. At some point in time, he remembered he had a wife and her name was Addy. She came to him in dreams. She always stood at the door of a cabin as if she'd been waiting for him. It wasn't his cabin, and each time he saw her, the cabin was different from the one before. Sometimes there were children behind her, peeking out from behind her skirts, but they quickly disappeared without a sound, and he never could tell what they looked like, or their names, or what they wanted of him.

He remembered that when they loaded him and some others in the wagon, he'd counted seven men, including one who lay in the wagon bed, covered entirely with burlap. He'd wished he could find out how old each one was, and if they had cut down any trees and if they had, how many. On the slatted sides of the wagon that held hay at harvest time and now was put to another purpose, he'd counted ten slats on one side and five on the back and front and ten more on the other side, but when he counted them again, he'd come out with fewer than the last time. So he kept counting. He didn't know why his counting was important, except he connected it with being "sent south," a threat he'd heard all his life and now knew was reality.

The body on the floor of the wagon turned out to be that of a woman. She wasn't his Addy. He was glad of it, and desolate, too. Thin as a rake handle, the woman wrapped her wiry arms around her body as though to keep herself from further harm, carrying both grief and hardness in her eyes. She'd told him she'd been sold away from her child. She'd muttered the words so he could barely hear her. He'd nodded as though her tragedy had been prophesied. Her words awoke his empathy. He sat next to her and wouldn't leave her side. When the wagon arrived at the plantation and stopped at the Negro quarters, he'd helped her down.

They were put in the same cabin.

The row of cabins was bare of any character or greenery, each exactly alike—brown weathered wood surrounded by brown dusty earth. A half-barrel stood by a high gray-brown palisade of a fence that encompassed the Negro quarters and kept them hidden from sight of the big house. A chair stood outside one of the cabins, and it was here they were brought. Standing on the threshold and peering into the dark interior, James suddenly remembered Perry's cabin at Gaines's, the colorful quilts and rag rugs, the table Perry had hewn himself, the kettle from which stews and grits emerged. He thought of Elizabeth with her long smooth braid, and the children, his own Libby, and his newborn son. There was nothing in him but grief now. It was the remembering, and for a long time he wished with all his heart he hadn't remembered anything. Especially not Addy, sewing, pregnant with James, Jr., listening to his tales about life in his former enslavement, then lying on the birth bed as they said their marriage vows with Preacher Green. To whom would he tell the tale of the Burton household? His brief, sporadic, sweet knowledge of home. If he spoke of it, he might bring it to the light of day where it would no longer be the jewel it was. Thoughts had a way of being reduced by words.

When he'd gone outside, the deep scattering of stars reminded him of everything beyond his reach; he'd stepped into a night filled with the sounds of crickets and cicadas and frogs—life teeming around him—and sought the comfort of the chair. He'd put his hands to his face and wept.

That moment crept into his thoughts now as he picked cotton with stiff, sometimes bloody hands. Looking back over the time since he was captured, he felt he'd been wasting away. He did as he was told, but walked down the long, hot rows with damnation on his lips for every white soul that lived. He became the dull giant they'd announced at his auction. What no one could know, and what he couldn't himself see, was that he now lived almost entirely among his memories. Even when Sara, the woman he lived with, delivered his second daughter, even when she wept over the infant she called Leola with what he knew was gratitude and a regained sense of purpose, he simply stared. Not caring was worst of all. Only his anger let him know he was still alive.

MATTIE, 2000

---

*T*hat last summer in Dorchester keeps rollin' by me. I ain't free of it. I see what was me with my thoughts wanderin' through the night before first light and before the birds began, then wakin' up to rememberin', always the sharpest before my eyes even opened. Maybe that's what hell is right there on earth. Things you maybe could have done somethin' about, or done differently come back to haunt you. Sometime, if the diesel monster cut off, I'd stare into the dark and miss the noise, the company of it. In a long night, there'd be nothin' to do but listen to the quiet, waitin' for sleep to come. And now that I'm free to go anywhere and there ain't no sleep and no wakin' up either, I keep lingerin' where my shack used to be, bothered about things I can't change.

I see myself sittin' in my kitchen starin' at beet greens. The red veins reach out along the leaves in the same way tree branches do. *If there's a God's plan, this is it,* I thought. Families branch out in the same way, space between members widenin' until they no longer touch each other, their beginnin's forgotten. I lived long enough to know six generations, two behind me, my own, and three after me. It was a privilege, after all, to see so far in either direction. And now I can see much farther, all the way back to Africa and the Caribbean, the darkest places of stealin' and betrayin' they ever was. But I have to ask myself, was my time any better? The time to come I'm scared to look at, 'though it's there, comin' at me on the wind.

Anyway, I watched myself go out in the middle of the night to wash beet greens. My sink was propped up on cinder blocks in the yard and over it was an old hand pump. The sink's back corners were rounded off in smooth white curves like a sculpture catchin' the light of the moon. The holes where the faucets should've been, stared out at me, ghostlike. The most ordinary things now are postmarks of my time. I loved that sink. Strange how a mind sifts through things and filters everythin' away until the only thing left is somethin' beautiful. Like comfort. I could never explain it or tell anyone.

The night's hush was all around, so when I started pumpin' water, the sound cut into it like the rush of sudden rain. Soon the pot was on the stove and the smell of my Georgia home was back again. So from my old trunk that came with me on the train to New York and on the bus to Maryland, I pulled out my picture album and opened the book somewhere in the middle to a picture of my younger brother, John, my Bo Pete, who'd cut out separate letters and numbers from the newspaper to spell out *World War II, Willie Thomas, 1944*, and pasted them above Willie's picture. John fought the Germans and came home, but Willie fought the Japanese and didn't. It was the reason that Thunderbird in my yard had a bumper sticker on it that said *America is #1 thanks to American Veterans.* There was a picture of John after the war, a city man, steppin' out in a new suit, his feet planted wide, his hat jaunty, smilin' a little like he was unsure of himself, uncomfortable in those new clothes. His thumbs stuck out from the fists at his sides as if pointin' to his stance, and I remembered how he always did that. Little Bo Pete. How he hated the name. Tears come. I missed him.

Then there was a picture of Grandma Pattyroll. She looked out to the side behind thick glasses like the sun was hurtin' her eyes. She had on her striped housedress, one she always wore, and her hands was in her lap 'long with her pocketbook. White sand stuck to the toes of her black oxfords. She never wanted to talk about slavery, but she did once, with her lips tight and gathered like it took all her strength. She say, "My father'd been a freeman. They sent him to work in the cotton fields anyhow." Grandma never liked complainin', or *whinin'* as she called it. She say, *You do with what you got.* She disallowed words that made you sound like you was helpless. In the picture, she held her head high despite the strong sun. Even the scary name, *Pattyroll,* was chewed down to the barest bones to be a name we all loved. I always wondered if her father had another family somewhere from when he was free. Just suppose Grandma Pattyroll had some half brothers and half sisters somewhere, a whole other branch spreadin' like the bloodred veins on a beet green.

Lookin' through the album, I turned to my favorite picture—Mama, 'bout fifteen year old, dressed in a white dress like an angel, her short hair thick and wild and fluffed out 'bout five inches 'round her face, her eyes already holdin' sadness, her mouth half open—a chile holdin' the first of five chilren, Baby Willie. The wood on the boards of the cabin behind her looked brand new. It was 1910. I can see all of it now. I see her gettin' up after the picture was taken and rockin' the baby who's cryin' his soul out, him no more than a few weeks old, all wrinkled, his little face screwed up. At least he was good for the picture.

And then, in another picture, was them narrow eyes starin' out at me—my husband, Plato. Plato Higgs. A hard man if there ever was one.

I stayed with my Aunt Mary till I was sixteen year old. She was glad to have me but after Alace left, I was lonely. I wrote a letter to my other aunt, Aunt Lizzie in Dania, Florida, hoping she'd give me some money. She sent me a ticket, and they put me on a train. I was scared to death because I'd never been on a train before. So there I was in Dania, packin' green tomatoes in wooden crates to go up North, and pickin' string beans. I got fifty cent a hamper full.

Plato worked mostly in the orange groves, but when I met him, he was workin' a fruit stand. Me and him—it all happen so quick. Next thing I knew, I was married.

I had my son. Had him at home with a midwife. No hospital or anythin'. There weren't any for colored. The doctor would come if you had complications or if you died. That was it. The midwife come and she'd be happy with whatever you give her. Even if it were only a dollar and a half.

Plato beat me. He gambled, and when he lost, he'd come home and take it out on me. Had a baby girl and when she were but six weeks old, Plato come home one night fists a-flyin'. I tole 'im, "This the last time you'll do me like that," and I grabbed a pair of scissors lyin' on the table and stuck the blades in his gut, all the way up to the handles. He went out the door yellin' and bleedin', more surprised than anythin'. But I didn't know that then. I thought I'd killed him.

I didn't know what would happen, so I left the chilren with my aunt, and she give me money to take the train back to my papa's in Blakely, Georgia. I remember comin' home and standin' on the porch with my aunt's valise in my hand. When Papa saw me standin' there cryin', he said right off, "Now, chile, what have you done so bad you had to leave your chilren?" He was a very understandin' man. I could tell him anythin'.

When I tol' him what happen, he say, "Mattie, you got to get yourself up North to New York, and stay with some of our peoples there." He give me money to go, and I went, knowin' I wouldn't see my kids for a long while. It was so hard. I like to die.

They doctored Plato and he lived and married again and beat that wife up, too. When I saw him years later, he say, "Mattie, why you do me like that?" and I say, "Why you do *me* like that?" There weren't no help for women who got beat up back then. You just stayed and took it or you decided to do somethin' 'bout it.

In New York, I found a job workin' for Heinz Catsup. Worked on the line and watched for the bottles what weren't full and put 'em back on the line. Then I got a job workin' at the Roosevelt Hotel peelin' vegetables. Peoples treated me good. You could go wherever you want and nobody minded. Even let us sit with 'em in the movies, buyin' our ticket like everbody else 'stead of goin' to the back and havin' 'em throw it at us like we was dogs. Made good money, too. I even bought me a hand-tailored suit and had my picture taken. It was a whole lot nicer than in the South. We went to the Apollo Theater a lotta times. Big name peoples were there, and there was a lot of music and dancin'. It was the first time I seen colored doin' somethin' besides pickin' crops.

Then when the war broke out, they rounded us up. Roosevelt say he needed ever man, woman, and chile. We were glad to do our part. They say, "You want to lay railroad ties or work in the scrap yard?" I picked the scrap yard. It was good money and not as hard as layin' ties. We sorted scrap metal when it rolled in on freight trains—old stoves and cars and washin' machines. We had to pick out the cast iron for bombs, and that would go on one conveyor belt. The other iron, for guns, tanks, and jeeps, would go on another belt. This go here and that go there. We call ourselves the pickatinnies.

I thought I was comin' up in the world. But after the war, in 1945, I was back in the fields. Went to Texas. Then I hear they need help with the cantaloupes in Maryland. So I come with a bunch of 'em to what they called "The Cantaloupe Capital of the World." Fifty year ago, it weren't nothin' but a railroad station, a few houses, and a little school surrounded by wide fields. We spent winter in town buildin' the wooden packin' boxes and summer out in the fields pickin' and packin,' and then we'd load the boxes on the train cars. If this was the capital of anythin', it was because we made it so. That first summer, I figured it was more of the same as down south, but I was only partly right.

We weren't much better off than in slave times, doin' what we was told, livin' where we was told, bein' paid cheap, and only pretendin' to be free. They even paid us to vote the way they said. Hell, for twenty-five dollars we'd vote any way they tol' us. Way I see it, slaves in the old days were no threat, but a free black, now, has to be beaten down. What they don't know is neither black nor white can be free with this happenin'. Funny how a body can *think* they free and not be, standin' there with wool pulled over their eyes. With a woman now, she knows she's never free, black or white. It's the *hope* of freedom what gets 'em through, though. A long time I wondered what freedom was. None of us weren't never as free as the people we worked for.

Oh, yeah. New York made me hope for so much. And that, in the end, weren't good. Me or nobody else could see past that old brown skin even though it covered up many a good heart. Meanwhile, even though there's no lines drawn in the space I find myself now, in my deepest heart, if you could say I still have one, there's black, there's Africa. Everythin' I seen only made it blacker. Not in anger, no. Just more *us* than ever. But I tell you, one good thing 'bout whatever this is—this aftertime. I can see a world where we'll be all mixed in, however long it take for everbody to be light brown, a pale mustardy color like old paper, darker than sand and lighter than marsh mud. It gonna take a while, but it will happen. It may be the only thing what saves us.

I put the album back in the trunk. It hit me then. I wasn't the mother to my chilren like my mother been to me. Take away the scissors on the table and a drunken husband, I mighta been a good mother. For sure, I meant to be. My son, dead of diabetes in his fifties, came to stay with me one year when he was a teenager. We got along fine. He went to the local high school but said he liked the school in Florida better, so I sent him back to his aunt. I guessed he turned out okay, he bein' minister of the Holiness Sanctified Church right there in Dania.

And there was my daughter, Juanita, who was mad at me on visits home. When she was old enough to be tol' I was her real mother come to visit, she cried and cried when I had to leave. What did better pay mean to a chile? She never forgive me. I never even give her a good Christmas like my mama did me.

When my time come, I went to Juanita and I explained everythin' again. I tol' her I raised many a chile, changed many a diaper, and wiped many a tooth-less grin, and always, always thought of my own as though tryin' to see 'em through a wall I couldn't break through. Years later, when I tol' her 'bout it one more time, I could see it didn't matter no more.

And neither did the stabbin'. The sight of that bloody wound in Plato's gut, the slight, slidin' sound of the scissors goin' in him, goin' in farther and farther, his screams, tortured me for years. But now it was just another story. I could still see him comin' toward me with his fists clenched and sweat streamin' down his face, his eyes narrow, comin' closer and closer, not in a hurry, but enjoyin' the thought of what he had in store for me, all his mad at the world rolled up in his fist and comin' toward my face. I loved him once. That's what hurt. My foolishness in lovin' him I blamed on myself. I never let it happen again, that stupid softness I had back then. But what did I know? How did anyone know what someone might do? He used to call me *Baby*.

I never hurt anyone again. But then I not been around family much, which could be a special hurt, the kind that could hang on like a canker sore that never heals. I knowed some kind of circle would be closed when I went back down to be with Juanita when the time come, and it was. There were grandchilren and great-grands to meet, but I was scared I'd have nothin' to say to 'em. When I left the fields, there was nothin' left of me, 'cept for them—for family—and my broken part along the branches of relatives that reached out across the South. Maybe that was enough.

The nights were long when I couldn't sleep, so many thoughts rushin' by me and I couldn't hush 'em. I'd go out the door to sniff at the day just when a bright sliver of sun was comin' up. Then the diesel started. Water sprayed out in thin, silvery lines along the pipes, but there weren't no rainbow from where I stood. Lookin' down the years, there weren't no rainbows for any of us, not for James Spry or Elizabeth, or any with dark skin. But there were short bursts of happiness, and we hung on to those. Now I watch families, them goin' from one to the other, talkin', workin', and I watch myself leavin' my family with a pain I didn't know I had when I was livin' it. Heads under one roof—the happiest of times—enough to bear us through the evils. I watch, and I know what each one is feelin' without anyone sayin' a word: Perry, Elizabeth, Addy, Libby, and the other chilren, and James, too. I stayed outside my own family, all the while lon-gin' for it. Those what have family close, do they know how lucky they be? No matter what comes of peoples' troubles, to know when the next meal comes, to have a bed to lay down on, to learn how to get through the good and bad, we get an education. You can see it on faces all through time: people are glad to belong to somethin' and live with or against it. How else do we get to know who we are?

God knows, the time for families is short. A collection of folks what lasts a minute, everbody sittin' like seeds in a milkweed pod waitin' to be taken by the wind and planted in a new life someplace else, never knowin' till they look back at how good it was.

My Georgia ties—they the strongest and clearest even now in the always. But pretty soon, I have to leave 'em alone. I have to go back in time far as I can go, pass Mama and Grandma Pattyroll, pass James Spry, all the way back to Elizabeth and the ones she took care of.

THE LANGUAGE OF THE FIELDS, 1850

The storm came bumbling in with clouds so dark it felt like night was coming on. Elizabeth ran to close the shutters. She saw Perry and Daniel in the field hurriedly pulling off ripened ears of corn. The children hid and chased one another along the rows, then ran off to the woods only to reappear at the deer path. As the wind picked up and the leaves of the trees showed their silvery undersides, she shouted, "Get to the house!" The first branch of lightning reached down over the woods. The children, loving the danger, screamed as they lit out across the garden patch toward home. She worried about them nearing the well where lightning had struck twice before, as if their claim on the land was cause for the white God's wrath. No, she told herself, white or no, it was just the way of the earth.

Perry pitched the sacks of corn in the corncrib and ran in behind the children. Elizabeth sat in her chair and waited. "Come now," she said. "Hysh. Sit down by me, quiet. When the Spirit sends sunshine, we do our work and we make our noise, but when there's thunder and lightnin', we sit and listen."

With the children gathered around, Elizabeth felt Perry's eyes on her and knew he was reveling in the moment. They both hated the idea that as the children grew, they would be hired out and, more than likely, living elsewhere, like twigs broken off from the main stem. Libby had already gone to work for the Prouses and did not keep it a secret that she hated the whole idea, even though she was mostly in the big house taking care of the newest baby, away from fieldwork. Daniel, almost twelve, husky and muscular enough to be a real help, would be off soon, too. He was a Johnson, born of a mother who'd been raped by one of the gang of kidnappers down Crotcher's Ferry way. She'd taken off for the North, promising to be back for her son, a fact Daniel brought up to Perry whenever he got hardheaded about something that had to be done. Mostly, though, the boy was cooperative and smart, already learning arithmetic and his letters at the preacher's Sunday school. He had a spark that drew others to him, and he was always rounding them up for some sort of game, letting them win when he saw that losing was too much for them.

Eziah Fleming, just nine, was the curious one, full of questions about how a thing worked and why. He was good with the youngest, James, Jr., and would bring him things to play with, a dried gourd with the seeds inside to shake or a milkweed pod to explode into a white cloud of fluff. He was the tree climber, watching from his perch for long hours. If he was missing, they knew where to look—in a large oak at the edge of the woods. Irrepressible, he would tell them as he was doing now in a whisper even though Elizabeth had told them to hush, about how the bucks scraped the ground and grunted when they wanted a doe. A burst of thunder drowned him out.

"I'll tell you somethin' that you don't know," she began in a low voice. "When I were a girl, I remember my grandmother tellin' how her people did, how the deer gave them whatever they needed, meat, hide for their clothes, bones and antlers to make tools. Deer come by just like they do now, when the nuts come off the trees. But one time in late spring, when my grandmother was still a girl, she seen a fawn by the side of a clearin'. No sign of a doe. She thought the deer was next to holy and wanted one for herself. She picked up the fawn—it was lighter than she expected—and soon she was makin' her way to the cabins where her tribe was. Her father told her to put it back where she'd found it, that what she'd done wasn't a kindness. There was no way to save the fawn once the doe was gone, but maybe the doe would come back. She cried and cried because at first, the fawn followed her and licked her hand, likin' the salt, so she sneaked it into a storage cabin and tried to feed it. She petted and kissed it, loved its big eyes and tiny mouth, promised she would take good care to not let any harm come.

But it wouldn't eat what she brought and only sucked her fingers. Come dark, she had to leave it, though she hated to. When she come back in the mornin', it was dead, the turkey buzzards already circlin'. Her father tol' her, 'The world has its own laws, its own ways. We can't change anythin' or interrupt what is. We can only change our own ways, our own will.' He was a wise man. He lived well."

She smiled down at the upturned faces, the whites of their eyes clean as new snow. She thought about all the varying circumstances that brought each of them to this place, not only her own gathering of children, but also her grandparents with their feet in free soil, knowledgeable, cultured, left to run or be stirred into the dark race in a state of flux, owned or disowned, placed or displaced, all of them now with mixed faces, mixed lineage, mixed ideas, mixed fortunes, mixed religions. What would come of it? Secrets of endurance passed on, she decided, and a unity among them. And because of it, strength. A riptide.

The storm raged; thunder rolled. The children sat still, expectant, and asked for another story. She obliged them with one of her grandfather who, as he left these shores, took the bones of his ancestors across the Chesapeake to settle somewhere else, she didn't know where, leaving her and her mother who by then had a husband of Negro blood and would not leave. What she did not tell them was how her grandfather had stood on the sandy shore, his face like a stone made beautiful by the waters of his grief, then turned his back and boarded his fishing boat along with his wife. That he was torn between leaving and staying was evident. That his way of life could not be broken as easily as that of new generations was made evident in the insistent way he did not look back, but put the paddles in the water and silently, silently pushed ahead with the others, leaving no trace. She never forgot the silence, nor the strength of his resistance as the dugout traveled toward the horizon. Instead of her sadness, she told them how he cut saplings that would easily bend and used them to build a series of horseshoe-shaped stays that when he covered them with hide, made a house. She told them her people abandoned their cabins whenever they began to sink into the earth, and she told them how, after about five years, the people moved to new hunting grounds and found new places to forage and farm. She told them how the land was free and they were all free to use it.

Elizabeth missed Addy, who'd taken up with Chambers on the next farm over. Elizabeth didn't see her much except in the fields. By summertime, it was obvious that Addy was pregnant. Elizabeth knew it was a natural thing for a woman to seek comfort and a substitute for the coldness of her bed. When Addy's time came, Elizabeth was glad to be there for the birth, a boy named Thomas. Yet Elizabeth longed for Addy to be home. She found herself watching for Addy to appear at the door, the newborn wrapped in one of her quilts. Maybe the child would come to stay with them in time. But dear Addy, whose apron was always the whitest of white, whose plumpness and ready smile exuded warmth and easiness, was a woman any man would be taken with. Of all the children, Elizabeth had to admit that Addy would always be her favorite, hers but not hers, the first of the borrowed many, and with her came the realization of family. They'd been blessed. But Addy was not particular enough about who she stayed with. Her lonesome heart could never be satisfied. And too, Elizabeth understood Addy's pride, the struggle not to depend on her and Perry. In any case, Addy knew she and Perry would always be there to help out, and they'd take the new baby, too, if Addy couldn't find a way.

The shutters rattled and rain hammered the roof. In such a wind, the corn would be beaten down, roads would flood, and trees would fall, which was why she was humming now with the children still sitting before her, her song keeping time to the rhythmic squeak of her rocking chair. James, Jr., almost six and big for his age like Libby, was soon asleep in a heap on the floor.

Perry took out his knife and began to whittle. The chips flew away and soon the wood revealed a shape: a small skiff with oars. He'd made one for each of the boys. This one was for James, Jr., who, at the next clap of thunder, woke with a start.

The land was paid for. One-third of it was already cleared. They had a house, a mule and a cow, and seeds they kept in a tin against the mice and damp weather. They'd gathered wild blackberries and preserved them; apples lay in sand in the root cellar. From the knowledge of her ancestors, from her mother's side, from the nearby Indian village of Chicone, she knew where to gather *tuckahoe*, the tubers found in the wetlands along the shores of the river. She knew when the shad and herring would run, and that the nearly cleared ground would yield an abundance their first few years before the woody plants took hold, and then there would be the thickets that would come, yielding black cherry and wild grape. She knew about the many plants usable as greens in the spring, knew that young milkweed was edible as well as little barley, the *mattoume,* and that the roots of sassafras would produce tea. Before the corn came in was the hungriest time and they'd had to forage, but the variety of food was welcome. When more of the land was cleared, they would be able to plant wheat and oats. Meanwhile, they had enough from their labors. Next year they would have their own corn milled. It had been the best year of her life and Perry's, too.

Did he think much about the distance he'd come even if it was only just across the road? Where he once had to bow and scrape, he, a black man, owned land in a place where few black men owned anything. Owning made all the difference. Her Perry was born again. *Now* was what mattered and she hoped he'd forgotten the rest. The last payment had been made and the land was theirs, an idea that startled both of them as they remarked to each other in the night. Being free had meant keeping wages. True, it meant living in danger of being sold back, but then neither of them had ever expected to own land and now they did. All they needed was the deed.

She listened to the scrape of the knife on the toy boat in Perry's hands. He finished shaping the bow and began to hollow out the hull. James, Jr., crept to his side to watch.

"Not too close, boy, 'fore I cut off your nose," said Perry, and laughed softly, lifting his head to catch her eye.

LIBBY, 1850

The tremor of cicadas had begun, rising with the heat of midmorning, then lowering amidst the high, nervous pitch of crickets. Small brown moths, their wings slowly pulsing, rested in a cluster on the ground where Libby Spry, now twelve, stood barefoot. She set down the weighty basket of warm tomatoes as if she had all day, daring to steal a moment, pretending not to care if she did get caught. But she did care, of course, and she glanced around to see if anyone was watching, then stooped to get a closer look at the wings that were fine, intricate patchworks of black, yellow, and brown velvet, and she felt a secret, quiet joy that later she was to recall as happiness, at the luck of coming upon the moths fluttering in a full moon shape on her path.

Her attention was broken then by mosquitoes buzzing around her ears and the need to slap her cheek. She began a wild dance, waving her thin arms about her head and swiping one leg onto the other to brush off the swarm, the temptation to waste time thwarted. She retrieved the basket and continued hurriedly, toes sending up small puffs of dust as she walked. *The moths had dropped down like scattered corn seed,* she thought, like herself, with a plan laid out plain and hard and straightforward. She would have preferred to ask the why of things: why the moths had gathered like this and why she'd been sent to the Prouse farm with nothing to say about it. She was, after all, free.

"Hysh," Elizabeth had said. "Free, yes. But a free colored." And that was that.

The moths would soon die, probably with the rise of the new moon, in a sequence Libby knew well having watched carefully all her young life. Watching, Elizabeth had told her, was the way to save herself. But Libby's watching was different from Elizabeth's, which was concerned with larger views. Libby's was confined to the field or the path to the house or Mr. Eben Prouse's newest baby whose care fell to her. The certainty of her life of labor was fixed, yet her name was not—Burton or Barton, or Boston, or Buxton. It sounded different every time she'd heard it, although Elizabeth said Buh-nnn, one sound indistinguishable from another like the flow of a single note wandering through time and space, but Prouse said something like *button.*

"You needn't be worryin' about any of it," Elizabeth had told her. "Like I tol'you, I'm not your mama, chile. Your mama is Addy and your other name is Spry. Your daddy's a Spry and there ain't no denyin' that with your long fingers and big hands. You goin' to be tall like him." Now there was a nagging mystery. Was her father alive and living somewhere far away from them? Didn't he want to come home? She couldn't imagine he didn't want to be with them. He must be dead. Or he must be a slave. It was one of the questions no one could answer. And Preacher Green just set his mouth in a straight line and shook his head when she'd asked him.

But now Preacher Green said her name like she wanted to hear it, *Elizabeth,* and he would add *Burton* because that was who had raised her. The sounds rolled off his tongue and caught in his even white teeth as if the name had some bite to it, a shape she could see. The first time he'd said it, she didn't know he was speaking to her except he was studying her with eyes that considered her and she understood then why he was the preacher. He could hold people just with his eyes and he knew not only the meaning of words but also their true sounds. All her life she'd answered to Libby, yet she knew it was her name she heard when he said, *Elizabeth,* and she took it like a gift and laid back her shoulders.

Her father was gone. Her mother was hired out to other farms and often stayed in the slave cabins with the other help, only coming home when she was poorly, an occurrence that was repeated when the weather was the hottest. Then she began staying at Levin Chambers' cabin. Addy told Libby she could come live with them if she wanted to, that Chambers was a freeman with a cabin all to himself since his wife had died. Yet whenever Libby could get away, it was to Elizabeth and Perry's cabin she chose to go to. More than likely her mother would become a Chambers. Then surely Libby's name would be different from everyone around her but James, Jr. It would seem they belonged to no one. And she would be taken. But to have Elizabeth Burton's name made them all family, with a mother and a father and children and a house of their own. As they stood in the sun after church, Preacher Green nodded at her namesake, Elizabeth, the woman who'd raised her. Libby Spry glanced at Elizabeth, who shook her head, *no.*

"Now don't you be tellin' the chile that just because she want to hear it," said Elizabeth who tried to give the appearance of not doting on any of the children in her charge, for she'd only borrowed them and might have to give them back one day.

"Elizabeth," the preacher had said, "the Lord sent you this child after he took yours. There's a reason. And there'll be more if you'll have 'em. There's more comin', don't you know?"

"I don't mind the chile. What I mind is her dreamin' all the time, changin' names."

"All around us people change names. Run. Hide. There's worse she could be doin'. In the end, it may be the thing that saves her, her father not bein' free no more and her mother in the fields and poorly half the time."

They were better off than slaves. Elizabeth said so. It meant they paid rent, earned their keep, and fed themselves. But it meant, too, that if anything happened to her mother now that her father was gone, she would no longer be free. She'd be taken for sure. Indentured. Anyway, it was the same as being owned. *Take you to the Orphan Court,* the women in the field had warned. The thought of not being free sounded bad, although how it would be different Libby was not sure. She worked at the Prouse farm. While Perry worked for Mr. John Prouse, she worked for his brother, Mr. Eben Prouse, along with Elizabeth. But she, Libby, *stayed* with the Prouses. It was the *staying* she didn't like. She longed to be back in Elizabeth's cabin, sleeping on Elizabeth's floor, hearing Elizabeth call her before the sun came up, and drinking hot tea from Elizabeth's cup. Many a morning she'd wake up to a bow for her hair Elizabeth had made from scraps of cloth she'd woven herself. Once she woke up to a doll Elizabeth had made during the night. It had corn silk hair and was stuffed with milkweed from the seed pods she and Elizabeth had gathered in the field, for Elizabeth and Perry now had a field.

The acid-sweet steam of the tomatoes cooking on the porch kitchen beckoned as she dug her toes in the path and glanced sideways at the flat landscape beyond. Like her mother, combing the rows with a hoe would probably be her passage through this life. The sun was hot on her back. Perspiration ran down between her small breasts as if in answer to the cicadas' call. She was tall for her age, *You goin' be big like your Daddy*, Elizabeth told her. Her sudden burst of height this year seemed to be the reason Elizabeth stopped calling her *Baby*. "We're blessed," Elizabeth said. "The Prouses are good. Eben—he works hard, pays his debts, keeps his word, and works alongside his help. All the Prouses do the same way. 'Though John, he goin' to get in trouble one of these days, owin' everbody. But they all Methodists. None of them Prouses ever whipped their help, I know of. You quit your complainin', Libby. I'll make sure you treated fair. Go and earn your keep and ever cent we'll put aside. I promise you."

Skirting the moths at her feet, Libby walked toward the porch kitchen. The tomatoes in her basket were for the pot, not the wagon heading to the dock, where the steamer to Baltimore would soon arrive. She'd never tasted one; she'd heard they could make a person dreadful sick. Miz Prouse laughed at her and shook her head. The tomatoes were for catsup and canning whole, she said, and she would show Libby how. Two of the Prouse children played on the ground. She envied them, just playing. Then she heard the baby cry, and Miz Prouse holler, "Libby!" her face steaming red over the pot of boiling water as Libby hurried inside. The child pulled at her mother's skirt, but it was Libby who picked her up, Libby who made her laugh, Libby she clung to now, her fat hand patting Libby's thin arm.

"Take the pot off the fire, and put the tomatoes in the water while I nurse her. Then scoop them out one by one and start peelin'. Skin'll come right off." Miz Prouse, her brown hair escaping the knot behind her head, pulled the baby from Libby and sat down on a small, black rocker, the white of her breast like no white Libby had ever seen, like the moon let out behind pewter clouds, a white startlingly beautiful, but frightening too, a deadly omission on God's part, where everything else in the world was so full of color. She looked away. It was because of that whiteness that Miz Prouse was free, while she, Libby, was only free because her mother, Addy, was, and that only by luck if you could call it that. You could be set free because your master promised you would be when he died, or because someone paid for your freedom. She was free, but she had no papers. But even if she did have, if the pattyrollers caught you, they took your papers. They could sell you, and no one would care. No one would look for you or put a reward out unless you were owned. Like her father. No one looked for him, but he must have been worth a lot at auction. He was so strong he could lift her high in the air. He'd pick her up in his huge hands and move his arms up and down, up and down, and she'd be squealing and giggling like she was swinging from a good strong tree. It was all she could remember of him.

"How 'bout if you make my mama change her name to Burton?" she'd asked Elizabeth. "Then me and James could be Burtons, too."

But Elizabeth just laughed. "And what if your daddy shows up and says, 'Where's my family? Where's my wife, Addy Spry, and my daughter, Libby Spry, and my son, James Spry, Jr.?' What then?"

And for the first time Libby dared hope he'd be back. Elizabeth thought so and that was proof enough. He'd protect them all, big and strong as he was. But then what if her mother married Levin Chambers because she didn't know Libby's father was coming back?

Elizabeth just said, "Never mind thinkin' 'bout it and worryin' yourself to death! You just keep yourself safe. You never let on your daddy's gone or your mother neither and you always watch. There was a boy, near about ten, just playin' in his yard. Someone come up and snatched him right then and there without his mother even knowin' and he was sold to the Georgia man. So you watch, girl, and stay close."

Which was why after Miz Prouse gave the baby back to her, and while she changed the baby and washed and dried between the deep creases and rolls of her thick thighs, she was jealous that the baby girl was white. She would never need papers to prove anything at all, and Libby wondered deep inside her where she hoped it would never show, what kind of God would make white and dark skin and favor one over the other. And she, Libby Spry, alias Elizabeth Burton, had to say she loved the God of Preacher Green but didn't know if He loved her back, and fully expected to be struck dead on the spot. When it didn't happen, she smiled at the baby, and the baby, speaking in tongues, gurgled something back. She took her to the path, to the circle of moths still pulsing in the brown sand, and it was only when little Ebbie reached out to grab them that they dispersed into the air, unreachable. The baby shrieked, and Libby swatted a mosquito off her arm.

She felt safe holding her. No harm would come to her then. The baby was her shield against someone stealing her, an event that occurred nearly every night in her dreams, ever since Elizabeth told her about her father.

Just gone, Libby, without a trace 'cept for the scuffs on the ground. The silence of it haunted her.

"You can't hear 'em come up on you, sometime," the women in the field told her as they hoed or picked. The stories made Libby afraid. "They wrap the horse's hooves in burlap, so even the horse be quiet," they said. Libby wished the women would just sing as they worked, not talk, for then she herself was quieted as their singing flung into the breeze, filling her with purpose and hope.

There were other stories passed in the field, sometimes whispered into the young corn leaves as the women hoed, glancing around to see where Mr. Prouse was. For the ones who were hired out, most of the talk was about running, about those who'd tried and failed, and the ones who probably made it. For the ones who were free, it was the fear of being owned again and the anxiety of not knowing one's fate. Out of that grew the nobler cause: the desire to help their own kind, hide them, become part of the undercurrent toward freedom.

"You only have to get to Baltimore," they said. "Steamboat."

"Not without papers," they said.

"Walk to Delaware," they said, "then on up to Pennsylvania. People along the way take you in."

"There's some doin' it," they said.

"Passin' right through here."

"Some go the river way. Hide in the marsh grass."

"You need a skiff to go the river way."

"Wilmington ain't far enough now. Baltimore neither. They catch you they bring you back to the man 'cause you runaway *property*. You can't be free up to Pennsylvania or New York neither. Best if you can make it all the way to Canady."

"Lot of 'em leavin'."

"It just goin' to make the man madder, take it out on those what's free."

"Can't blame 'em what gets beat. That's reason enough."

"Man run a week ago. Up near the Delaware line."

"Hysh!"

Footsteps. The overseer. The woman whispered, "They got 'im."

Now Libby hung onto the baby as she walked toward the farmhouse. It was Saturday. She'd get paid and maybe Perry would come by for her. She hoped she could stay with Elizabeth until Sunday night. She would listen to the talk at Preacher Green's church Sunday morning. There would be more stories, more singing, and the promises. She would sing with the rest: *Moses, I hear the horses comin', Praise God!* She wasn't sure if that meant she could hear the horses coming to get her and she'd have time enough to hide, or horses that would bring release. And then afterward, there would be the lessons. She could already write her name. She would think about that. She would lay her worry aside.

She loved Preacher Green because he knew the Way that no one would say out loud. But Libby knew. Because where had the children come from? The ones Elizabeth took in without a word, whose parents had been stolen or run away in the night, children whose names were not always connected with people they knew, like Eziah and Daniel. Some hung onto the promise they'd be sent for later. Some accepted their fate with the next meal. Elizabeth shielded them all. If Perry didn't come by Saturday night, he would get her for church and with the children gathered around her, Elizabeth would say, "Libby, where you been, girl?" and hold her to her heart. The same tired dark eyes would look at her, eyes that believed in work like it was something holy. Elizabeth. Who'd weaved and sewed and hoed until she could buy Perry, who worked as hard as Perry so they could get the land. Well, almost. Except for the deed. "That's what bein' free is, Libby," Elizabeth had said, "Ownin' land."

Didn't the Bible say it? To be a good servant was noble and she was lucky. She'd never been whipped. None of them were ever whipped. Maybe that was what being free meant, that you didn't get whipped.

"Libby!" She brought the baby back to Miz Prouse and waited. Eben Prouse came up the porch steps, his shirt wet with perspiration and his face dotted with mosquitoes which he furiously brushed away. He leaned over the railing and spit. "Goddamn 'squitoes. Time a man opens his mouth they rush in. I need you in the field, Libby. Them tomatoes need to be picked."

A few weeks ago, Prouse took time to explain that tomatoes weren't poisonous as Addy and the rest of the help believed. That was when he picked one off the vine and ate it in front of them.

"Oh, Mr. Prouse, sir, you goin' be dead by mornin'!" Libby called out.

He shook his head and laughed. "Miz Prouse thought that, too, at first," he said. "I read about it in the papers. George Washington had them in his garden. One thing you can't do, though, is eat them from a pewter plate. Acid in the tomato draws out the lead in the plate and that's what poisons you."

She didn't know what a pewter plate was or acid either, and now he was saying, "Libby, you stay over Sunday. We have to get the tomatoes off the field. Too many split because of the rain." Plans of a day at Elizabeth's disappeared down the long rows in front of her where the vines sat in tangled lumps, reaching stray branches across the rows. The women and children scattered with their baskets. She set hers down at her feet, her disappointment exhausting her. On the first plant was a caterpillar, fatter than any she'd ever seen, and as long as her middle finger. She screamed and recoiled, then feeling foolish, carefully reached between the leaves for the first tomato of the long weeks that stretched through all of summer.

THE FIRE, 1852

---·•·---

August Woodson, wheelwright, worked alone in his shop this morning, sweeping shavings from the day before, the sleeves of his upper arms tight against muscle. The smell of newly cut oak rose from the dirt floor, but he no longer smelled it. The air in any other place smelled strange to him as though it were missing an essential element. He worked without a fire, thankful for the cool of November. There were no mosquitoes now, and the trees revealed themselves as the last of the leaves fluttered down, standing plain and simple, like truth. He loved the sight of a bare tree, for his concern was the wood. He stood with his hands on his hips and gazed at the great white oak that stood beside his shop. He often talked to it, the tree being his closest avenue to a kind of religion, or maybe it *was* God for all he knew. Certainly a tree made a man look up to things greater than he.

He'd brought in the logs at his feet the day before, and he was already deciding which of these he would use for hubs. They had to be cut precisely into sixteen-inch pieces and left with the bark on to season for years, sometimes as many as eight, depending on the type. The wood could not be rushed even though he hollowed out each piece with the auger to help in the drying. Choosing the wood for a hub was like reaching into the future, for everything about a wheel depended on the hub. Leaving his work on earth, a man could reach into a time he might not see, which didn't matter so long as what reached into the coming years was as good as it could be.

A son reached into the future, too. But sons had their own ways. They didn't always follow the way of the father, and there was nothing he could do about that. Still, he taught his own how it was with him at every opportunity, and one day, his son would choose. Knowing how to make a good wheel would stand him in good stead, a bit of perfection to work for. He watched the boy run from the cabin with a warm biscuit, his dark hair falling about his eager, slim face that resembled his mother's. He had her large, gray eyes as well. He was still too young to hold the other end of the saw for the cutting of logs. August worried that his son had no meat on his bones, his future strength not even hinted at.

"Sweep the rest of those chips, eh?" he said to the large eyes that seemed to take up half the boy's face. The boy nodded and offered the biscuit, which August took, the warmth of it reminding him that the air had grown damp, and he had better build a fire in the shop, not for himself or the boy but for the sake of the wheels already begun. Later, he would show his son how to use the two-handed saw, let him lay his hands on one end so he could feel the motion as his father worked.

William. The boy's name was William. August had been afraid to use it after all the sons he'd lost, as if he were under some kind of curse where naming was an assumption that didn't apply to him. Five of them had died at birth. Once, he'd asked the tree why all but one of his sons had died, but the tree only stirred in the wind, its leaves turning this way and that.

The next morning, the wind changed, bringing the stench of pigs and erasing the smell of clean wood. The village was called Slab Town, and for all Woodson's hard work and dignity, it angered him to live in a place that was named after the dwellings of pigs. He enjoyed saying his was the first business in these parts, the wood expert who had settled here before the pig keepers, and he'd declare to whoever would listen that the noble task of making wheels overpowered the ignoble stench of raising pigs. Spinning wheels, wagon wheels, oxcart wheels, and now, the order for a paddle wheel for the grist mill would become Woodson's largest and most challenging undertaking. How could a man be taken seriously about his work in a place called Slab Town, named for the slabs of wood that sheltered pigs, a place where foul odors could knock down a full-grown man?

As he turned a small hub of wood on his lathe, he thought he'd try to change the name of the town he lived in, but soon forgot his intentions when he became absorbed in the cylinder's transformation into a hub shape, the bulged middle and narrowed ends like a spool thick with cord. He loved the light, fragile curls of wood shavings that dropped at his feet, the pure, delicate wood whose quality extended from strength to ephemeral—from wheels to ashes. Like man. Suddenly he looked up, his pleasure ruined by the overpowering stench. The name of the town was as insidious as the odor, and he would press for a change in the name to Williamsburg after his son, to good purpose and promise for the boy's legacy. Despite his intentions to dwell on something good this morning, there remained an undercurrent of anger, a darkness spilling into his day and tainting it.

In the night, he'd heard a man running. Through the window, he could see the figure was dark as the moonless night itself, barefoot, breathing heavily as though he'd run a long way. The man stepped out of the trees and ran toward the road. He passed directly under August's tree, the one beside the shop. Taking stock of the house and its surrounding, he appeared to be looking for a place to hide. A few others had stopped here, mistaking his house for the one up the road, one that would take in runaways for a day or two and then help them to the next "station," but his wasn't one of those. He admired the black man's daring. Fear made a man weak, and August knew about fear. It seemed to him he was born afraid. He never remembered a time when he was free of it except maybe in the long hours in his shop with his hands busy and his mind occupied. At dusk, it would come again. It would descend with the night and strangle him in his dreams. Yes, he knew fear.

Last night, he was startled by the first faint bark, so faint the sound could barely be recognized. His mind filled in the rest, the advancing dogs, the men behind them, an enslaved man running, his capture, and his cries replicating the sounds of the dogs, a circle of sound unbroken by anything rational or kind. The dogs, in a frenzy, their constant yips and cries and steady oncoming progress through the woods frightened them all, Kay, his wife, and the boy, and although August wished to appear gruff and merely annoyed, his heart fluttered wildly so that he was no help to either Kay or his son. He broke out in a sweat.

He'd wanted to open the doors to his shop and home. He wanted to tell the man to hide among the half-finished wheels or the pile of wood scraps, or to jump in one of the barrels that held bark soaking for the tanner. If he could have commanded the wind to change at that moment so that the pig stench would erase traces of man scent, he would have. But he could not open his door. He would not jeopardize that for which he'd worked, or his small family. He could not change the face of his fear nor answer it.

So the anger he felt this morning after the predictable outcome, was mostly directed at himself, but some of it was at the ones who kept others in fear. He knew them, the patrollers who hung around Crotcher's Ferry on a Saturday night. He knew the roughness of their ways and the stealth of what they did that hovered over everything. It was worse than the pig smell. He turned the hub-shape and ran his hands over the widest part to see if it was ready to be mortised and receive the oak he'd so carefully seasoned for the spokes. He forced his mind to focus on the hub, to see if it was ready for the pit that would hold it while he gouged out the holes where the spokes would be imbedded. With a great deal of effort, he thought only of the spokes, only of the shape of the hub, only of the mortising, only of what there was to do next. He clung to the wood. It made sense, and held a reliability his mind and heart could not harbor. There couldn't be anything that asked more of him than a wheel. Center, balance, precision, the character of the wood, the exact curves of the felloes—even the tools he'd made were beautiful. The traveler's wheel that measured the circumference of the circle had to be perfect, and it was. He'd made it himself. The plane had to be perfect, too, and he loved the reddish glow of the handle that fit smoothly in the palm of his hand, almost like something he could worship. He'd made that, too, and the spoke-hammer, pulling his arm in an arc as it swung over the spokes to secure them into the hub. Did God know sour gum would be best for the hub, that oak would become the spokes and axles, hickory for the felloes? Was that why all those trees were in abundance for the taking on these shores?

If that was so, he must be part of the plan, too, even though his guess was that it was all too self-centered, too egotistical to imagine the world was made for man. Surely, it was the other way around. Still, if a man's life could be measured in how well he fit into that world and used its gifts, he'd fulfilled a mission.

He had secrets about wheels he would never share except with his own son. Secrets hard won—his understanding of how the combinations of wood he chose would work together in the wheel and how each kind of wood would season and what had to be done for it to reach optimum strength and weathering. The second hub before him, seasoned and augured, he would mortise, and it would be ready to receive the spokes by dusk and then he would leave it. Now with the short, stubby handle of the mortise chisel, he began the rectangular cuts carefully marked and evenly spaced around the hub, pushing with his hand and shoulder which pained him at intervals. He kept on.

August worked through the winter. By May, wheels in various stages rested here and there in his shop, the distinctive color of each piece of wood naming it. Six new wheels stood ready for the blacksmith, and he looked forward to the drive tomorrow with the boy by his side when they'd go to the smithy in town.

The trees, replenished, gave green to the landscape and shade to hot roads. Puffs of warm wind played with new rye and brought the green-yellow pine pollen that settled itself everywhere. Good, clean oak planks, stripped of their bark to hasten the drying, lay in the sun. He loved the color of new wood, white-yellow inside the rough bark, just waiting to be free of it. He'd stop at the smithy and bring the bark to the tanner, drive on to the mill north of town to see about hickory. Even though thick woods went on for miles behind his land, nowhere could he find the essential hickory.

He hungered for news. His world was his shop. He was well satisfied with it. His house, which stood but a few feet away and his place on this shore between two rivers seemed peaceful enough. When he left it for the necessary trips to town, the rumblings in his own heart were so loud they often became a cacophony of unbearable sound. Then, he was brought face-to-face with the auction market and the strange dilemma would begin: his own macabre fascination and his valiant attempt to ignore it. He tried to ignore, too, the slave trad-ers who traveled through and he searched their faces, wondering if any one of them would be familiar. There was talk among the farmers that free Negroes were brought to town and hidden in one of the houses, chained to the walls until they could be taken south—another one of those recurring thoughts that plagued him.

The town of East New Market was a well-ordered place. Two roads entered at right angles and crossed where Indian fur traders made their deals and stage-coaches came through in the old days. The Episcopal Church stood on the western end of town and the Methodist on the eastern, as if proclaiming to all residents the limits to which civilized society should adhere. The town had solidarity, a long history, and upstanding citizens who were models for all. He admired the large brick homes of the doctors, lawyers, and landowners that lined the streets. Set back from the road, Friendship Hall was the grandest of them all, a plantation dwelling said to be built of bricks used as ballast on the ships from England. Behind the house lay a racetrack of commendable size.

On Main Street, visitors and slave traders were likely to be found at the tav-ern. Just across the street, holding its own in defiance of debauchery, stood the white-framed Temperance House, where members (mostly women and the few men they could persuade) were sworn to sobriety. The female seminary had just opened for educating the daughters of the wealthy, and next to it was the funeral home with its ornate carriages, one painted white for carrying the very young, others painted black. Side by side, with its twin harmonies of noise and smells, stood the smithy and the tannery, places where the men were likely to congregate while the women frequented the grocery and open market.

August wanted to feel reassured about the righteousness of his world, yet his bane was not only to doubt but also to keep his doubts to himself. He was alone in a crowd of men, perhaps even more so then. In such a mood, it would be best to avoid town this morning. Things were as they were, he told himself. If men of means sometimes sold their Negroes for the cotton fields in Georgia and slave traders watched for possible sales of human flesh to fill the ships that left the small town of Vienna for the South, why should he criticize them? He had his own devilment on his conscience. It was the way the world worked. And for some, it worked well. Outside of town stood Colored Town, far enough from the center of things but near enough for its population to serve the big houses. He would go to the colored smithy there who didn't charge as much.

After packing the wheels and lunch in his wagon, August drove along the green fields with the boy sitting silently by his side. He'd have the wheels he'd made banded with iron, which would tighten the wooden fittings and lock them together for all time. It was a compromise. He'd made hundreds of wheels with wooden shoes. Succumbing to metal felt like he was giving up something of his skill.

By the time they arrived at the shop, the day's heat had descended, made even warmer by the explosive fire that belched out of the furnace. The Negro had opened its door and pulled out red hot iron that would be a horseshoe. Shirtless, and wearing a leather apron over his overalls, the man's body glowed like the metal.

"You're Preacher Green's son, aren't you?" August asked.

Sam Green, Jr. nodded. "Learnin' the trade," he said. His eyes looked sideways, not directly. Never directly. Just before he began hammering, and quickly, before the metal cooled, he said, "Mr. Moore be back soon, sir. Just stepped out a minute." He pronounced his words carefully, as if the sound of them mattered. A preacher's son. Then he began hammering, and the sharp ringing began its rhythm while August and the boy watched. The iron took shape. Then holding the tongs that bit the cooling metal, Green returned to the furnace to heat the metal again, turning enough for August to see the stripes across his back and upper arms, rivers of dark slashes, flesh that had mended into hard cords. August could not pull his eyes away as if the least he could do was acknowledge the scars, feel them in some way.

The blacksmith, Moore, entered his shop. He nodded at the wheelwright as he turned to slip the strap of his leather apron over his head.

"Hear the news, sir?" he said, shouting over the hammering.

August shook his head.

"Cambridge courthouse been burnin' since yesterday afternoon. All the records are gone. People'll be scramblin' about their deeds and all."

Sam Green, Jr.'s eyes stayed on his work. August knew the full story would come if he was patient. The network of information, like the river at high tide, would have spilled over with the news during the night. Negroes knew more than they would reveal, but Moore was unusually talkative this morning.

"Sounds suspicious to me," Moore said. "Maybe somebody set that fire, wantin' to get rid of some papers."

August waited.

"You hear 'bout the case in the court?"

August shook his head.

Moore went on. "Woman named Green was s'posed to be freed at forty-five. She never been tol' and now she be sixty. Don't make no difference no how. She ain't never gonna win, papers or no papers. She might be a relative of his, don't know," and he nodded toward Sam Green, Jr.

How did Moore know he, August, would sympathize? How did Moore know he was connected in the way all men are connected to what is just? Did Moore know of his guilt? August almost succeeded in aloofness until he again noticed the stripes on Green's back.

Moore went on. "They callin' for wills now, copies of anythin' you got." Maybe it was the fire that had excited him. Fire was in his blood, especially the knowledge of how fire could even change iron. His was a life of respectability. He was one of the trustees for Mount Zion Church. A rarity, he was a free black man with a business.

"How many wheels you got there, sir?"

The hammering had begun again, so August held up eight fingers, then walked to the wagon, and as he carried the wheels into the shop, he was careful to avoid looking at the man with the scars.

On their way to the mill, he and the boy had to drive through town. The women floated on the sidewalks in their wide skirts and waved to the people in the gigs and surreys. The young girls, on their way home from the seminary, called to one another. The town went on about its business. The giant sycamores along the streets made a tunnel of green, doors slammed, horses clopped, water splashed from a small fountain into a trough, a gentle breeze stirred the roses and plum trees, and all the while, August wondered if God cared about the man with the scars. How had He chosen who was to suffer? Even with a God in attendance, men put scars on another man's back. Unless God had nothing to do with it. No, the question was, *who are we?* He was confounded.

On his left, he noticed the figure of a woman surrounded by children. She walked in the street, the children close, her head held high, her slim body erect, her long braid down her back as she strode toward market with an armful of quilts. He would recognize her anywhere, at any age. Her name was Elizabeth, and because his heart had skipped a beat, he knew seeing her was still an enormous pleasure although one without hope or promise, without sense or reason, impossible and inopportune but still *there.*

A BARGAIN KEPT, 1852

———•———

*J*uly settled in with a vengeance. With day after day of unrelenting heat, the scorched earth and dry winds plagued the corn until it shriveled. Elizabeth watched Perry who was ahead of the others, watched him hoe with his back bent, shirt sleeves rolled up. Rivulets of sweat ran down his temples, neck, and chest. She noticed that he began to tremble, and the trembling wouldn't stop even though he stood to wipe his brow and take a deep breath. He trudged down the row toward the edge of the field, toward the bucket of water she'd brought that morning. As he bent forward to pick up the dipper, he groaned. His pains must have begun again. He had a swelling on his chest like a knot in a tree, and soon there were others, across his chest and down his side. She didn't know what caused them, only saw that the pain took his breath away and he was weak. He sat down, and at that moment, she knew he would not get up again.

She hurried toward him. "Perry?"

He shook his head. He motioned toward the rows and simply said, "I cain't."

She'd never heard those words from him before. "Come on, Perry. Come on. We goin' home." The words didn't sound like her words, her voice like someone frightened. It couldn't be his time. Surely, not. He'd not yet gotten the deed in his hand. She knew he dreamed about one day sitting down in front of it, folding his hands and studying the words, the mystery of the letters and the beauty of what they would mean, all his.

She called to the others, to Daniel, now fifteen, and Eziah, twelve, and they half-carried him to Prouse's wagon. In air yellow and dense with humidity, she drove him home, taking the boys with her to help, and when they laid him on the straw mattress in the cabin, he stayed there, only his eyes alive, watching her. James, Jr. fetched water from the well and soaked a rag to cool him. "Where's Addy?" he said, not remembering. A day later, Addy came and sat with him, her apron high with Chambers' child. She couldn't sacrifice wages, so when Prouse came for her, she left and promised to come back as soon as she could.

He nodded at her and managed a smile, knowing he'd not see her again in this life. His body shrank with each passing day, and one evening as Elizabeth came back from the fields, he said, "I'm ready to go. The Lord can have me."

She did not leave his side then, but lay with him and held him while he moaned, his shirt soaked with sweat. To help him rest, she gave him laudanum and offered tea, but he would have none of it.

"You get the deed, Betsy. That's all you need worry 'bout. The deed. The Lord will watch over you and do the rest. If you got land, you'll be all right."

She would not let him see any tears.

A week later, in the middle of a hot, breathless afternoon with cicadas winding their tight call, he took his last breath, his hand in hers. For a long while, she sat quietly and stared at him, unable to cry or move, unwilling for this moment to be over. The boys and Addy came in from the fields and found her sitting beside him, calm, still holding his hand in hers. She watched over him for two more days, and when, finally, the moment had come for him to be moved, she emptied the straw from the ticking on which he'd lain and wept because it was black with mildew from the sweat of his pain and the unbearable days.

Preacher Green offered a plot at the church graveyard, but Elizabeth was bent on keeping Perry on the land. "It's his, bought and paid for. He belongs here." The words came from way back, from her grandmother's roots where the land was the link between the dead and the living. She would keep his spirit close, and from his spirit world he would advise her, comfort her. There was only the land under her feet, she would tell herself, not a distant heaven. She couldn't tell Preacher Green that, of course, nor Addy, since they were so sure about a heaven in the clouds. As far as Elizabeth could see, the land was heaven and hell, too, enduring with seasons and ways she could understand. They buried Perry before harvest time. He would be with them through harvest and in the quiet time, and in all the years to come.

When John Prouse came, she was sewing. Subdued, the children had quietly finished up their chores while she rocked, the stitches naming the hours and her thoughts, each loop of thread a record of their moments together, hers and Perry's. The quilts on the beds were from different times, the birthing time, the arrival of Libby, and James, Jr., and the others. She'd made a quilt for each of them. She heard footsteps approach and rose from her chair. She'd heard Prouse had been poorly, but the sight of him frightened her. He was pale and too thin, plagued by fevers that kept returning, weakening him.

"Lord, I do miss him, 'Lizabeth," he said. "Seems like I never had a harvest without old Perry, although there's plenty head to do the scythin'."

She nodded. "I've got somethin to ax you," she said. "It about the deed."

"I haven't forgotten. In any case, you have the receipts for payment. The deed is comin' and it's also written up in my will. If need be, Sophie will...see to it...when the time comes."

He said it with a hesitancy decipherable only by a slight pause. She understood. He was not well, and that frightened her. He had become her protection in the white world. To outward appearances, he still owned the land, and maybe it was better that way. The receipts were only that; the deed might never be hers. In the end, to be a free colored woman who owned land might not be such a good thing. She was just a woman who owned something any white man could claim if he wanted to. Still, it *was* only right. Her right.

The thought deepened her sorrow now as she stood in the doorway with John Prouse leaving and the silhouetted figures of the children in the sunset. She worried about the tobacco leaves that would have to be gathered and hung in the shed, and getting in the feed corn. Daniel would help her with the pig. She looked out over the field. Her field. No, still Perry's. He would be there in all she harvested. And then the field would be all there was of him.

She was better off than most. But would the receipts be enough? They lay in the tin along with Perry's manumission papers and the seeds. At least there was no debt. Nothing but the hollow in her heart.

When the hearing notice for the transfer of the deed arrived in its great white envelope, her name spelled differently than she was used to, her hand trembled. She carried it to Preacher Green who helped her read: "Conveyance of land, September 9, 1852, John Prouse to Elizabeth Boston, 1:00 pm at the County Courthouse in Cambridge, Maryland."

She looked up at him, counting on him like she'd counted on Perry. "I'll bring you," he said. "Got to see to a few things in town on that day anyway." He spoke in his quiet way, but he seemed worried. Was it about her? Her new vulnerability? People would know the land was hers now. The notice would be in the newspaper. She was both prideful and frightened.

Then at church on Sunday, he drew her aside.

"Don't want to trouble you none, Betsy," he said. She winced at the name Perry had called her. "But I got to leave awhile. State convention in Baltimore. I'll be takin' the steamer out of Secretary tomorrow. But don't worry. I'll be back in a few days."

She stared at him, not able to think what he wanted from her. She knew little of him except in his role as preacher, but now she felt something would be asked that was of great weight.

"The convention is church business," he said, "to make things better for us all. The man is just makin' things tighter all the time. Some of those who call themselves Methodists still own slaves. The church is scared to take a stand. The way I see it, we've got to stand together. What I have to ask, though"——and he came closer, his face leaning into hers—"is that Harriet might be comin' through while Kitty and I are gone. There'll be a few comin' with her. Says she can't wait for winter, the long nights. It has to be now. If they come, you be ready. It's the dogs I worry about." His voice trailed off as he looked at her.

Harriet Tubman, he meant, the woman who helped runaways. Elizabeth stood still, breathing deeply, trying to quiet her thundering heart. She had suspected it, but now he'd given the secret a voice.

"It'll be a Saturday night most likely since there're no papers on Sunday for the notices," he whispered. "They'll get a head start that way. No tellin' exactly where they'll come through. Be ready, Betsy. The Lord'll be with you. And not a word to a livin' soul."

He expected no commitment from her about the Lord. He probably sensed her beliefs were not his. He was a good man with depths she knew little of. Two faces, two lives. Like a face painted half white from somewhere in the old Indian time, or the long hair the men grew on one side of their head and shaved on the other. She knew of the runaways because Kitty had told her. Harriet had taken out her own niece and her niece's children, and then a few months later, her brother and two others, and at Christmas, that little spit of a woman had guided eleven slaves north. Unbelievable. Elizabeth felt it was the only good news out of a whole lot of bad. But this was the first time Preacher Green asked anything of her. He knew her well. He knew what would keep her going.

She nodded. She drew in her breath and straightened her shoulders. She'd do it. For Preacher Green, she'd send up a prayer: *Yes, oh yes, Lord. Let me!*

Meanwhile, her deed was conveyed and she made her mark on the paper which was read to her, listened as her name was announced right there at the courthouse in Cambridge: *Elizabeth Burton, free Negress.* She obsessed over the thought of Perry being gone, and there was only her name on the deed. She hated the singleness of it. The land was hers. She'd never consider it so. She'd never forget. With the deed in hand, she walked the field out to Perry's grave and talked to him. "It ours," she said to the wooden cross and the bare ground. "And it will be the chilren's someday. We done good in this life, Perry. We leavin' somethin' for 'em."

She waited for runaways, but no one came. To harbor them wouldn't be a shared responsibility, but hers alone. Soon Preacher Green returned, and nothing further was said about being ready for runaways, but his words had made her part of a dangerous, hopeful secret. There was a Way and knowing about it gave her confidence. That was why when she was on the road to town one after-noon and saw a paper posted, even though she could read nothing but the word *Reward,* she reached up and tore it from the tree. She was, when all was told, a landowner, which no longer frightened her as it had a while ago. Word would get around. It always did. When she heard a few days later that Harriet took away nine more she thought that whenever they came again, she'd be ready.

Addy stayed to help Elizabeth. Hired out to Thomas Prouse and Jefferson Wallace, she either brought the baby with her or left him with Elizabeth. How-ever, as soon as the tobacco was in and hung to dry, and the fodder stored for the cow, she returned to Chambers' cabin. "Addy, Addy," Elizabeth said, wanting to keep them both close, but Addy, with the baby in her arms, determined to have her own cabin after all this time, only said, "I'll come back when I can. He needs me, too," and took off across the field, her skirts whipping about her in the bitter wind.

Elizabeth knew there'd be no talk of marriage with the likes of Chambers, but there was the bare cabin that called to Addy, and Chambers' warm bed, things Addy so wanted to call her own. She knew, too, that in a little while, Addy would be pregnant again. And she was. No matter how hard Elizabeth tried, she couldn't be sad about that.

MATTIE, 2000

I keep hoverin' over Dorchester land as if I could guard it. I cain't leave it yet. Too much time with my feet in the soil, my hands on the crops, watchin' things from the peach tree. I see what happen long before my time, and I don't have too much feelin' about it other than bein' satisfied with the knowin'. But those last years in Dorchester tug at my heart because the older I got, the more I sat takin' it all in, me and the cat and the geraniums and the old Thunderbird. Did I leave my soul there? I know I made a friend or two, and that's one place you leave part of your soul if you got no family.

I had chickens right up to the very end. They were good company. When I had one to kill, I'd cook it in the pot on the burner. But one time I had a taste for roast chicken, so when Fran come by, I axed her if she'd cook the chicken in her oven since I didn't have one.

So I plucked out the chicken and when it was ready, I called her on the phone. I had the chicken in my biggest pot with the lid on and she took it home. Next thing I know, she call me. "Mattie," she say, "The chicken's in the oven, but I don't know what to do with these yellow balls of different sizes, seven of 'em, and the feet. I never cooked feet before."

I told her the balls was eggs not ready yet and you could tell which one would be laid the next day, and the next by the size.

"What do you do with 'em?" she axed.

"Just give 'em back to me along with the feet. I'll make soup."

Fran didn't know. That surprised me. She weren't dumb, but she was ignorant and there's a difference. Ignorant was what white people thought of me, but it only meant I didn't have the same experiences they did, so it weren't as bad as bein' dumb. That's what you are when you're not payin' attention.

Take Gordy now. Peoples used to say he was dumber'n stone. But he was only dumb in front of white folks. Didn't know nothin' then. He was good at shruggin'. He wouldn't tell 'em one thing. He tol' me it was his way of payin' back.

But he knew things. He lived long enough to see many a field around Dorchester pass from father to son. He say he seen land pass from a man to his woman, too, and it took some gettin' used to for them women, all a them acres to take care of, to say nothin' of how they was goin' to feed the chilren. Take them twenty-two acres 'cross the way, next to where Gordy lived. He'd tell 'bout Elizabeth, the deed goin' directly to her from John Prouse 'cause the husband died and she the only colored to ever own it, and she takin' care of chilren besides. After her, it was Miss Nettie, a white woman whose husband built the house there now. When her husband died, Miss Nettie made out by rentin' the land to Webster's grandfather and sellin' eggs. Come Saturday, she'd put on her white gloves and hat like she was goin' to church, and pack the old pickup with eggs to sell in town.

Gordy work for Miss Nettie, and other peoples, too, wherever he could pick up a few dollars. He got hit in the face with a chain once, so his face was bunched up on one side. Could be scary if you didn't know 'im. But he a good soul, just real tight with money. He and Margerite's cabin is still there. Empty now. Gordy was somethin'. The only thing he was generous 'bout was stories.

He say, "The onliest thing 'bout a woman ownin' land is the man come along thinkin' he can take it—thinkin' it'd be easy to take from a woman, 'specially a colored. For the man, there's always a way to get it. Like Webster. Wanted Miss Nettie's land and kept inchin' over with the plowin' ever year. Seen it myself. Plowed that field right up to her back door. Now I know that piece was always twenty-two acres, but even from the first surveyin', it was twenty-two acres *more or less*. And gettin' less each spring."

But how the land got passed from white to black and back again, neither one of us could figure out. Gordy believed Elizabeth come to no good. I suspected it, but he could throw a whole lot into one story: kidnappin', rape, murder, whippin', drownin', lyin', stealin', cheatin', and I didn't know what to believe. I figured it was the beer. Now I know.

He sure could tell a tale. One he'd heard about was a slave who chopped off another slave's head with a hoe in an argument over how dry the corn was. And the one about babies put in a trough at the edge of the field while the mothers picked and there come a storm with a heavy downpour and when the mothers ran back to their babies, they found 'em drowned in the trough. Oh, he could tell some stories. Some made me cry.

Then I'd tell the one about a young man who got lynched right there in town, the same year I come to Maryland. None of the colored would go down there but the white peoples did. The boy was accused of rapin' a white girl, but later, they found out a white boy did it. My friend, Mary, in town, tol' me 'bout it—how they brung the boy to the colored funeral home and how my friend seen him with her own eyes and swore it was the truth even though none of it got in the papers. But now I know. Ever word was true.

Gordy loved to tell 'bout Sam Green, the preacher man. "He sly. He outfoxed 'em," he say. "Live right down the road there. That little church with the steeple? He carryin' on like a good ol' Bible stompin' man and all the while, he helpin' them slaves go to the North. Now that's brave. Some kinda practicin' what he believe. You cain't help but admire that. Funny thing, though, you never hear tell of it nowheres. You say Sam Green and people say, 'Who?' And he livin' right down the road. And when his story got in the papers and all, white peoples still sayin', 'Who?' because they don't want to know and don't want nobody else knowin' either. 'Specially 'bout runaways. White peoples spreadin' sech foolishness 'bout Negroes bein' so happy."

Sometime Gordy would stop talkin' all of a sudden. "Sometime I think it do no good, all the rememberin'," he'd say, drawin' on his pipe. And we'd both finish the beer and look up at the stars like we could hitch up to somethin' good, somethin' for keeps.

Then I started talkin' 'bout my home in Georgia and Christmas time, things what lasted me a lifetime. I didn't want to forget nothin'—Mama killin' a chicken, pluckin' it out, and havin' it in the pot after she work all day in the fields—Papa puttin' milk down the well to keep it cool in summertime. Made me feel good just thinkin' 'bout it. It a shame I never got to tell my own kids how we did them days. But sittin' there and rememberin', Gordy and me, what we never guessed was it don't all disappear. Only from human eyes.

Elizabeth, like me, was diaperin' and feedin' babies that weren't hers. Don't matter, I guess. It all come out the same. Puttin' people in the world. You just hope they turn out good. My aunt did all right by my kids. Got a granddaughter down there in Florida now, who's goin' to college. Takin' up computers. Imagine that.

Her name Dory Collins, case you meet up with her. She one of the reasons I'm glad we survived. A better day is comin' for her, don't you know?

ADDY'S JOURNEY

A few years ago, Levin Chambers had a wife, Julia, a lean, quiet woman from what Addy could remember. The summer she was pregnant, Julia worked in the field beside Levin until labor started. By the time he got her to their cabin, she'd already started to deliver. As soon as Elizabeth heard, she ran across the fields to help, but the baby was stillborn, and Julia developed childbed fever. Elizabeth helplessly stood by. Later, she worried that Levin Chambers held the deaths against her. It was true he had cause for bitterness, even anger, but he directed it toward Elizabeth and never changed his sullen attitude toward her. Mother and baby were buried together in the cemetery close by, and all the neighbors went to the funeral. Julia had been faithful in Preacher Green's church. Since then, Levin's cabin stood empty and forlorn at the edge of Jefferson Wallace's field, while Levin took to wandering at night and drinking heavily.

Although Addy was not attracted to him in a physical way, she felt sorry for him. He'd been born not only blacker than black, but with legs so bandied he could barely walk, a gait so swayed it made him slow. It could be said there was a certain safety in his deformity. He was not worth much as kidnapped merchandise. He'd never done anything but picking and hoeing.

She could make him a home. Maybe that would change him. He was lonely, without purpose, set adrift without woman or child. Their agreement was made quickly and almost carelessly as they hoed on Wallace's farm, and she moved in with him the next day. She hoped for much as she cleaned his place, made corn bread, and started a garden, pleased to show him she could change the loneliness in his life. She kept her apron white, but in a short while began to wonder if he ever noticed.

That first siege surprised her with him coming through the door, stinking drunk, swinging his fists. She ducked and then fought back which only made him insane with fury, his coal blackness stone cold to the touch. He hit her. She felt the blood trickle down her cheek, watched dully as she saw the stains spread down her apron. He stepped back and seemed to study her without expression. "Bed now," he said, and without touching her again, lay down on the pallet and patted the place beside him. When the moon rose, she did as well. She soaked her apron in water and rubbed at the bloodstains, crying to herself and stifling her sobs as Chambers snored peacefully. She knew what the future held, but there was the cabin and the garden and Thomas, not even a year old, and her unborn child, and all the food she'd preserved. She hated to leave.

But the second time he came in growling and swinging, her heart turned to stone. He'd been beaten at Crotcher's again, judging by the bruises on his chin and the bleeding stump where his thumb used to be. She had no desire to nurse him, fear blowing away all thoughts of kindness, and vowed to return to Elizabeth's. She would walk across the field in the night while he bled on his bed. She wouldn't feel sorry. She had children to raise. The children. The thought kept her going over the frozen field through the midnight hours, Thomas heavier in her arms with each passing minute. The baby under her heart stirred and stirred. She could always say her time had come, and she needed to be under Elizabeth's roof.

Two women and a house full of children were better than one lone woman and one beaten up by a drunk. Would the Lord provide like Preacher Green said? *Put your faith in the Lord,* he'd said. *There was the strength of what was right,* he'd said. And what was right was mightier than some old drunk, even if he did have a cabin. That was all he had, no crop, no chickens, no order to his life, not even a trickle of hope. She'd done it all, got some chickens and a goat, cooked and sewed and split wood. All he had to offer was a run-down old cabin, his jug and whatever he could steal.

Damn him, she breathed into the cold air, and immediately sought the Lord's forgiveness. He would come after her. In a drunken state, he'd threatened to bring her down to Crotcher's Ferry and sell her to the trader man, saying, "I'd get a good price for you, two for the price of one." He'd demand his children and he'd threaten Elizabeth. And then again, he might just go back to Crotcher's in the blind search for his manhood and drink enough to forget his maimed heart and body, getting and giving beatings he somehow felt were justified. As she walked, she wept, *James, oh James. If you could see me now.*

"What's he done to you?" Elizabeth said, her eyes searching Addy's face. But she needed no words to tell her. So Addy stayed, and although Chambers asked about her, he did not approach the house. The baby, Mary, came sooner than expected, and Chambers did not make an attempt to lay eyes on her.

Elizabeth had to admit Addy had not been right since the baby was born. There was something wild in her deep-set eyes that had not been there before. Chambers began to stalk her along the wooded Indian path on her way to town. She couldn't go anywhere without Chambers following and threatening. The fact that she could outrun him was her only defense. He was inclined to strike when he got hold of her.

He found her before sunup as she milked the cow and said he wanted her to come back to his cabin. When she refused and said Elizabeth needed her, he hit her and knocked over the precious bucket of milk with a swift kick. Addy decided she had to leave.

With tears running down her round cheeks, she said to Elizabeth, "I'll be back. Don't worry. You're my mama far back as I know and a powerful woman but not even you can stop the devil."

"Stay away from where he might be, the road to town."

Addy nodded. "I'll go the other way, toward the river."

"Not too close to the Marshyhope, either. Go to the wheelwright, August Woodson," Elizabeth said. By daybreak, Addy was gone.

Elizabeth trusted Woodson. Although unaccustomed to taking chances, Woodson was on the path the runaways took. He was a good man. One above the rest. There was dignity about him. A slow carefulness. An empathy or questioning about the way things were that she came to trust. From the time she was young and went to town on Saturdays on her way to the Prouses, she would see him. He watched her. At first she was frightened, but then Miss Mari asked her to bring him her spinning wheel to be repaired. She had to approach him. From the first, there'd been a strange connection between them. She couldn't deny it. There was a catch in her throat whenever she saw him, but they remained innocent of each other. She was grateful. She sensed that somewhere in the man's past he'd begun a guilt that wouldn't stop. She didn't know why. He regarded colored and white equally kindly, maybe colored even more kindly—and that would come of guilt. It came from the same place as the sorrow he carried in his eyes and hunched posture.

The barn doors had frozen shut, the bolt iced to its latch. August could hear the horses stomping within, excited by his approach. With the lantern raised to warm the bolt, he waited and looked up into the night, the stars so many they appeared in strands of faint clouds. Too soon he would raise the bolt and events would begin whether he wanted them to or not, whether he could help it or not. Glancing back at the darkened house behind him, he wondered why he would leave wife and bed for such purpose. He must be mad.

The woman had come just before sunrise, trembling from the cold, and alone. She'd left her children, she said, sleeping in the cabin of the woman who'd raised her. Not her mother, she said, but a woman called Elizabeth Burton, a good five miles south from his place. So that was it, then. It was because of Elizabeth this woman sought him out. Yet, the woman who appeared before him with her head wrapped in faded homespun he did not know. The blacks were a dark blur; they came and went. They worked here and there, never in one place too long, following crops, the seasons, and the need. Hired themselves out if they were free, or were hired out if they were not. But a few like Elizabeth were skilled and therefore constant in their own homes. Despite himself, he thought of her hair that was like black silk, her narrow nose, her light skin. She was part Indian, but with the Christian name, Elizabeth. Yet this woman, the one who had been hiding in the bottom of his wagon since daybreak and through noon sun, wrapped in a quilt his wife had made, to whom he had brought a hot sweet potato for supper, was dark as coal, and she was running.

Speaking through swollen lips, she said, "Can you help me get to Baltimore?"

"Baltimore?" She should have gone in the opposite direction, toward the steamboat landing on the Choptank River. "Why did you come this way?" he asked her.

"I'm afraid of the way to town," she said. "Elizabeth say to head north and I come straight, not goin' by either the Choptank or the Marshyhope. Elizabeth say pattyrollers follow along the marsh."

He would have to travel northwest, farther up the Choptank and along one of the creeks to find her safe passage. There was only one thing to do, head toward the Quaker's place near the old mill. He didn't know if the trip was worth the danger.

At last, he could withdraw the bolt. He pushed open the huge groaning doors against banked snow. In answer, the horses heaved billows of steam into the air and threw their heads up, wild-eyed.

"Hello," he said into the cold, "I've come to hitch up the horses." From within the hay stacked in the wagon, he heard her muffled, "Lord, Lord! I thank you." He worried as the wind whipped across the open fields, about the roads that had had sun on them in the afternoon. Where the snow melted just enough to freeze at sundown, they would be slippery. The horses would exhaust themselves against the icy wind, and the night could bring patrollers, acquaintances of his, men of questionable purpose against whom he'd now pit himself or at least make one small protest.

It was a pitiful protest at best and one in which he doubted he could make a difference, except maybe for the one in his wagon, a mother. What desperation had precipitated a woman leaving her children and going alone he didn't know or want to know, but he doubted she would make it. The new laws made everyone a slave catcher. It was the law to return them. And if they were free, the impulse was to doubt them.

The horses burst from the barn's opening, restless, steaming, winter-coated Morgans, muscular and massive with huge clumps of hair about their hooves. His pride. They gave him courage as they broke into a steady trot, muffled by the snow, their rhythms calming him, recalling right and reason, and yes, good purpose. He was surer now as they fled toward Linchester Mill where the safe houses were spaced along the road to Wilmington like stars in familiar design.

"Quakers, yes," she said, nodding when he told her the route he'd chosen. "Please, sir," she said, her eyes tearing. "I'm free, but not free." He didn't know what to make of her.

Once he thought he heard hooves, or were they only an echo of his own horses? It was a flimsy excuse, the delivery of hay at this time of night. Still, maybe he'd be lucky. The moon, caught in tree branches as he passed by, seemed to move with him, and he realized he was plain as day in its light. He was a fool to try this. He understood the fear the runaways must have because of what now gripped him. He was not a part of what was known as the Underground Railroad. How had she known she could approach him? Unless she'd simply become lost. No, with a full moon, the way was well lit. It was Elizabeth, of course. Elizabeth knew the tender side of him. And why they had chosen a moonlit night, the woman, Addy, appearing so suddenly before him in the shadows as he milked early in the morning, he could hardly think. He'd been nervous all day with the woman hiding in his barn. He wouldn't have relented had she not been so badly beaten about the face, her right eye swollen shut, her cheek a deep purple-black and cut slantwise, her lips so puffed she could barely speak. He cringed at the sight and had Kay, his wife, see to the wounds.

Suddenly out of the night, Elizabeth's face appeared before him, her honey-eyed complexion, her thin-lipped mystery. At one time in his youth he had wanted her. It was a shameful thing to him and the fact that the opportunity had never presented itself was something he was now grateful for. His was a tidy life, and he had a wife he loved. But he and Elizabeth had exchanged words, many of them, and he harbored a depth of feeling he didn't know he had. He had had business with Gaines, her husband's owner, and she had been in Gaines's house sewing when he'd delivered the spinning wheel he'd made. He was so taken with her. Dare he think of her as beautiful? That he could feel so much for a woman of mixed race shocked him. For a time, he sought her out whenever he could, in town, at Prouse's, at the mill, and even once in the field. He had watched her from the road for a long time that day, dreamy and stupid. And the feeling returned to him despite his best intentions, as it did on the day he saw her in East New Market. In a different time, different place, a relationship with such a woman could flourish. But not here, not now.

They were almost there. They traveled across the bridge by the lower mill to a dip in the road that was uncommon in the infinite flatness, and on toward Hunting Creek. He passed the mill and the path that led from mill to creek where he knew many runaways had slipped through unnoticed. The shallow creeks that lined the jagged edges of land were the way to cross, but a woman alone had best be taken to Quakers. He did not think they would be turned away.

It was the road to the safe house he worried about now. Not a tree in sight to cover the road, only the bare fields with the stately house in the middle of a sea of white. The house cast a distinct shadow in the moonlight. On the first floor was a single lighted window as if someone expected them, which he knew they did not. The barn door was open; he drove the wagon directly inside and waited in the dark. Soon he saw the light of a lantern and someone step toward him with a coat thrown over his nightshirt, his face heavily lined, eyebrows that showered over his eyes, his voice coming from deep sleep, gruff, hoarse, yet surprised. "Who is it? That you, August Woodson?"

Relieved because the Quaker, Jacobs, had recognized him, he said, "I've got a woman named Addy in the wagon. Was a Wilson. Was raised by Elizabeth Burton down to the old Indian trail. Free, I think."

"Free or bound, the danger is the same. Kidnappers like the free ones. I thank you kindly, August. I know you are not in the habit of trips on moonlit nights," said Jacobs, smiling.

They pulled the hay aside. The woman slept, one arm underneath her head, the other clutching her shawl. August shook her.

"Wake up, Addy! Wake up! Have you any papers?" He hadn't thought to ask her before.

"Uh!" she said, startled, her high forehead shining in the light of the lantern. She shook her head, one side of her face still a deep purple-black and swollen, her left eye shut.

"It's all right, all right. Hush now. You're safe. Follow me up to the big house. You'll stay till tomorrow's sundown," said Jacobs, and nodded at August.

"My husband had papers," she said in a half whisper. "Didn't do him no good. Have you seen 'im? His name James. James Spry. People say he been taken. But I don't believe it. He was too big—with the fire of the Lord in him—to be taken so easy. And he had the paper. I always ask everone if they remember James Spry. But he gone. Ten year ago. I hate to leave without him. He left me, but I don't think he meant to." Her words came in a torrent now, hysterical. "Disappeared on his way to find work. They got him. And they'll get me, too. They goin' to find me and sell me South, free or owned, because I got no papers. I tol' Elizabeth, I'm goin'. I'll be back for the chilren, but I gots to go."

"Who beat you?"

"The man I stay with and left. He find me again and again no matter where I go. In the fields, in the woods, on the road. Can't hide from him. He not my husband. He say he was goin' to kidnap me for the trader. A way for him to make some money, he tol' me, and I don't doubt him."

August stared at the woman, her words menacing in their directness as she stood in terror, her figure shadowed against the wood grain of the barn and the dull yellow of his memory. He wanted her to be gone, safe—yes, but gone from him because he could no longer look at her, her with good enough reason to leave her children and head to Baltimore without a paper tucked in her pocket and nothing to save her. A fugitive, a *free* fugitive. He was sickened. What had plagued him all these years had come back to haunt him. Because the man he and his brother had kidnapped had been free. As they lay in wait for him, they dreamt their dreams of home and hearth and horses and a farm and the staying of their hunger and cold. There had been several bad years in a row, which was no excuse, or maybe it was. He no longer knew.

Oh, God. His conscience was on fire, rekindled into a blaze, just when he thought he'd forgiven himself, when he'd about forgotten, when he'd finally been able to distract himself with enough of a life that was proper and whole.

With the ship waiting at the dock in Vienna, a dealer had appeared down at the Ordinary at Crotcher's Ferry that November night. He had a dark mustache and his hands were tucked in his vest pockets. He spoke with an authority they weren't used to at Crotcher's. He made a promise to the drunken men who could barely remember what he'd said, "You haul 'em off down to the ship, day or night, no matter. One— two thousand dollars, depending on how fit they be. Five hundred for breeders."

August had only done it once. The paper the Negro had carefully kept in his pocket, he had burned in the woods and covered the few ashes with soil. *Certificate of Freedom*, it had said. *James Spry.* Now he knew why this night had happened. He'd hoped for some sort of atonement. Now he could plainly see there'd never be one. He hated who he had been, the place he'd been born to poisoning him, his soul tainted by the era of his allotted time, and he, a part of everything he disdained. He saw in that dimly lit moment that there would be no peace for him ever, no matter how many Addys showed up at his door. He climbed up to the seat of his wagon. Tipping his hat to the woman and the man who would guide her, he went off into the night, no longer proud of the horses that had been purchased with part of the slave trader's money, along with his farm, shop, and home, even the wagon in which he now sat. All of it. For the moment, he could feel the wrath of God and believed in a just world. There was a God and he was doomed, a thought he rarely allowed himself. But there it was, as sure as his black shadow perched atop the wagon shadow pulled by horse shadows, all of which were reminders of his shame.

It was Elizabeth. She'd conjured it. She damn well knew everything that went beyond words. Had looked into his soul with those dark, mournful eyes, behind which lay the dead center calm he had never possessed. Yet he'd never made the connection between her and the deed he'd done. He'd never heard her say the name Spry. He knew little about her ties.

After this, his guilt might lift a little. He'd harbor whoever else would come to him whenever they appeared, and he'd bring them to Jacob's. He could see how in his heart he could be a Quaker since they professed a rightful duty toward humankind. He wondered how long it would take for his sin to be washed away, how many fugitives he'd rescue before he was cleansed. No. He would never be free of the man called James Spry.

The Quaker man spoke. "Addy Wilson, you say, ma'am?"

"Adelaine Wilson Spry," she said.

"How many children have you?"

"Four, sir. One still at the breast."

He raised the lantern high the better to see her facial wound. Then he said, "You'll have to go back or your children will be taken no matter who you've left them with. They'll be back in slavery in no time."

She winced. "How many beatin's I gotta take for those chilren?" she heard herself say, astonished at her outburst.

He shook his head. "For now, rest. If you decide different in the morning you can go back. Otherwise, I'll take you to the steamer at Leonard's Wharf. You'll be wanting to go to Baltimore, but I doubt you'll want to be going far from those babies for too long."

She hadn't thought of how she would get there. Like a rabbit changing directions in split seconds, her only thought had been to escape the hand of Chambers.

"I got no passage."

"I'll give you the two dollars. You pay me when you can."

"I got no papers."

"I'll give you a note. It'll say you're free, that you were in my employ, that now you're looking for a job and a place to stay. You show it to the stevedore named Elbert Stanley and he'll tell you where to go. There's a church where you'll be going. And when you're ready, you come back home and take care of those children, hear? You're free and with that goes responsibility."

He shook his head. "Sorry. I didn't mean to lecture you, tell you what you already know." He spoke like a man grown weary of the strife around him, although his empathy was a kind of love, too. She had not had the courage to look him in the face, but she did now. "I don't know why you helpin' me, but I thanks you with every breath."

He nodded. "No need for that," he said quietly.

Midmorning, she sat in the back of his wagon surrounded by sheaves of tobacco bound for Baltimore as they made their way to Leonard's Wharf. The Quaker said it would be a short ride to the dock just west of the mill, and once she was on the steamer, she would be secreted under Elbert's watchful eye.

"But stay below, hear? Don't go wandering on the main deck, especially around any of the ports."

For the rest of her life, the smell of tobacco would bring back the ride to the river and the great unknown that contained her wildest hopes. The closer they came to the wharf, through the sounds of Mr. Jacobs's horse plodding on the frozen ground, the pitch and roll of the wagon, the crack in the sideboard through which she could see the ground, the horizon, the passing stripes of gray-wintered trees and the soft browns and yellows of the marsh—the more she missed home and ached for her baby. Too soon, the river, the mournful sound of the ship's horn, the loading and unloading of cargo, to which she now belonged. She'd never been away from home, never had any cause to go to the banks of the river, be on a boat, or walk among strangers. She'd never seen more than thirty people at one time. She thought she'd pass along from quiet town to quiet town, house to house, from the hands of one kind of Elizabeth to another, in a safe wandering. She hadn't imagined drifting on deep water, severed from the land, from all she knew, and now she panicked at her own not knowing. It was only the pain in her swollen face that let her know she must do this. Jacobs had given her a scarf. He held it out to her in his pale hand, and she'd received it in her trembling one. Of all he'd done for her, this was the kindest, the gift that brought tears. She pulled the scarf across her face to hide her wound.

She clutched her breast where the note lay against her skin and sat still, waiting to be told what to do while the stevedore helped load the tobacco. There was no more than a look that passed between Jacobs and the man she thought was probably Elbert. Then Jacobs raised his hand to help her down from the wagon and she followed Elbert on board.

"You'll be fine now, miss," he said, and led her below to steerage where two others sat quietly clutching their belongings wrapped in burlap. Dully, they watched the men rake out ashes with long hoes and feed coal into the boiler. Addy wondered if these workers were slaves, and if not, why they would choose to work in a place so like hell.

Elbert Stanley showed her a berth in a curtained cubicle apart from the men. All through the day she stayed there, seeing nothing, waiting for the sound of something brushing against the hull of the boat, which would mean they were approaching a bank or shallows, where they would stop again to load and unload. She dozed, and when heavy sleep took her, she dreamed she lay in a coffin with the baby at her breast. When she woke, her blouse was wet. Never had she been so filled with doubt. By the time they pulled into Baltimore, she was seasick.

With Elbert's guidance, she passed easily and without challenge among the city's population and with growing confidence, made her way to the church of Elbert's bidding. There were many kind faces, especially that of Preacher Lakes. She soon found work, telling herself she would see how things went. Maybe stay just till payday. She'd decide what to do then, whether to stay another week or two, or a few months. At two dollars a week, it would take three weeks for her to get enough for passage home after feeding herself and renting the room. And while she had quickly found a niche for herself in the work, the noises and smells of the city, the constant coming and going, the hordes of unfriendly, strange faces parading by her in the street left her bereft for the quiet of Elizabeth's cabin, for her small baby, and the open sky and fields.

Old man Gaines had left his shotgun in the barn where Daniel found it one day, lying on a rafter just under the roof. It must have been left there after the last pig slaughter when Perry was still alive, the day he and Gaines had talked about Perry's freedom. Gaines had never liked a gun in the house, which Perry thought odd. He'd told Elizabeth that Gaines gave the job of slaughtering to Perry because her husband was a man with a soft heart.

"That was what wore out first on him, too," Perry had said.

They took a chance having the gun, of course, but Miss Mari wasn't the kind to pay a gun any mind. She would never use it and had no doubt forgotten it was there, said Daniel when he showed it to Elizabeth. He'd cleaned it with a bit of lamp oil and got it working again, admiring the smooth click of the hammer when it was pulled back. In the cabin he aimed at things, making Elizabeth nervous.

She quietly took the gun from Daniel. "We'll keep it hidden. If we don't talk 'bout having it, Miss Mari will never know. And sometime, when we need it, we'll both know where it is. I mean really need it, and not till then. Heah?"

So when Chambers came by looking for Addy, she was ready. He swayed in the yard, shouting and wailing, "Addy, you bitch. Get on out here 'fore I come in after ye. Ad—dy!" The drunken, dangerous fool. Elizabeth stood in the doorway then, with the shotgun across her chest, hoping she wouldn't have to fire it.

He stood there, surprised, but daring her, too, so she pointed it at him. Then he seemed to shrink like a squash withered on the vine after frost and walked away, unsteadily, cursing her.

Addy's reasons for leaving were plain, and Elizabeth didn't blame her. She had to save herself. But having no news worried Elizabeth. She lifted the cornbread off the fire and spread it with bacon grease for the boys. She looked at their faces, James, Jr., Eziah, and Daniel, old in the way they held themselves, already subdued by a life of work since Perry died, just like Libby who had remained with the Prouses. She taught them always to be watchful, to stay together, to look out for James, Jr. who carried water to the field for the hands, and she instructed them to come home before dark. They were never to stay anywhere but her cabin. She allowed Daniel and Eziah to be hired out only to the farms adjacent to hers, to Loomis, Morris, Thompson, and Wallace. It was Wallace who hired the boys most frequently, although he often didn't pay. Still, whenever he called, they'd plow and hoe the bare fields, earth hard as stone between the parched corn, heat like hell itself. What was she raising them for? More of the same, like her, working in the fields all day for others, tending her own at night.

Mr. Wallace was the worst of the lot, yet he came to her politely and asked if she needed anything, to which she always answered, *no*. She'd be dependent on no one, least of all a man who didn't pay his help even if they were only half grown. When she asked him about it, he'd say, "When the crops come in." He came asking about her corn or wheat, how it was coming on and if she needed help clearing. *He could see himself how it was coming on*, she thought, not trusting his friendliness. "No, thank you, sir," she said again and again. Once, he wanted to know if she had enough to pay the rent.

"I don't pay rent. This my land," she said to him and worried then if she should have said so. But surely he knew it was her land. He was fishing.

"Well then, are you paying the taxes?" he said. She knew about the taxes. Preacher Green had seen her name in the paper and told her what she owed.

"They put those who owe in the paper." He'd said it like a threat, knowing she could not read, yet he must have known full well she owned the land. Her heart stopped. She knew she did not have enough money saved for taxes.

"Yes, sir," she lied.

And here he was again, just after she'd given the boys their supper. He drove up her lane in his black stovepipe hat and black suit, a lawyer's uniform, in a gig drawn by a fine black gelding. He was a man to be reckoned with. She watched him from her window as he approached and steeled herself for an encounter with danger, a reasoning and intricacy she might not understand. He would try to trick her, she was sure. Her heart pounded at the sound of his heavy step outside her door and his clamorous knock. She opened the door and because it was cold, asked him in.

He glanced around the cabin, taking in the preserves on the shelves, the ax and adz in the corner where Perry kept them, the dwindling fire in the fireplace and the rag rug before it. She saw what he saw: her shoes lined up by the door with the children's, her small loom that held the threads of the weaving she'd been working, and her sewing in the basket beside it. The boys ate silently as they sat on the floor near the fire; the baby began a whine that could not be hushed despite her caresses. He looked at her with eyes that saw only his advantage and then, as she expected, he began his persuasion. He came as a friend, he said, and wanted to know if she needed a guardian for the land. If she'd put the land, all twenty-two acres, in his hands he would see to it. He would till and plant and harvest in the coming year in return for the work of the boys. "There are four now," he said, pointing to them. "And what do you have here, not walking yet?" He nodded at the baby. She would get half the profit. Instead of rent, he'd pay her taxes. Same thing. She'd still own everything, of course. But a woman alone needed help.

"I'll think on it, Mr. Wallace," she said, knowing if she gave an inch she'd be cheated. Because he didn't pay his help, he probably was not likely to give her half the profit either. Still, the boys might be safer working for a neighbor in payment for land and crops. Then again, he might take them, could very well take them anyway no matter what she consented to, or didn't. They didn't have parents as he well knew. They were only in her care and she was a widow up in years. In the end, she stubbornly refused. She would hold out as long as she could.

He tipped his hat to her and left, his boots clattering down the wooden steps.

When the boys were finished eating, she took the bowls outdoors and washed them in the snow. She looked back at her cabin, at the steps worn from going in and out. The boards of the house had turned as gray as she had this year, she and the house together. Nonetheless, Perry's hand was on every board, there in every mark of Miss Mari's ax.

The door opened and Eziah poked out his head. She heard the baby cry. She could see through the door frame to the window opposite and knew every inch of space with her eyes shut. The house was filled with life and still she was lonely. She longed for Perry's warm hand on her back. Instead, she wore his shirt over her dress, the one she'd made him for Sundays, remembering how he'd left the collar open except during church. Had his God paid attention to such respect?

"I'm comin'," she called to Eziah.

"It's not Christian charity on his mind," she said later to the preacher. "He a turkey buzzard, bidin' his time, circlin' overhead, waitin' for me to roll over dead."

"Hold on, Betsy. We'll get the congregation to help if you get in a bind," he said. "Besides, you never know when we'll be needin' your station. You don't want a white man on your land unless you truly can't help it."

She took comfort in the fact that they had enough food to last the season, enough flour, corn meal, pickled pork, and smoked bacon. It was early spring that was the hardest, just before growing time. She wanted Libby home, fifteen now and ready for babies. She needed to keep a close eye even though Thomas Prouse had promised to. Yet, you never knew. And Addy, God knows where Addy was—if she'd even made it. Elizabeth had to admit there were fewer to feed this way and felt bad thinking it. Now, the added worry over taxes.

Calling out to Daniel to split wood and James, Jr. to find kindling, she thought of Miss Mari alone in the house across the way and sent Eziah to do her bidding. She hadn't but two hogs left. Elizabeth was not as alone as some. With the young ones, she had some hope. But guarding them as they grew was a fearful task, when a devil like Chambers could betray his own to say nothing about the traders hungry for money or the planters who indentured children and didn't feed or clothe them properly, whipping them as they would a slave. How she longed again for Perry's comfort.

She would ask August Woodson the next time she saw him. She knew she could ask anything of him. He was a thoughtful man, a man who hesitated, a man who would bend like a willow this way or that. She would ask if Addy had stopped there. If the answer was yes and she was assured Addy was given safety, she would then ask him if he needed an apprentice, if he would let Daniel work beside him because only a skill would save Daniel from the fields. And with August, she knew Daniel would not be beaten or starved like some.

August Woodson took to drink. After dark, he'd hitched the horse to his wagon, leaving his fire and his wife to frequent the Ordinary at Crotcher's Ferry. The inn stood on the embankment of the Marshyhope, where the river turned and wound its peaceful way north. Snow had outlined the skeleton of a ship that rose out of the trees before him. The shape of its keel, propped on scaffolding, gleamed in the moonlight as he tied his horse to a post. He thought about the audacity and skill of men in building something so fine out of a mere tree. He felt a kinship with them although it occurred to him he might just be looking for a reason to justify his dallying in such a place as Crotcher's on Saturday night. While he stood in the white quiet, he watched as a Negro came toward him, one whose body swayed side to side in a difficult walk.

To his knowledge, no Negro dared approach Crotcher's. This one was lame and in this light, his face was blue-black. As he considered the man's dark face and bandied legs, it appeared to August that some must feel that God was a monster, gleeful in his plot to make a black man's lot in life uneven from the start. The man's attitude of anger seemed as glaring as the moon on the snow, his station in life a mockery of all that whiteness where not even the brightness of the moon could lighten him. To August, in this moment, the moon created other ghosts as the ship arose before them out of the snow, proof of a possibility to which only a chosen few were allowed. All was part of a strange plan, if there was one, the moon so perfectly round, the inn so warm and well lit, everything in its place but entirely without a place for the man before him who was left to his own devices in the hard cruelty of his life. Beyond, a barge lay tied to the pier where new lumber had been piled. It was Saturday, payday, when rum and whiskey had been delivered that very afternoon. It was probably the black man's knowledge of it that had driven him through the snow this night.

Then he heard him say, "You seen a woman called Addy Spry? Been walkin' a long way lookin for her."

Before he could answer, the door to the inn flew open and two men rolled out. There was the dull thud of a fist hitting a chest, a man choking, steam rising into the cold air, then a struggle to stand, blood seeping into the snow. The Negro grinned as if he were coming home.

August recognized the one they called Shadrack, pinned to the ground, his face now turned toward the Negro. "Chambers, git 'im," he growled. "Git the bastard," as though he were siccing a dog.

Two of them rolled on the ground, one on top, one underneath, both white, young, strong, and each with money enough to be drunk. With a savagery all the long years had taught him, the Negro responded and pounced on Shadrack and his opponent, on the two-backed animal that grunted and rolled and steamed with an outpouring of hate and release, after which one man might buy the other a drink, become his protector out of gratitude. August understood that scenes like this had been played out many times before. This was the Negro's only faith, for if nothing else, he could fight, although his loyalty depended on who was on bottom and who he could trust to buy him a drink and say this time, just this time, it was okay for a black man to hit a white man. August saw Chambers' hands wind around the white man's throat, and when the white man gasped, he stopped just short of killing him, rolled him over, and punched at his face. He kept pummeling until he was stopped.

A crowd had gathered. "Here, now," someone said. Then a roar. A Negro was hitting a white man, even if he was doing their bidding. They could lynch him, depending on their mood. In this precarious moment, so much depended on the balance of things, on the white men and their power over one another. Shadrack Morris rose out of the snow, bloodied, swaying, his arms raised and waving as though to wipe the slate clean, and gestured a drink with his hand tipped to his mouth. "Bring two," he said in a raspy voice over the senseless body of his opponent.

Spellbound, August stood by his wagon and waited while the others went back to the inn. Shadrack and Chambers stood in the snow looking past each other out over the frozen river. Neither spoke, till finally Shadrack said, "Figure that was worth a bottle?"

Chambers nodded. Soon he would not feel anything.

"I'll put it outside the door. Then you get out of here. Hear me?"

Chambers nodded again. "We both free," he said into the biting cold, but it was probably only courage born of the promise of a drink. Still, August felt the man wanted to declare equal footing, even though his blackness forever separated him from Shadrack, a man he'd just defended and might've given his life for. No, no maybe about it. Free or not, black men were expected to give their lives.

Shadrack turned away and kicked the man he'd fought. "Come on, now. Up with ye 'fore you freeze to death." The man moaned.

But Chambers had more to say to Shadrack, the patroller.

"Elizabeth Burton? She got a gun. I been lookin' for my wife and when I went to her place, she wouldn't let me in, just stood there in the doorway with a shotgun."

"Oh, yeah? She should know better. No black's allowed firearms, especially no damn woman."

It was clear now what Chambers had in mind. He'd pass on what he knew and in so doing, he'd be equal in the eyes of the law and commonality.

"Right, sir," he said, but he spoke as though there was no glory in it. Black against white, man against woman. Whose side was he on? Opportunity changed everything.

Shadrack opened the door of the ordinary. The roar of the crowd inside poured out into the night. August, too, entered the inn, leaving Chambers waiting in the dark. He hoped the bottle would appear before the man on the ground awoke.

Later, when August had had his fill, he rode home with a nagging worry about Elizabeth. Somewhere along the road, he passed a man lying in the snow. It was Chambers, lying curled around a bottle. Despite his former empathy, he decided not to stop. It was the least he could do for the woman called Addy. With dismay, he realized there was nothing he could do about what might lay ahead for Elizabeth.

Preacher Sam Green received a letter from Preacher Lakes, an acquaintance of his in Baltimore. At first, he thought it might be an invitation to attend another conference. That he was often invited amazed him, for he was a simple man, a farmer, with little knowledge of politics and certainly not a man who would in any way cause consternation or the slightest ripple. But he could read and his sermons were passionate, a fact not lost on visiting ministers on the Methodist circuit.

The letter said Addy had found work washing dishes at an inn. "Said woman, Addy Spry of your parish, asked me to pass word to Elizabeth Burton that she will send what she can," was the message. One dollar was enclosed in the envelope. That Sunday he handed the letter and money to Elizabeth and leaned over her shoulder while he read it to her.

"Can you write back, Preacher?" she said. "Tell Addy Chambers is dead. They found 'im on the road between my place and Crotcher's yesterday mornin'. Pattyrollers got 'im. They say now there's one less free black, not worth the dirt what stuck to 'im. I cain't say I'm sorry."

"Elizabeth, a sad soul has gone to his Lord. That's all you can say. There's none of us can know another's heart."

"He beat Addy."

"I know. The Lord will take it into account."

"Tell Addy to come home. I need her. The children need her—the baby can't get milk. She keeps throwing up the cow's milk I give her. It's not been three weeks since Addy left. If she comes soon, her milk might would come back."

Preacher Green posted the letter in town the next day, passing by the black-smith shop where Sam Green, Jr. worked. His son glanced up at him and nod-ded, but returned to his work. That was all. Disappointed, Green went on his way, admonishing himself because he couldn't afford to buy his son. The price would be even higher now that Sam, Jr. was skilled. *This world,* thought Green. *This old beleaguered world.* He looked to the right and left of him, at the homes of brick and mortar that were like fortresses, their permanence insulating those who owned them from the strife in their midst. He saw his own tribulation as a mere grain of sand in the configuration of things. Best not to dwell on it. Only on that which he could do something about.

A week later, another letter waited at the post office for Preacher Green. Addy was coming home and due to arrive on the steamer on Wednesday. He didn't have a way to let Elizabeth know without riding out to her cabin, so he and his wife, Kitty, met Addy at the landing. "I almost stayed," she told Kitty. "I was workin' but I couldn't stand the sound of my baby cryin'. I could hear her all through the day and night. My milk never stopped." She was thin and there was a deep wound on her cheek that would probably scar. Her employer gave her a signed paper so she could pass. She didn't like Baltimore, she said, "Even though

I was makin' good money." Kitty put a shawl around Addy's shoulders as she sat in the back of Preacher Green's wagon. The mule cantered on the cold ground and filled the air with sounds of homecoming. Addy was silent. Kitty began to hum a hymn Addy loved. All the way along the old Indian road to Elizabeth's cabin, she sang. *Wake up, Jacob, Day's a breakin', I'm on my way! When I die, I want to go to heaven, Wake up Jacob, Wake up.*

"I guess the Lord do provide, Preacher," Addy said. "Such kindness with us. I believe the Lord take care of us in this way."

The closer to home they drew, Addy watched for sight of Libby and James, Jr, Eziah and Daniel, and Thomas. Running in from the field, they chased the preacher's wagon, little Thomas toddling behind them. Libby cried out, "Mama! Oh, Mama!" Elizabeth came to the door with the baby in her arms and with a broad smile, silently handed her to Addy.

To follow the law that said they were to be home by dark, Preacher Green and his wife could not linger. They left as soon as the mule was watered. They should be home before the patrollers, before the dogs came running, before the wind picked up. They huddled together on the wagon, buffered, side by side. Elizabeth could not help but envy their twosome as they drove off.

It was early spring when the flour and cornmeal ran out. They'd had the last of the fatback from fall when she finally allowed Daniel to load the shotgun.

"Stay away from the road," she said, "and go way back till you get to the stream. I don't have to tell you, if somebody come, leave the gun and take off. Don't let 'em find you with it in your hand, heah?" At dusk, she watched him stride toward the woods like a man. He almost was, and she worried he'd be a target for those who were evil bent. But they were hungry, all of them except the baby, and anything he brought home would be appreciated. He shot two rabbits and handed them to her with a bright smile, the first she'd seen on him in many a day. He went out two more times and used up the last of the powder and shot. With the powder gone, Elizabeth placed the gun out of sight and told him when she got money for more, he could hunt again. He'd done as she bade him and had been careful to go deep in the woods, far from the road, and often stayed in the trees for hours so he wouldn't be noticed. His hunting saved them that early spring. Otherwise, the rifle stayed in the rafters except for the one time she'd had to scare Levin Chambers off. It was still in the rafters when the patrollers came. *They must have seen Daniel,* she thought.

The one called Shadrack strode right into the cabin without a knock. The baby began to cry and the boys cowered in the corner, all except Daniel, who'd been expecting trouble and appeared ready to meet it. He stood up now facing the man who'd intruded, his hands knotted at his sides.

"You know it's against the law, don't you—for you to have a weapon of any kind? You know that full well, so don't be lookin' like you have anythin' to say. Nothing worse than havin' the likes of you armed, so don't be sayin' anythin'."

He was answered by silence. Even the baby hushed as Addy pressed her close.

Finally, Elizabeth spoke, her voice raised in anger and her hands trembling. With the conviction born of her landowner status, she drew herself up and held her head high. "Sir, we gets rabbits with it sometime when we're hungry."

Shadrack glanced around the cabin. "You're doing more than that and you know it. You were seen threatenin' one of your own kind. Next thing you know, it'll be a white man."

She stood staunch, arms folded across her breasts. There was no use to counsel his fear. It traveled hand in hand with hate. She wanted no trouble. She thought of Preacher Green and understood the times he'd backed down, kept his mouth shut, even seemed to cower. It was only playacting. Meanwhile, the river of souls kept flowing and one of these days it would flow right through this cabin on its way north. If it weren't for the land, she'd go too.

"Get the gun for him, Daniel. It take a big man to take one off a hongry woman with chilren."

It was Chambers' final say. What good would it do to remember she was raising his seed? She only hoped that the poison in him hadn't been passed on. As for Shadrack, he'd be back. He'd work on having the last word. Her only regret was she wished she was better at playacting as she watched the back of him with the shotgun in hand. *Daniel, oh Daniel, my sweet boy. You can give in and stand tall both.*

A WILL AND A WAY, 1854

---

*P*reacher Green was surprised to see her that day in spring, the one whose mother had the same surname as he before she married. He knew her as Minty Ross, but now she'd taken her mother's first name, which was Harriet, and when she'd married, she became Harriet Tubman. She'd appeared as an old woman with a shawl draped over her head, walking through town with a cane. She beckoned to him right there on the street, brazen-like. He dared not speak to her, but climbed aboard his gig and began to follow her as she walked directly under a poster calling for a reward for her capture. She'd been known to lead runaways to safe routes north, and it was known, too, among the black community that she'd never lost a single one. That she kept coming back to get more fugitives was a miracle only God could accomplish. Her disguise was one of many; she was slippery as a greased wheel. And quick. The stern, serious, determined look on her high cheek-boned face never left her.

He'd first seen her name on a notice four years ago under **THREE HUN-DRED DOLLARS REWARD,** and then, farther on down, after her brothers, *Harry* and *Ben,* there appeared the words, *Minty, aged about 27 years, is of a chestnut color, fine looking, and about 5 feet high.* Of late, she was called Moses by some. She was fearless and he marveled at her daring. He whispered a prayer to God and to the power and glory that had produced such a miracle. He helped her whenever she asked, and he guessed she was about to ask again. In his gig, he slowly followed the tiny figure, then soon overtook her and waited at the edge of town.

"I'm here for your boy," she said in a hoarse whisper. He nodded. "I know it's time even though to have him near has been a comfort to Kitty. Still, he's been beaten awful bad sometimes. It pains me."

"He needs to go all the way to Canady. Not Philadelphia or Baltimore. None of it safe now. This a bad time. Winter is best. If he can wait, I'll come for him then. If he cain't, I'm goin' to tell him the way."

So it was planned that Sam Green, Jr. would run, and Preacher Green dared not even tell Kitty. He knew the next beating would be his son's last. Within a few days, he stood in the blacksmith shop, tears in his eyes at the sight of the open wounds on his son's back.

"Son," was all he could manage. He stared into Sam, Jr.'s eyes, which were bloodshot and narrow with pain. He whispered to him, "I'll tell Harriet. You wait for her. She'll know the way. Don't stop to say farewell. Go quickly. The Lord be with you."

He knew full well that when news spread about a fugitive son, the seed of suspicion would be cast and he, the trusted exhorter, would walk in its shadow. But that did not matter in light of the greater need.

Elizabeth felt something was up, way off in the woods like she was. The patrollers came by more often now, but thankfully did not stop again at her cabin. Led by Shadrack Morris who lived in the vicinity, they kept a search out along the sweetwater marshes of the Marshyhope. Once, digging along the shore of the river for tubers of tuckahoe, she saw the men on horseback, dogs in tow, and she hid in the rushes with her basket as if she was guilty of something, though it was feeding the children she was after. She worried about the boys who were off on their own down at the grist mill netting fish. There'd been little meat since the last two rabbits, and they clamored to go off to the creek where the herring were spawning. Still, she hated to let them out of her sight.

She was grateful for Preacher Green who stopped by occasionally and Mr. Prouse, too, just to see if they had enough to eat and with advice about when she should plant. John Prouse loaned her a plow, brought in on his wagon along with a bundle of sewing for Elizabeth to do.

But then in the beginning of May, just when the dogwood bloomed, and in the middle of corn planting, John Prouse took ill with ague. It came on suddenly and forcefully, producing chills and fever and sweat in turn. What kind and the cause, no one knew. His wife stood helplessly by with the children near, silent and frightened. His heart gave out and he died four days later at the age of forty. In those last moments, they watched in panic, although they'd known for a while he'd been frail.

He was deep in debt. He owed John Webster for land, his brother Thomas for seed, Jefferson Wallace for hay, Shadrack Morris for lumber, Loomis for the new hogshead, and God knows how many others. Libby was sent for to help with the young ones, and Addy to help with the washing and cooking. Elizabeth helped to lay him out.

Soon after the funeral, Elizabeth returned to the Prouses, borrowing Miss Mari's wagon to return the plow, which would surely be auctioned off to pay debts. The house needed repair. John Prouse had probably meant to mend the roof in the spring; the shingles were piled nearby. There were fence posts dipped in lime and ready to be set before the rains came, lying near the corn shed. She thought about Perry's corn and wheat left to her and the boys to help with harvest, about the flow of work that never ended, the struggle that united them all. But she'd been fortunate. Miss Sophie had nothing but debt before her.

Approaching the Prouse's house, she did not know what she would say. She began with, "I'm awful sorry for your trouble, ma'am."

Sophie Prouse was stoic as she stood on her porch with the youngest child. She beckoned for Elizabeth to join her on the porch, and although she looked stern, she said, "Funny how things turn out. You get your land free and clear while I get what's left after all is said and done. I 'spect it'll take everythin' down to the last kettle to pay the debts. I don't know what'll become of us." Her voice cracked.

"He was a good man, ma'am. He did right by our family."

Sophie nodded. "Yes," she said softly. "At least there was that."

Elizabeth handed her the corn cakes from the last of her meal and the salted herring wrapped in one of her cloths. Sophie's thin hair, undone and unkempt, hung over her face, her demeanor that of someone painfully aware of her new station, grateful to receive gifts from a colored.

"Elizabeth," she said, "There's always some who are ready to take what you have. They're already sniffin' around your land. Heard talk of it, you bein' alone with only half-grown boys to help and you not able to use the land proper. Now that some of it's cleared, there are those very willin' to relieve you of it. I'd make a will if I was you, so everythin' is legal."

She'd not thought of a will. The land was her subsistence, and in her mind her ownership had permanence. She'd never have to worry. She had a cow and the old mule. She and the children were still maneuvering around the remaining stumps, but they were planting well. Wallace had bought the corn last year, and she hoped he would again this year. She'd kept aside some for her own use, but Wallace got the rest. It was against the law to sell crops as a free colored, and Wallace let her know he was doing her a favor to add her corn to his. He was a long time in paying, but he came through when Christmas was long past. They were doing just fine.

Out loud, she said, "How do you do that, make a will?"

"You just write out what you want and give it to somebody you trust. John wrote out his and gave it to his brother, Eben, to keep. When the time come, Eben took it to the courthouse."

So Preacher Green wrote out the will according to Elizabeth's dictate: *Being well in body and mind, on this eighteenth date of July, 1854, I bequeath to Adelaine Wilson Spry, the coulered Girl I have raised, all of my estate both real and personal.* With the preacher's help, she wrote her name and he folded the paper carefully.

"You keep it for me, Preacher," she said.

He shook his head. "No, Betsy, best do like John Prouse did. Give it to Mr. Eben Prouse. We have no count with the law."

Late summer brought thick clouds of gnats and mosquitoes. Trees withered from lack of rain. There was heat enough to make a man crazy. August stopped his work for a moment and stood in the shade of his tree, then bent to turn a wheel and spin it on an axle. It was not balanced. In disgust, he sat down on a log and hung his head over his lap. How much was a man worth? More now than ever before, say forty pigs, twenty oxen, hundreds of acres of good farm-land. How much for a husband, a father, a living, breathing being with love in his heart—and hate? Surely hate, and curses for those who'd stolen his freedom. A person whose flesh and blood he, August Woodson, had used to pay for his land. It was another man's future he'd held, and no less an evil than taking a life with a gun.

His labor had always brought him pleasure, but this morning it became his punishment. He drove himself into a frenzy, finishing parts carelessly and piling them up, turning wood he had laid aside for proper curing into hubs and spokes and felloes, wheel parts he knew would not fit one another or warp later because of his haste and lack of concentration. He knew and he didn't care. He was in a spell. He was cursed.

Why should he be the one to suffer so? The men who'd kept Negroes chained to the walls with horseshoes cemented into the bricks, did they suffer from their doings? And the cries of the women and children as they stood on the block—did they prick the conscience of these men? Sometimes the silence of the Negroes grieved him more than the cries. Children were desirable—half-grown boys sold for the cheapest price and young girls they called *breeders,* for a bit more. He'd seen a trade a few days before, cash money passed hand to hand for a young boy naked to the waist and trembling. The sight sickened him.

Many were running now. They should. They should run and run from this hell, run from these flat, mosquito-drenched, parched fields, run for their lives. He'd heard a woman was leading them out. A woman! When he did not even have the courage to offer his place as a station. He hated his weakness. His desire for status had overridden his heart and his sense of right.

He looked up at his tree, the white oak that shaded his shop and yard, its mighty boughs filled with masses of dark green leaves that hid the sky. He couldn't fathom its mysteries. This morning it brought him no peace.

On the next trip to the smithy, he heard that Sam Green, Jr., the preacher's son, had left. He pictured him running, breathless, wading with his arms held high against the tide, rowing, or lying in the marsh grass, hiding in corn cribs and potato holes, napping in the loft of a trusted family, running through briars, through swamps filled with mosquitoes, in corn rows, running up through Delaware, following the star and direction someone who'd made the trip before told him of, sleeping in the day, but all night running, running, climbing aboard a moving train in the dark and lying on the roof under the stars so he could watch them and keep his faith, each step of the way a fearful glory. To Wilmington. To men a hundred times braver than August Woodson.

Several times a week the preacher met the "gentlemen," as they called themselves, while they crisscrossed the county, patrolling the roads and swamps. They rode their horses through woods and dusty fields in a fury that matched the heat of the sun. There was bounty to be had. Rewards from the wealthy. Why a man would leave his farm during harvest to search was more than Preacher Green could fathom. Their wrath grew and they took it out on the free ones, stopping to chastise them, search their homes and fodder houses. Shadrack Morris led the way. He was proud of their number, proud of their power to take matters into their own hands like they'd done with Levin Chambers.

They stopped at Mount Zion Church one Sunday and walked in on one of Green's sermons. With what felt like an ice pick in his heart, he looked up from the Bible as he watched two of them enter and sit down. "Where is he?" one of them called out.

He bowed his head. "Lord, Lord," he prayed. "These men, dear Lord, are tryin' to do what is right—bring property back to the one who's lost it. Forgive us, Lord, the way we trespass one another, the one who ran and the one who owned him." The last phrase slipped out unintentionally. He quickly went on praising the Lord and led his congregation into song: *Steal away, steal away to Jesus,* a chorus that seemed to him to leap from the windows and up the short, white steeple, out to the heavens, the rhythms mesmerizing the congregation as they swayed in one body, one motion, sending Sam Green, Jr. safely on his way. The white men left, slinking, wordless, not knowing what to make of it, not wanting to interrupt a prayer to the Almighty.

The searches went on for weeks. Rewards increased as time passed. Notices were sent through newspapers as far as Dover, Delaware. Posters were nailed to the trees. The preacher kept track of them whenever he could obtain a newspaper. The patrollers rode all night just behind the dogs and in the day, too, despite the harvest.

When he saw the death notice in the paper, he thought the patrollers must have stopped in their tracks at the sight. Along the road to Federalsburg, from the magnificent oak tree that stood outside August Wilson's shop, a rope swung bearing his lifeless body. The newspaper said the wheelwright's wagon stood nearby, the horses still hitched. The debris of wheels half made was strewn about the yard. They cut Woodson down and rode on to tell his wife and son, who were helping in a neighbor's wheat field. The patrollers must have puzzled over his death and regarded him as the man who'd always held himself apart, above them in skill and therefore better than they. But, surely mad.

The rain finally came at the end of summer and with it, high winds. In the forest, mold multiplied, as well as mushrooms, huge white funnel-shapes and orange domes for Libby to wonder about. The trees revived, but many branches crashed to the ground, and the ones that were mostly dead fell across pathways. The corn still shriveled in the too-late rain. The fodder turned black with mold, and chokeberry stained the ground purple. Moss turned bright green again, and lichen bloomed in its strange way.

Libby had grown. Although she was now sixteen, she still longed to go back to Elizabeth's. Since the youngest of Thomas Prouse's girls was now four, Libby was sent to the fields more often. Not only Prouse's fields, but she was loaded on a wagon with the others to work any field, any time, harvesting watermelons, winnowing wheat, gathering fodder, spreading guano. But it was the cornfield she hated most. She feared she would be taken down, as many had, among the stalks where no one would know. The pattyrollers were everywhere, sometimes even on foot in the corn rows.

Thomas Prouse seemed pleased with her, a fact that gave her the courage to approach him to ask to work in the house and help the Missus. "Libby, you do as you're told. You've got no special dispensation," he said, glaring at her.

"I don't know what that mean, sir," she told him, the words coming as slow as she dared so she could judge how they were landing on him.

"Favor," he said angrily. "You've got no special favor with me."

She bowed her head. It was not like him to speak so rough. Maybe it was the sight of ruined crops and the poor corn harvest. Or maybe he worried that his help would leave because he couldn't pay them. But he should know there was no wildness in her. The only place she wanted to run to was Elizabeth's cabin. Her mother, Addy, was back home now and her true brother, James, Jr., was there, too. The land was Elizabeth's, the field almost cleared, corn was plentiful, and two pigs were fattening up. It was home. Surely, she could work there and learn to weave and sew like Elizabeth. Throughout the yellow air of August turning into September, it was all she could think about. Just five miles east. That was all. She could easily walk it in a morning.

She told her wishes to Elizabeth as they worked together in the field along with Daniel and Eziah, cutting late wheat. Elizabeth's hair was tied up in a scrap of cloth. The scarf and her skin were covered with particles of grain like gold dust. She looked up at Libby.

"You been beaten? You eatin' good?" she said.

"I eat good as they do but sometime there ain't enough. But I've not been beat."

"Then wait, chile," was all Elizabeth would say. "I'll talk to 'im. You just keep doin' like you're s'posed to. We never signed papers for indenture so he has no right. But what I don't know is if it go accordin' to just his say-so."

So Libby waited.

The light in the cabin grew dim, the surrounding trees so dark Elizabeth had to turn the lamp on early. They had had the last of the salted herring for supper and she was thirsty. She looked forward to cold weather and readying the hogs. Bacon, soon. And corn cakes. She'd seen a wild turkey with a half-grown brood come out of the woods, and she tried to throw a quilt over them, but the mama squawked, feisty and mean. *The size of it!* Its head was up to her elbow. She let it go for the time being. In colder weather, she'd tell Daniel or James to hunt the hen down and then pen the young ones.

Not all the corn was in yet, what little there was. They'd worked beyond sundown on moonlit nights. The fodder still had to be gathered for the animals. Soon there'd be the slaughtering and the curing of meat, the making of sausage. Used to be, she didn't mind the work, one day slipping into the other, labor giving her purpose, distracting her from worry. Harvest was always satisfying. But the coming months of darkness and the news of August Woodson's strange death had spread an ominous cloud over her so that she found herself staring out the window as she sat in her rocker, wondering if she could have done Mr. Woodson a good turn or offered a kind word and if that would have made a difference.

"Betsy, you got the mopes," said Addy. "You feelin' all right?"

She nodded and watched Addy's needle go in the side of Daniel's shirt, and out, and in again, as she wove the threads to a patch.

"You're a good girl, Addy. Always have been," she said and her eyes filled. Addy couldn't ever remember seeing Betsy cry. She dropped the shirt and came to her side. "We're all right, Betsy. Don't worry so."

"It's the gun what scares me. What Mr. Morris don't know is it belong to Miss Mari. If word gets out, what Miss Mari goin' to think? She goin' to claim it—and then what? Worse than havin' the gun is I *stole* it."

"You didn't. Daniel did."

"Either way, what's the difference? One or both, thrown in jail. It'll be the end of this here homestead. You know if you spend anytime in jail, it just a good excuse to put you up to auction. Sell you south, free or not."

"I'm goin' to pray on it," said Addy and she did. Her head turned toward the candle and away, toward and away, and her eyes stayed open as if the Lord himself was in the room. Elizabeth heard the familiar words, the words saved especially for prayer, words like "kingdom," "power," "praise," "love," "glory," "blessed," and "true." She watched the shadows grow and recede across Addy's face and concentrated on the mellow sound of her voice. Light and shadow, sound and silence—through it she could allow herself to be unburdened. Give it all to the Lord, Addy would say and Perry would have, too. But Elizabeth would give it all to Addy, the only place she was sure of, the only one she could see. She rested then and was soon asleep.

She awoke to a knock on the door. It was a beginning, if you could divide a life into beginnings and endings of which there were many when you thought about it, gains and losses within a year, a day, even minute by minute, people coming together at different times in a life, each belonging to their own time in a person's memory. Now there were four of them, men she did not know who huddled around the steps, their faces lit by the opened door and the dimming light within. They'd been running and were breathing hard. The sound both frightened and thrilled her. They stood outside her door, expectant and hopeful. She was ready. With Addy and the children already gone to bed, she welcomed the men inside. They sat on her bare floor and told her Preacher Green had sent them. Could she hide them for a day? *Just a day, till tomorrow's dark?* She nodded and then two of them crept to the corn crib and one to the fodder shed. The young one climbed to the loft to stay with the boys.

She belonged to Preacher Green now. While his faith in God could not be hers, his brave faith in the Way was empowering. It was a privilege to be a part of something so large, so clandestine. He connected them all to one another. No one could lay back. This was community in its truest sense and she was now a part of it. She felt more hopeful than she ever had. How had she lived so long without hope? Merely to survive had never been enough.

"Not a word," she said to Addy and the boys in the morning. "This the most important thing you ever goin' do in your life, keepin' quiet, doin' some good, heah?" And she sent them to the runaways with freshly baked sweet potatoes, one for each, one hideout at a time, and bade the boys to watch as they'd never watched in their whole lives.

It was a beginning. The gun diminished in importance, belonging as it did to the *before* of things and now she was in the *after.* You could say she was right in the middle of the river, looking beyond herself and Addy and the children, all of them carried along by the tide, watching the shore, where whole congregations of people seemed as snarled as eels in a net, knotting themselves in and out of the holes, unaware of what they had wrought. She wondered what God thought of it all, or whether He'd washed his hands of them. Maybe he was a black God, one of their own. In her unquiet heart, she thought it just to believe God held no man image at all.

On a sunny December afternoon, warm enough to be outdoors without her shawl, Libby leaned against a post on Mr. Thomas Prouse's porch. The air was still, the trees bare against a cloudless sky. A black line appeared like a silk scarf waving from the east along the horizon. Blackbirds. She'd been waiting for them. Their fluid formation drew first nearer then farther away, then swooped down to earth and up again to the heavens. The designs they made changed every second: a fish, a ribbon, a platter, a bit of paper curled in the window widening into a broad banner that rippled and rolled in on itself, then swelling into a cloud. At some unseen signal, the flock spiraled and turned suddenly, specks in the sky, and then turned again into distinct bird bodies with beating wings, evenly spaced. Closer and closer they came, until at last they swarmed into the nearby trees and settled on the branches, thick as leaves and full of chatter. She stood motionless against the post, knowing full well they'd flare up at the slightest movement or sound. Maybe they carried prayers, collecting them for delivery to the Lord, in which case she would send one with them about being as free as they were and part of some great, wonderful expanse she knew nothing about—instead of stuck here in the soil. Did they know the secret that pointed the way to heaven?

Miss Marna, wife of Thomas Prouse, opened the door. The birds stopped their chatter as if of one mind and in the next instant, flared off in a whirring rush. The trees stood empty and lonesome.

"Libby," said Miss Marna softly. "He's breathin' heavy. Sit with him while I see to supper."

"Water, Libby. There's a good 'un," he said when she came to his bedside. Mr. Thomas would normally work in the barn fixing tools or be outdoors splitting wood in December. Now his face was flushed with fever and almost as red as his hair. Studying him, she was sad for him and for all of them. Perry was gone, and Mr. John Prouse, and Mr. Woodson, all the ones who'd treated them kindly. And now, Mr. Thomas Prouse. Did the birds wait to carry off his soul? She glanced out the window where she could still see them or part of them through the narrow glass as they flowed in an endless meandering stream, widening and narrowing in the near distance. She wrung out the cloth Miss Marna had left and wet Mr. Thomas's lips, then rinsed and wrung it out again to lay it on his brow. She waited silently, watching him. His skin was shiny, puffed, and he breathed as though each breath was a labor greater than he'd ever known. Then, without a word, he turned his head to one side and the air came rushing out of his body. Then all was still as the trees without the birds. She called out, *Jesus, Lord,* and ran for Miss Marna.

She thought about the birds after that, about Mr. Prouse dying and her wish to be free and to be sent back to Elizabeth. His dying did not mean she would be sent home, but it could mean she would be sent elsewhere. After the funeral, Miss Marna said, "I need you more than ever, Libby." She'd been selfish to want to go home. The birds had taken Mr. Prouse's soul. It wasn't her fault he died; it wasn't wishes or prayers the birds carried, she told herself. Or was it?

Just before Christmas, Elizabeth came in her Sunday dress and shawl, her face placid and her chin high. Libby caught sight of her from the second-story window and leapt down the stairs. But Elizabeth's eyes remained stern and narrow as she stood on the porch as if any softening in attitude would jeopardize the task she'd taken on. She carried a basket of corncakes for Miss Marna along with one of the turkeys, cleaned and wrapped in a cloth.

"Elizabeth!" Libby cried. She slipped into her arms, the basket set now on the porch floor. Elizabeth had come for her, she was certain. She pulled away and went to let Miss Marna know. The mule waited beyond the gate, its neck slunk down between its shoulder blades.

"I'd like for Libby to come home now," she heard Elizabeth say when Miss Marna appeared. "Her mother need her and so do I."

Libby held her breath. No telling what would happen with Mr. Thomas gone. There would be the payment of debts, an auction, Miss Marna figuring how to pay everybody and thinking maybe she could sell what didn't belong to her.

Miss Marna, the flesh under her chin trembling, said, "Now Elizabeth. She has to stay till the end of the year. That's the way the accounts are set up."

Libby watched Elizabeth pull her thin lips into a line that wouldn't be crossed. "No, ma'am," she said. "Libby need to come home now."

"I say after Christmas we'll look at the accounts and let you know."

"She free and her mama free and that mean she can come home when she need to." Elizabeth held out the basket. "I'm sorry for your troubles, Miss Marna. But I'm takin' the chile now. No papers were signed. She not an orphan. She got a home. And no wages been sent for months now."

"Of course, I can't hold her," said Miss Marna, taking the basket. "I only appeal to your sense of what is right."

"I come to fetch her," insisted Elizabeth.

Without further word, without a thank you or any civility, Miss Marna turned and pushed the door open with her knee, the heavy basket filling her arms. "I'll not forget this, Elizabeth," she hissed to the door. "Libby! Get your things!" she shrieked.

For a while they walked silently, one on either side of the mule. Libby turned often to look behind her at the Prouses' bare, gray cabin. There was nothing to say about any of it. She was sorry for Miss Marna. She watched the sandy road under her feet till Elizabeth said, "Libby, I'll ride the mule now. I'm tired." Libby rested the burlap bag that held her Sunday dress on the ground and knelt on one knee so Elizabeth could boost herself onto the mule. They were far enough along the road out of sight of the house now. The trees began to thicken and the road ahead disappeared into the woods. Libby handed the sack to Elizabeth and giggled and danced, raising dust.

"Oh, Elizabeth, I'm so glad to be goin' home with you."

"I know, chile. We got a house with three women and three generations plantin' come spring. Perry'd be proud. I think he know. I think he watchin' us."

"We goin' be together under one roof."

It was like the settling down of the blackbirds, this moment of happiness come to Libby, and it stretched out across the sky. She'd be hired out again surely, but each night she would come back to Elizabeth's cabin and Elizabeth's field. Someday, it would all be Addy's (Elizabeth said so) and they'd stay free. As long as they paid the taxes, Elizabeth said. And she would pay her share and work alongside her mother and Elizabeth, and she would belong to them because that was what being free meant—staying with your own people on your own land.

MATTIE, 2000

—•—

Now I settle in the woods near 'bout where James was taken, maybe because it was the moment when everythin' changed. I can see it clear. No need for explainin' or thinkin' about it, no *what-ifs*. No chance for a way out. No chance for lyin'. Simple. Clear. He got stole. I wonder if he know I hang 'round. I wonder if he come by, restless as I am, wantin' to know what happen and who did it, and if it helps to know. He must. So I settle in the woods where nothin' and everythin' changed without questions of anythin' bein' fair. It different with animals. They got to live—deer nestlin' in the clearin', raccoons chasin' possums, owls swoopin' down on mice, fox stealin' birds. But a man stealin' a man now, that's different. It a branch broken off. An empty place. But I'm piecin' it together.

The woods help me 'cause they the same as they always was. Lots of places are covered over with cement, but these Dorchester woods mostly stay wild.

You see what's happenin'? I stay in Dorchester. I could go anywhere, but I don't. Instead, I jump across time like it was nothin' but a blink. I see Fran sometime, the mail girl. I almost want to go and see if I got any mail but the box ain't there no more. Still, Fran rides by.

I remember one time before I died, there was a dozen crabs in the mailbox, all steamed and wrapped in newspaper. I sat right under the peach tree and ate 'em, suckin' that sweet meat out from the claws, my favorite. Fran left 'em. When her husband had a good catch and she had extra, she'd leave some for me. At the

136

same time, though, a letter come stuck in there, and all I could make out was it come from the gov'ment.

So the next day, when Fran come by again, I hailed her down to thank her for the crabs. I had some cantaloupe for her that she said she was glad to get. But I had somethin' else on my mind.

"Fran," I say. "I hate to bother you, but I needs you to read me this letter from the gov'ment. I 'most threw it out, but then I thought it might be somethin' important."

She was always willin'. A nicer woman you'd never meet. If I forgot to get my mail a day or two, she'd stop by to see if I was all right. She kept her eye on people and helped me make out money orders for my hospital payments. Come to find out, the letter said the gov'ment was goin' to send me money. They got my name from the census. All the peoples born between 1917 and 1926 didn't get paid the right Social Security so they were talkin' 'bout payin' us five thousand dollars. A lot of 'em already dead. After that, I got a handful of letters, one axin' me if they should send me so much once a month, or send it all at once. Fran helped me fill out the paper, and I say, "Send it to me. All of it at one time!" Then they wanted me to send money to support the passin' of the bill. It was called the Hatch Act. Fran said, "Don't send anything, Mattie."

I waited a long time for that money. I planned to go to Florida and visit Juanita, maybe get a new coat or somethin' that wasn't man's clothes. Ever once in a while I'd ask Fran, "You think the gov'ment goin' to send me that money?" She never said yes and she never said no, but she'd get this look in her eye that tol' me she was doubtful. All she say was, "I sure hope it does, Mattie. If anybody deserves a check in the mail, it's you, the way you been feeding everybody that comes through here."

My electric wasn't but twenty-eight dollars a month. I never wanted a stove because then I'd have to pay a gas bill. I had a hot plate and an electric fry pan and a toaster oven. That and the telephone were my only bills. But I could have used that money from the gov'ment. I never did get it. I got along just fine, but I have to admit there weren't a day went by I didn't go to that mailbox thinkin' this was gonna be the day.

I shoulda known. Nobody gets money dropped in their mailbox. And even if they did, they don't get to keep it for long. It goes back somehow. Taxes. Bills. Like land—you only borrow it for a while 'fore somebody get it from you. The thing that somebody didn't know was they be only borrowin' it, too. The land'll be there long after each of us has a turn, ownin' or just scratchin' the soil. Elizabeth had that field for only a little while and then it was somebody else's. Lady what came after her, Miss Nettie, she thought her ownin' was good and permanent, too. People have a hard time thinkin' about their passin' and what come after.

Home, we sharecropped. Like Preacher Green, we worked the land, but we didn't own it. We planted cotton with a walkin' planter then, and the mule pulled it. We didn't set out tomato plants like they did here. We planted seeds just like we did for barley and wheat. Tobacco, the same way, and peanuts. When we picked the cotton, Papa would sell it. So many loads he'd carry on that little cart and haul to town. There was a gin there where we took the cotton and they'd get the seeds out and bale it. People would come and buy it right there at the mill.

When the tobacco got ripe, we had to break the stems and strip the leaves off. We put 'em in a cart and hauled it to the barn where we had sticks. My brother and I would hand three leaves at a time to my mama and my oldest sister, who'd string crisscross back over the sticks and tie up the leaves. Then my oldest brother and Papa would hang 'em up in the barn. When we got that done, Papa'd make a fire in the kiln to dry the tobacco. When it was ready, he'd take the tobacco to auction and the buyer would come out and all the white peoples and colored peoples and sharecroppers would be there and the auction man would roll those sounds out, singin' away, *sixty-five, seventy, seventy-five—who'll gimme more?* In the biddin', the white man got the money, and then he say you got to pay for seed and fertilizer, and when he got done, we never got nothin' and we owed him besides.

We always had a good crop of peanuts. Papa would plow 'em up and let us shake 'em out. We'd turn 'em up so that the tops would be down and the peanuts would be up and they could dry. Then he'd take 'em in the cart up to the barn and we'd pick the peanuts off and put 'em in a bag for winter. He tried to sell some of the peanuts after he saved some for seed and fed the hogs. We'd put the peanuts in one-hundred-pound bags and Papa would carry 'em to the market. They didn't really buy the peanuts. They wouldn't give you much for 'em. It was like they took 'em from you and didn't pay you. Papa would just stand there and they'd take 'em. Lord, we'd be standing there dumb-like. It seems funny now, always expectin' this time it might be better and we'd get some decent money, but we never did and we never said anythin'. Lookin' back, I still can't believe we let it happen that way. It'd be different now. It took me a while, but I learned to say, "No, you don't," good and loud.

One time, Gordy and me was out fishin' along the bank of the Choptank and I slipped in the mud under a tree root. Well, my arm got hung up and no matter how I tried, I couldn't break free. Gordy tried to help me ever which way and the more he tried, the worse it got. Finally, I wrenched my arm free, but it was broke bad. Mangled. Gordy took me to the hospital and the doctor say my arm had to come off. I started makin' noise then. When I drew myself up I was way bigger than he was. "No, you don't," I hollered. The doctor backed off. Nothin' like seein' a bit o' fright in a white man's eyes. The doctor started talkin' 'bout gettin' me up to John Hopkins in a helicopter, with me still yellin', "No, you don't!" Finally, Gordy called the man we was workin' for, and he carried me to another hospital in his pickup. I was in traction for nineteen days, but I still had both arms. Stickin' up for yourself good and loud, that's what you gotta do.

Somethin' not fair can make you crazy at the time. But now, it all just a story. In this aftertime, I can watch myself under that peach tree, so glad to tell my stories to anybody who'd listen, me just sittin' there, leanin' on my cane, chewin', satisfied. I'd go on and on, just like me and Gordy used to do. All them faces rollin' before me—I knew what helped me say *no* was Luther King and his people. So maybe that's what freedom is, the chance to say no, in which case I figure it somethin' you have to steal and treat right when you got it. And before there was Luther King? Peoples stole themselves. Runaways. Imagine that.

It takes a lot a doin' not to be afraid.

Lord, take segregation. How they killed peoples down there in Mississippi and Alabama. Oh, Lord. Honest peoples, church peoples, little chilren gettin' killed. Lord, there's a lot of hate for colored folks. The president that freed the slaves, they killed him because he did. They killed both the Kennedys. And they killed Dr. King.

It was better in Maryland than down south. Pickin' crops here we got good money compared to what we got in Georgia. Down there, I got fifty cent a day. In Maryland, I got fifty cent an hour, so that's where I stayed. Besides the cantaloupes, there was plenty of work when the tomatoes come in. You'd have a bucket with a number on it, and when you filled that bucket, you put it at the end of the row and the man would tally up how many buckets you picked. Then you got paid.

Ever tomato that got put in a can was peeled by hand. We worked in the fields all day and peeled tomatoes till eleven at night. Sometime, we peeled till we got done. In the morning, I got to the fields at daybreak. There was no time for yourself when the tomatoes were in. Come Friday night, there'd be an old school bus the white man owned and he drove us to the beer gardens in Cambridge for twenty five cent a head. We got giblet stew there and had a drink or two. Twelve o'clock the bus would come 'round again. We had to get off where we got on.

There were beer gardens all around then. One in Rhodesdale where you could buy meat, hot dogs, pork chops, eggs, flour, and beer you could drink right there. There was another one in East New Market where the colored went in at the back of the store and the white go in the front. There'd be tables where the colored could sit and drink. And there was one down at Whitely's in Williamsburg, one side for white and one for colored. There was James's Place in Vienna. It a church now. No white ate in there.

We didn't go to the movies in Cambridge, but we'd go to a drive-in. You could park anywhere at a drive-in. That's if somebody had a car.

We didn't go down to the river much except to fish. Sometime now I go with the breezes right over the Choptank River. Now there's motors in the workboats and you don't see oyster tongin' much no more. But on the way to the river, not five miles from the shore, is where Preacher Green's farm was and that old church, Mount Zion. High tide, the river reaches inland and that old preacher knowed news traveled the same way. Stories come off that river he couldn't read in no newspaper, what with them big workboats and schooners and steamboats travelin' up and down. He knew what was happenin', Gordy say. What was seen was soon said and passed along from river to creek to swamp to road to the preacher house. I see where plenty of skiffs from long ago hid in the rushes at high tide. A man could lay down in the grasses in the daytime and run by night. And he'd know which way to go and who to ax for help. That Preacher Green, he right in the middle of it. And nobody ever knew.

CURRENTS, 1855

---

*I*n the dead of night, Preacher Green often sat by his fire and listened for a man called Josiah Bailey, a friend of his son's, who, when he could, rowed across the river from Jamaica Point and ran with news for a good portion of the night. Josiah, despite his job as overseer for the harvesting and hauling of timber down river for the shipbuilder and landowner, Hughlett, was one of the many who Green knew flirted with escape. It wouldn't be long, he told himself. Like Sam, Jr., Josiah was often beaten by his master. The one fortunate circumstance was that because Hughlett's land was on both sides of the Choptank, Josiah had access to his master's skiff along with many of the secrets of the Way. Green worried about the chances Josiah took in stealing his nights for the cause, yet Josiah often confided that he felt fortunate. He could have been assigned to the fields like his wife and three daughters, all of whom were also owned by Hughlett.

Only a few weeks after Sam, Jr.'s escape, news rippled through the congregation at Mount Zion of his safe arrival in Canada. Josiah had brought the letter that said, "Come one, come all, plenty of friends, plenty to eat, and plenty to drink." Green tucked the often-read, wrinkled letter in his Bible. It was his most treasured possession.

And after the last shipment of white oak down river, much to Green's delight, Josiah knew exactly when Harriet was passing through. Her parents lived at Poplar Neck, not far up river. It was one of the more favored stations along the Way. As he told the story later, Josiah "borrowed" Hughlett's skiff, paddled the mile across river, and set off on foot to Green's house. In less than an hour, he was at the door with news.

Christmas was close at hand. Green thought about its heavenly message—how sweet it was, but not the earthly realities his parishioners would have to endure. The congregation would swell with slaves and free alike because they'd be given a day or two off to visit relatives, but it was also the time of year when owners settled their accounts and took stock of their situation. Many of the farmers he knew owed for land and expenses, and those who had borrowed more than they could repay used their slaves for financial leverage even though they'd promised manumission to keep their help satisfied. They'd sell their field hands if they needed cash, and the number of slave auctions would increase. More families would be broken.

However, there was another message this Christmas and it was *be ready.* He couldn't say it from the pulpit, but he didn't have to. The song told the story: *When the good old ship of Zion comes along, be ready to step aboard,* Harriet herself at the helm. The white population didn't know much about this slight woman and her power, but to Preacher Green, she was larger than life. Hers was a story as stirring as those in the Bible and one he loved. She was called Moses now. How she accomplished what she did was testimony to God. He'd chosen one of theirs to be the new Moses and He'd spoken to her. Preacher Green was in awe of how God watched over her and how every escape was successful. She said the Lord did it, her mouth set in a firmness not to be argued with. She was one of them, poor and proud, but in her determination, strong as a man. She'd once suffered a head wound so grave it was thought she'd die from it. A slave owner had thrown an iron weight at her, but she healed to proclaim the glory of God. She was a little woman who'd been scarred by the white man, yet she was afraid of nothing.

As the year drew to its close, he saw an ad in the Cambridge paper for an upcoming sale and realized the widow Brodess would sell Harriet's brothers. He knew, then, Harriet would be back. He watched for her. When members of his congregation asked him privately if he'd heard anything about her, he denied any knowledge. His people were greedy for gossip and hungered after good news, but he had to ignore their curiosity. They guessed she would be back and whispered to one another that she would get through, of that they were sure, the way she read the stars and knew all the safe houses and had visions from God Himself who spoke to her. His signals kept her and her travelers safe. There was a price on her head, too, but they were never going to catch her, not with the Lord watching.

To his congregation, he affirmed nothing, although they were right about all of it. When he returned to his house on Sunday evening, he shut the door while he listened to the wind. He could not distract himself as he sat by the fire, glancing at Kitty and watching the lamp burn low. He could not read the Bible or settle his mind. Even though all of him waited, when he heard the soft knock and the half-whisper, *Preacher! Preacher Green!* He jumped. He knew it was not Harriet because she never called him Preacher. He was unsure about opening the door with the children upstairs. Kitty glanced at him above her sewing with a flash of worry, yet there was no question that he'd open the door. He'd heard no horses and knew it could not be the white "committee," four or five of them stealing up to the house, guns at the ready, wanting to search. No, it wasn't them.

He opened the door. Crouched before him was Josiah, his bald head shining in the light from the fire that accented the scar on his cheek. There was a furtive urgency in Josiah's stooped figure.

Once inside the cabin, his words came in a torrent. "Robert Ross, Harriet's brother? He left, and Ben Ross, Jr. and Henry Ross, too, and a woman, Jane, but Robert held back, his wife havin' a baby just as he was about to leave. Christmas night, it was, with the baby just born and the mother cryin', suspicionin' something. Then Robert say he goin' to hire himself out for Christmas Day. She say, cryin', *I'll not see you again, sure,* and the two boys standin' there watchin'. Robert scared to leave, scared not to, knowin' he'd be sold south and he not seein' his family either way. Then he run, without tellin' her the truth, the others already there, forty mile away at his mother's—old Rit's house, but hidin' from her, too, fearin' she'd raise a storm in her excitement with seein' 'em home for Christmas and draw attention. So ol' Rit waited for 'em, rockin' in her chair and smokin' her corncob pipe not knowin' her chilren were right there in the fodder shed, and old Ben—he never saw 'em either, 'cause he covered his eyes when they come so he could honestly say he never seen his own flesh and blood. Robert come on Christmas Day—it rainin' hard—and waited with 'em in the fodder, and when darkness come, they took off, the woman dressed like a man, and Harriet leadin' 'em out with old Ben walkin', two sons helpin' him far as he could go with his eyes blindfolded so he couldn't lie. They probly went up Denton way from Poplar Neck, or maybe Federalsburg way—nobody know for sure, nor would say if they did."

He was out of breath with the running and the telling, perspiration trickling down his cheeks and neck. Lit by the fire, his face twitched. He glared at Preacher Green, his eyes reflecting the flames, or was it another flame that lit him? The preacher could tell when a man had decided, when he was approaching the moment of decision, when in his head he truly became free, when nearly all of his thoughts were of planning and scheming the way north. Claiming a man's freedom occurred way before the act of running ever took place. Josiah wet his lips as though he could already taste freedom, could imagine it, dream it for himself, and therein lay the difference between those who'd make it out and those who'd be broken in the trying.

"Man what work on the water sent word up to Harriet her brothers would be sold and sent south after Christmas Day. I heard 'bout it when I was haulin' timber," Josiah said. "So Harriet sent a letter to Jacob Jackson, who was workin' down there where the brothers be a short way away, it written so the postmaster not catch on, 'cause the postmaster, you know, he read everythin' sent to free ones, 'specially Jackson. They suspectin' somethin', bein' he can read and write. But Jackson say he don't know what the letter mean, comin' from somebody named William Henry Jackson, and sayin', *Tell my brothers to be watchin', when the good old ship of Zion comes along, be ready to step aboard.* He played dumb even though he knowed full well what it mean. And he tole Harriet's brothers to get ready. No time to waste. Then she met 'em at Ben and Rit's cabin up there to Poplar Neck." He paused, finally, and sat calm in the light of the fire. "So many goin'. It give me the idea."

"Tonight?"

"No. Not yet. I want to have a little in my pocket beforehand."

"I got another letter from Sam." The preacher pulled a wrinkled paper out of his Bible. "This part is for you, *Tell Jackson to come on, Josiah Bailey come on. Come more.*"

"He workin'?"

The preacher nodded and read him the rest of the letter, how Sam, Jr. had gotten work at a sawmill after arriving in Canada on September 5, how he was earning close to a dollar a day. *I live in a vilage coold Chip Way in Canaday.* The words rhymed a song, one the father got to humming to himself at odd moments.

Josiah, seated now, elbows on knees, swung his head side to side as he smiled. "That's good. That's real good."

He stared into the fire for a while and then glanced back at Green. "Got to get back 'fore they miss me. I been beat for less. Been beat just for beatin' sake, seem to me. I been a good worker, savin' the man money so he don't have to hire white to oversee, but sometime, more I hear, I cain't stop thinkin' 'bout takin' off. Ol' Sammy made it though." He laughed then, and got up. "I be damned. Excuse me, Preacher."

With that, Josiah disappeared into tree shadows. He would stop only to listen and Green prayed he would hear nothing but the beating of his own heart.

When at last he lay beside Kitty and closed his eyes, he prayed again for Moses, a name rightly chosen, and the runaways and for Ben and Rit who would be under as much suspicion for their sons' escapes as he was for Sam, Jr.'s. The white planters would be stirred up and come knocking more furiously than ever, but for him to have an enslaved son who'd made it out was like blowing seeds to the wind. There was much wild hope in it, and pride. *Forgive me, Lord, but I am proud to the bone.*

In the darkness, he began to plan how he would go to Canada, traveling in broad daylight as a free man to see his free son. It was as grand a statement as he could make. But he had to come back—there was his daughter, Sarah, married now but still enslaved, and there were his grandchildren and the children who stayed with him and Kitty, his congregation, his white clapboard church with the steeple high above the surrounding cabins. He had a duty.

He knew there would be reprisals. He knew he'd be watched closely because of his son's escape, but he never suspected anger over the escape would touch his beloved daughter, Sarah. Then came the news like an ax swung to his heart in the midst of his dreaming and planning, in his pride in his son. There came the punishment beyond all, the knock on the door, the gasped words, the news. Sarah had been sold. Taken from her husband and children, she was sent to the frontier border of Missouri. A long way away. Kitty would be inconsolable. The grandchildren, too, were enslaved and though he and Kitty might raise them now, it would be the same. The raising and the taking again someday. When he told his wife, it was the hardest thing he ever had to do.

Through their tears he told her the Lord would see them through. *Hear me, Kitty.* But anger burned his insides. He would go to Canada. He would see how it was. He might even stay. Take Kitty and the children. And the rest of it be damned.

He went out to split wood. He swung the ax high overhead and down with a vengeance, sighing and yelling out in turn, naming his grief. The boy, Edward, whom he and Kitty cared for, watched with astonishment. He told Edward to collect the split wood and pile it on the wagon. He knew the boy would take pride in neat arrangements and keep a record. In subsequent days, Edward marked on the fence post the number of cords he'd delivered, which amounted to twenty-three, then forty-eight, then sixty cords of wood. Each wagonload went to the neighboring farmer. On the last day, with the final shipment of wood on the ground, the farmer gave Edward two dollars. At first Edward said he thought the money was for him with payment to be made to Preacher Green later, but he soon learned the money was not for him.

"This is for the preacher," said the farmer.

When the boy returned and handed the money to Green, anger once again consumed him. Two dollars for sixty cords. He would ask for more. He deserved more. Yet when he considered that his request would be scoffed at, he gave up the thought.

Help me grow above it, Lord. Meanwhile, Canada grew grander.

They'd come in the late evening from a farm ten miles away, four more of them, ragged and barefoot, having started out just before the first star appeared. Elizabeth shared leftover corn cakes from supper, which they ate quickly as they listened to her instructions.

"You go directly north and stay on this side of the Marshyhope. You don't want to cross that river—there's evil on the other side. They'll get you sure if you put one foot on the land 'cross from Crotcher's Ferry. No—stay straight north—watch the stars—to the next road—it'll be the one to the Quaker meetin' house." The preacher had told her the Way, and the directions were etched on her brain.

She looked at the youngest one. "You be the same age as Daniel," she said. "You can stay till your daddy sends for you." The boy shook his head. Slowly, so low she could barely hear him, he said, "I can keep up. I'm goin' with my father." She wrapped him an extra cake. He was going to fill out soon, be a man. His voice was on the verge of going deep.

"Go," she said, "Keep your eyes open."

Daniel was in the field tending the root fires started that day. He'd been beside her all this time, clearing. They'd been able to hitch the mule to the root plow for a large section of the field, and where the plow wouldn't go through, Daniel and Eziah had dug down and pulled up roots. She and Addy raked them into piles for burning. Nearly three acres were cleared for wheat now, one for each year owned. Daniel had built a shelter for the pigs, split wood, taught Eziah, and given her what he could when he was hired out. Eziah, the same. They were good boys, just like sons.

She remembered that first day Daniel came to her. Crusted with dirt, his skin cracked and gray, he stood before her and cried silently, without expression, his eyes filling with tears. She took him down to the stream and began to wash him, running the cloth and soap over his small, thin body, and marveled at its perfection, while she crooned softly, "It be all right. Your mama come back for you sometime. And I'm here. I be your mama for a while. That be all right now, won't it? And after we get done here, I got a corn cake for you and a little syrup." He merely watched her, detached as if nothing in the world could ever belong to him again, but she kept on scrubbing. Then she dried him off and rubbed him down with tallow to make him shine like a chestnut newly out of its husk. When she was finished, she pulled a long shirt that had belonged to Perry over his head.

"You be all right now, chile. There be plenty to eat." The stream of tears ceased. He let the last of them drip off his chin. She wiped his face. "You'll see your mama again sometime, I promise." But it was an empty promise, one she hoped he didn't remember. A little while later, Eziah was left with her, and Daniel came down to the stream with them and told Eziah, "You all ashy, but don't you worry. Betsy be your mama now. She take care of you same as your mama would."

Lord, that child was sweet.

Could she claim any right to them now that they'd been with her through their growing? No. There was no debt unless it was hers to them, no owning, no ties save her love for them. She would miss them when they left. She'd wait until Daniel asked to go, and if he asked to go north, she would see to that, too. She knew the Way now. Times were dangerous and at the same time promising. The black river was seeping north. She did not know that soon it would be rushing like the unstoppable power of water.

Libby, a major source of income now, was hired out to Eben Prouse, the youngest and the only one left of the three Prouse brothers. Elizabeth allowed it only because of the money but took a firm stand about where Libby stayed.

"She glad to work in the fields with your girls, but don't put her in a cabin by herself, Mr. Eben. I ax you, please. She work for Prouses all her young life, and she do anythin' she has to. But if she not livin' home, then she need protection." Mr. Eben had agreed, and a cot was prepared for her in the corner of the kitchen. Miss Leah, Mr. Eben's wife, was glad for the help since the youngest of their five daughters, still a baby at the breast, was sickly, and Miss Leah herself did not fare well after the birth.

However, the household was a bustling, cheerful place with the high-spirited older girls, all with hair the color of flame. They often included Libby in guessing games and chases when she was through with her chores. Every one of them could read, and Libby begged to be taught. Mr. Eben didn't seem to mind.

The oldest, Lydia, just Libby's age, often read to them in the evening by the fire while the girls sewed. This night, she sat on the floor with the newspaper, *The Cambridge Eagle*, spread in front of her, and read out loud an announcement about a lecture to be held at the Methodist church on Sunday evening.

"It's going to be about *electricity*. Please, please, Papa, can we go?" It was hard for Mr. Eben to deny his girls anything, although he was strict when it came to work. He was not likely to do something just for their sake, but the word "electricity" aroused a curiosity that permeated the room. Libby wasn't sure what they were talking about, so she bent her head over her sewing, feeling fortunate to be included in the gathering around the fire and being read to, too. Once her father said yes, Lydia begged to have Libby come along. Embarrassed at the prospect of riding in the wagon with the girls and entering a white church, Libby kept silent. She had hoped to go to Elizabeth's on Sunday. In the end, Mr. Eben insisted she go along with the girls to church, saying it was part of her education.

On Sunday evening, despite a fierce wind and imminent snow, Mr. Eben hitched up his hay wagon to drive his four oldest daughters and Libby the two miles to town. As he helped each one onto the wagon, he called out, "Hup, now. There you go! Huddle up, girls!" He often said he wished he'd had five boys instead of girls, but it looked to Libby like his broad smile showed great pride in his family. She thought there was nothing so endearing to him as the voices of his daughters, especially when they were excited as they were now. The air was cold, the wind fresh, but no one complained. Libby hunkered down in the back of the wagon and listened to the voices as she pulled a blanket tight around her and stared into the night.

When they approached town, Mr. Eben slowed the horses and the girls quieted. They listened to the voices of the townspeople calling to each other along
Main Street like echoes traveling through time, flirting, teasing, and proclaiming
hopes for a snow that would pack the roads solid enough for a good sleigh ride.
The lighted windows glowed with the promise of warmth and cheer. Laughter
exploded from an opened door as two young women floated out along the side-
walk where the muddy footprints of midday had frozen. The uneven ground
caused the women to step gingerly and reach out to one another. The trees
swayed, the wind picked up, and snow began. The figures of the Prouse girls jos-
tled in time to the wagon's rhythm. The closer they came to the church, Libby's
apprehension grew. The strangeness of privilege. To be *allowed* after being denied
was confusing. It brought false hope. Momentary pretense. She wondered what
Elizabeth had made for supper, and if Daniel, taking care of things, ever missed
her like she missed him.

Suddenly, Lydia called out, "Emily!" One of the young women turned and
waved. Pleased, Lydia laughed and said to her younger sister, "You know her,
don't you? I see her in church all the time. Her father's a doctor, and she lives in
that big house over there."

To Libby, the town, with its auction block and staunch brick houses where
she'd heard slaves were kept until trade or auction, was a fearful place, yet she
realized to the Prouse girls, it spelled enchantment. Mr. Eben was not rich. He
was a carpenter at the mill and a farmer in the field. Libby was his only Negro
and she was free as well. But those who lived in the big houses with porch
kitchens and slave quarters, smoke houses and liveries, high windows filled with
candlelight, immense fireplaces and fine horses and carriages, they were powerful—those doctors, lawyers, businessmen, traders, gentlemen farmers—men
who'd owned much of the land and who had all the say-so. Their sons *inherited.*
And their daughters went to school and went to parties. They were different
from the Prouse girls, who never tired of stories about the goings-on in town.
Mr. Eben said it was all a bit of foolishness, that those in town were safely
guarded from reality and were blindly accepting despite meaning well. He said
he was glad his girls didn't fit into town society. "Look at you, my lovelies. You're

all ruddy-complexioned and sturdy. You can do anything on the farm that needs to be done. You'll be good wives one day."

But Libby heard them talk when Mr. Eben wasn't around. They all wanted to be in town, wanted *entertainments*, which meant tea served to them mid-afternoon. They longed for visits back and forth for card games, dances, and parties. And they wanted to attend the women's seminary, and wear hoop skirts and kid gloves. Who wouldn't? Lydia had said, "I'd just love to be in a place where farm work was for somebody else," and she glanced at Libby. "Wouldn't you, Libby?" The gulf between them had widened. Libby looked down without answering, tasting bitterness.

Now Lydia chatted about her friend. "You know, she doesn't dress herself, but has a Negro dress her? One time she complained because she had to do it herself. I wouldn't want anyone dressing me. And she's a very fine seamstress. She's making a bed screen for when she marries. She's already got someone picked out, a doctor's son, only he doesn't know it yet. And she plays the piano. She has a ballroom in her house and sometimes holds dances. She knows how to dance a hoedown. She said she'd teach me."

Yes, there was Emily in her blue wool coat and matching hat, arm in arm with her best friend, about to enter the church.

Lydia went on. "And just last week, her father brought home oranges that came by steamboat. She let me have one."

Libby's mouth watered. She'd had an orange once. It was the Christmas the preacher in Cambridge gave a basketful to Preacher Green, and he'd shared the fruit with his parishioners.

The talk went on and on—about the new teacher from the North who'd come to teach at the school for ladies, and how Emily had been the first to ride in Mr. Wright's new carriage, about rain so heavy they'd had to spend the night at Emily's best friend's, about sitting on the settee with her young man. Oh, all of it was grand to Lydia. For Libby, a window had been opened to a world she knew nothing about, while Lydia pined for it.

Nattering on, Lydia said, "And you know, Papa? She said the most beautiful words to me, so beautiful I memorized them, 'The aim of one's life should be to cultivate a love, find the beautiful in nature and art, to educate one's better nature and virtues, overcome evil thoughts and words, and to shun all things of hidden evil.' Don't you agree, Papa? Isn't that the most beautiful thing you ever heard?"

Mr. Eben nodded as snowflakes caught on the brim of his hat.

At the church, the girls spilled out of the wagon in their haste to enter while Libby covered her head and remained in the corner.

"Come on there, Libby. It's too cold for you to sit out here."

Libby shook her head.

"I said for you to come on. What's the matter with you?"

"I don't belong."

"Well, don't look at it that way. God is the same everywhere."

She doubted it. Her eyes filled with tears. Mr. Eben did not seem to notice as he held out his hand for her to climb down. There was nothing else to do.

Inside, she stood in the back of the hall as the sisters took their seats. After the lecture, Emily and her friend stood on the small stage and held out their hands to the electric current, gave a little scream, then a laugh. Frightened, Libby hung back. She felt Mr. Eben glance at her, but she never lifted her eyes.

Afterward, the young women gathered in a small circle and talked. Anxious to be heading home because of the snow, she and Mr. Eben waited in the wagon until his impatience took hold, and he called in a voice he seldom used with them. Maybe he thought his daughters envied the young women in town a bit too much. Maybe he wanted to tell them to erase from their minds any thoughts of belonging to town society, that the rift was too great and they were better off with their own kind. What he said to them was, "Don't go gettin' ideas. There's rightfulness and grace in knowin' one's place."

She heard Lydia mutter, "'Less we find somebody fancy to marry."

Indeed. She wondered if anybody in town knew or cared how the people who served them lived, or even if they saw them at all. Society took care to regenerate itself. Townspeople didn't ask questions. No reason to, everything going their way. Maybe the Prouses had questioned some things and maybe that was why they remained separate. She listened to the wagon wheels squeak through the swiftly gathering snow. The wheels for the way things were had been set in motion a long time ago and could not be slowed down enough to change direction. The girls, huddled under shawls and quilts in the open wagon, were quiet and sleepy in the falling snow. A peaceful scene, one Libby was thankful for, where girlish chatter would not break the silence. But as they passed under a street lamp, a poster tied to the pole shuddered in the wind and told its story: "Reward for Runaway, a Negress, twenty-nine." That she could read it was little comfort.

THE ALPHA AND OMEGA
SEASONS, 1856

───·•·───

*P*reacher Green walked behind his plow, his arms molded to plow-iron as though he and the plow and the mule were one, sinking into wet brown earth together. Maybe he ought to wait with the plowing until the ground had dried. He turned to look behind him. His eyes followed the long, dark furrows impressed with his footprints in lonely, purposeful stride. All of a man's work should be as clear to him. In an ideal world. Plain and simple. Instead of sneaking and hiding. Two more came through last night. He led them near the mill to the Quakers up near Hunting Creek, but the last time they came through, the patrollers had dogs, and he'd had to take the runaways across the creek, wading through marshland just as the tide was coming in. He hoped their tracks were covered and, for their safety, led them in a circuitous route.

He told his people that during planting time he could not hold Sunday school at the church. It was only partly true. If he were to be caught teaching the young to read on a Sunday morning during a surprise visit by the "committee," matters would be worse. Assisting the runaways in the dark of night was different. He knew what he knew. All of his prayers were for them, and if the Lord ignored his beseeching it certainly was not for lack of trying on his part. An article in the paper proclaimed the black man's happiness and contentment to serve. "The Negroes are well looked after. The relationship between colored and white is all to the good." He couldn't show his growing anger, could never lay it out like his footprints behind him.

The unity he sought was not in his church, the one place he expected to find it. The church had split into two factions over ten years ago, Methodist Episcopal South and Methodist Episcopal North. There were many slaveholders in Dorchester's ME North and although they didn't have many slaves, they were rebuked by abolitionists and fellow church members who were against slavery. At first, there were heated debates at the conventions, and then silence took over. The issue became the great unsolvable, not to be spoken of in polite company. Still, he knew about undercurrents. They simply did not go away.

The plow lodged a stone. The mule strained; the plow dragged. He stooped to dislodge the rock when from the distant woods he heard the barking of dogs. His flesh crawled. He unhitched the mule and headed home, leaving the plow in the last furrow, something he'd never done before. The bitter truth was that he was afraid. Underhandedness was his only weapon. It wasn't that he wasn't grateful, Lord, that he'd been able to serve, but when he'd worked every inch of the soil he stood on and he was shaken by the sound of dogs barking, it generated for him scenes of men being caught and whipped.

Forgive me, Lord, for my impatience and doubt. I will listen for Your plan, lay down my fears and put my trust in You, Lord.

Daniel and Eziah held the plows, working beside each other in Wallace's field. James, Jr. and Thomas carried drinking water and watched waves of heat rising from the earth. It had rained last night and the air was again thick with mosquitoes. Elizabeth followed the plows, driving holes for the corn seed with the back end of a hoe. Addy followed, dropping seed. Libby, home from Mr. Eben's for the planting, was on her knees, covering the seeds, while the child, Mary, followed dreamily. As Elizabeth crossed the furrow and began to work behind Eziah's plow, she noticed that Libby would straighten up from the planting and follow Daniel with her eyes. If he noticed her, he never let on. Those two. For hours now, Elizabeth had stepped back and forth between the two plows, entertaining herself with thoughts of Libby and Daniel. Maybe someday.

They'd work Wallace's field till just before sundown, and after supper they'd plant their own while the earth was still wet and receiving. She stopped for a minute to watch Daniel, his arms thick as a man's. Too good for fieldwork, although she'd never tell him that. None of them were too good for anything, she decided, although she promised herself she'd take him with her to market next time in the hope he might hang around the blacksmith there and make himself useful since he liked smithery.

The heat was high for May. Could be it was too wet in which case the seeds would never leave the ground. Just wait. August would be dry and the crops would wither. The rains would not be held in the sandy soil long enough to do any good. Happened every year.

Wallace was watching from the edge of the field, his tall, bean-pole body high in the saddle. She didn't like him watching as if he didn't trust them to do the work and didn't appreciate him saying he'd keep an account of their hours and pay the tax bill.

"No," she'd said. "No. You pay us cash, and we pay our own tax bill." For that she had to depend on Preacher Green's watching for the notice in the newspaper and letting her know how much. She hoped she could keep the war between herself and Wallace down to a chicken fight. In the end, he would probably win but her power lay in her persistence, which was like the steady mosquito buzzing in her ears. For now, she'd keep on making his damned holes while she owned the morning, smelled the damp earth and thought about the willingness of things to grow. Owning her land made her strong, made her a rival and kept things even, because all of them, black and white, needed rain the same.

There would be a full moon tonight. Corn was best planted then as was any vegetable that grew above ground. The wheat was already planted. Not much, but enough for the mill and a sack or two for winter. Potatoes and beets were planted best under a new moon. Dark nights suited them, Perry always said. Peas had already come on and between the crops and what they got out of the river, they ate well. A couple of wild turkey babies had been penned for fall and there were a few chickens. Saturdays, she would swap eggs in town for coffee. They were making it, by God.

They kept to themselves. She cautioned the children to keep silent near strangers. "The white man don't like us ownin' land," she said simply. "Keep low, stay quiet. Don't cause trouble, heah? No need to remind 'em we're doin' good or they'll run us out of here. Or worse yet, round you up to chase hogs through the pines again." They nodded and looked at the ground, remembering how Perry used to talk about losing his way in the woods while herding Gaines's pigs, about hating the dark woods where dogs would suddenly appear followed by white men with guns.

The old days. Perry. She'd go to his place in the field as the sun rose and tell him everything. His spirit would be pleased. All she knew was that he was not in the white man's heaven nor the black man's either. She believed in the physicality of things, especially in change, as it caused a body to turn into something the earth could use and be replenished by. A giving back. Memory, the images that stayed behind the eyelids, could be God. She didn't know. But in the end it was enough to know something was left. In time, she would experience the Great Change as her people called it, and her spirit would be with Perry. And what would be left then? The children, and what she'd tried to teach them about survival. She'd shown them how to hold together and work their land. What it meant to be free.

Many were leaving, but staying, Elizabeth thought, *staying was the hardest.* The land held her to its heart as if she were a tree with roots that went down deep. The rhythms of the earth and seasons in this particular place—the growing children left in her care—she would never leave. Oh, no. What comfort she found when she walked her field, the soil having been marked long ago by Perry's footprints. Christian ways said Perry had gone to heaven, but her Indian ways told her the dead lingered and watched over them, their souls owning a place in your heart as long as you had breath.

The year before, Mr. Prouse had given Addy a few tomatoes and she'd saved the seeds. Now she planted them just outside the cabin door where she could keep an eye on them. She carefully pricked the soil around the fuzzy stems until the blossoms appeared and then tied up the vines to stick poles. As the summer wore on, the tomatoes were plentiful and lush, thriving in the dry weather. Blackberries, too, grew into clusters of plump, seedy beads. Picking them was happiness itself. All the family drifted among the tree stumps to gather blackberries. Later, they sank down under the shade of the few remaining trees along the road to taste the harvest, saving some for preserves and some to sell at market. The boys chased each other, their mouths red with berry juice, their fingers stained purple.

By the time the blackberries were scarce, Mr. Thomas's crops were ready, and the Burton family helped to gather in the hay and dig for potatoes. Evenings, they tended their own crop and set their potatoes in dugouts for the winter. There were enough tomatoes for Addy to can, a treasure like none other, and she set the jars alongside the blackberry preserves high on a shelf Daniel had made.

There was a week of extreme hot weather when the air seemed to lull them all into a stupor. On the hottest day, Addy sickened in the heat and had to be sent home. "Heat stroke," said Elizabeth, and she confined Addy to the cabin for a day, never mind lost wages.

And while she lay on her pallet, her eyes closed, with an earthen pitcher of water by her side, she thought she'd heard a scuffle, a soft scrape of boot on dry ground that awakened every nerve. She listened, tense, head aching, and help-less, unable to see what was coming, but knowing. Oh God, yes. Knowing that despite the good land, despite the rows of growing corn, the pride of tomato vines by the door and canned fruit on the shelf, despite the free babies born to her, despite sorrows and all the making do, despite labor and praying and minding one's own business, a woman alone would come to no good end. She could see fate, recognized its heavy footfall and braced to meet it. As he hit her again and again, she covered her face with her hands. When he tore at her clothes and roughly entered her, she silently thanked God it was her and not Libby—it could have been Libby. And afterward, the gray-white face with the graying stubble that had burned her, turned away. As he left, he grabbed a jar of toma-toes from the shelf that Daniel—sweet Daniel—had made, and the tomatoes with the sun still in them he took and with them, all the sun within her.

She did not know why she should be bleeding. Even after Elizabeth and the children came back from the fields, she wondered, too weak to rise and take care of herself. And when Elizabeth asked, "Who? For God's sakes, Addy, who?" only then did she begin to sob in sounds foreign to her own ears.

Who, indeed. She did not know, only thought maybe she'd seen him in one of the patrols once along the road, riding in a lazy, loose kind of way, like he didn't care, and it was all the same to him. In his hand he held a rope that led to one of the field hands, a trembling black man who was barefoot, with his shirt torn off his back, his hands tied and held high before him while his legs tried to keep the pace of the horse, stumbling, stumbling, and finally on his knees, dragged. She did not really look at the man on the horse, her glance skimming quick as lightning over the one on horseback to the one who was tied. She'd looked away, not wanting to know how it might have been with James long ago, the defeated, unmasked look of the captured, a man taken as James had been. She was ashamed then, and felt as powerless as she did now after the rape. She'd wanted to be associated only with safety, with owning land, with dignity and pride, as one who had somehow risen above the treachery. Was that why the Lord had punished her? For her pride and her wanting to forget?

"No," said Preacher Green when he came to see her. "The Lord had nothin' to do with it. Do you hear me, Addy? Nothin'. We'll pray now, for the Lord to heal you, sister."

But it might have been him, the one on horseback, might, she thought, but she could not remember having seen him before. Yet he must have known she'd left the field alone. One of the men working for Wallace? It could have been any one of them. It didn't matter. Nothing to be done anyhow. But she would never forget his face and it haunted her worse than the image of James taken—all through the fever that blurred everything and the bleeding that would not stop.

A few days later, Preacher Green recognized Elizabeth coming toward him across the field. Shoulders back, her head held high, she approached him without greeting but with grief in her eyes and bitterness that was rock hard.

"Addy's gone," she said. She spoke in his terms out of respect for him. "She been taken by the Lord." She'd had bleeding and high fever the likes of which Elizabeth had never seen before and was powerless to cure. The grief that had no outlet was huge and silent. There was no way for the sun to warm her. He reached for her arm and only then did she moan and sink to the ground in a tearless grieving. Addy. He would go immediately, Kitty by his side, and tend to things.

When he entered Elizabeth's cabin, Addy lay on her pallet surrounded by her children. She'd been there a whole day. Elizabeth had thought to wash Addy's apron and put it around her waist. The youngest, Mary, clung to it.

"She's with the Lord, now, children," he said. "In heaven. Surely, in heaven. And we're goin' to pray now, our best prayers."

Before they put her in the pine box Daniel had made, Libby asked about the apron. "Can I have it?"

Elizabeth said, "I'll make you another."

"It's for Mary," Libby quickly added, and Elizabeth relented.

Although he offered the church cemetery, Elizabeth insisted on burying Addy on their land next to Perry. "We're family," she said. "We keep our own close, their bones in our soil. Their spirit keeps us strong."

After the funeral, Elizabeth stood in the cabin and wept, finally, at the losses come to her. When she was done crying, she looked at the faces of those who needed her. They were her comfort. She was only an instrument for the next generation. She and Perry had paved the way. She would leave this earth content if they could remain free. In time, the children would own the land. It was a proud legacy. And because she saw that all good came from a single source, a place where all the rivers of spirits ran together, she said, *Thank you. Thank you for the day Addy came into my life.*

Soon after, Daniel left. He'd made the coffin from boards he took off the corn crib and then split a load of wood for winter, all the while appearing like the calm before a storm. When he was done with the firewood, he passed the ax to Eziah. Two days later, he announced he'd walk to town and talk to the blacksmith.

"Take the woods road behind the town and go in by Creamery Road. Stay close to the smithy," Elizabeth said. "Don't you go marchin' up there on Main

Street. Traders are lookin' for young and strong like you. They'll drag you to the ship or put you on the auction block faster'n you can blink. Heah?"

He was eighteen. He knew to be watchful and to keep to the heavily wooded Indian trail. Once he was within sight of the steeple of the white Methodist church, he turned toward Mr. Moore's shop, which lay nestled among a few cabins on the southern side of town. Except for the blacksmith, the shop was empty of people when he arrived, unusual for a weekday morning. With the music of iron hammering in his ears, he stood quietly by and waited.

"I seen you hangin' 'round. I ain't lookin' for no boy," said Moore, his hand traveling down the leg of the bay before him, readying the horse to lift its hoof for shoeing. The bay tossed its head and stomped the ground.

"Can I hold him steady for you?"

Moore straightened up. "Time I can't shoe a horse by myself be time I quit." He studied Daniel now, drew up his mouth, and nodded as if the question he was about to ask he already knew the answer to. "You a Johnson, ain't ya? You stay with Elizabeth."

"Yessir."

"She say you been wantin' to learn. No pay till I see how you do. Right off you'll be splittin' wood, haulin' coal for the forge, and sweepin' ashes.

Daniel began then, the break away from all he'd known. Under the watchful eye of a free black man like Moore, a trustee of Sam Green's church, he tended the fire in the forge, sometimes sleeping by its comfort at night and sometimes sleeping in the shed out back. Elizabeth was proud. Daniel was done with the fields. The next time she saw him he'd been trusted with the hammer and tongs and was bending iron. Sometime after he left, she found his name etched in the bottom board of the corn crib. Thanks to Preacher Green, he could write his name and there it was, *Daniel Johnson*, plain as day. She'd always thought of him as a Burton, but what she saw now was his declaration of the name *Johnson*.

When the leaves began to turn, Preacher Green's trip to Philadelphia was at hand. Kitty received her papers in time so she could travel with him, and together they took off on the steamboat one bright morning in October for the National

Colored Convention in Philadelphia. With the river still as a mirror, the boat slipped through the water's calm without so much as a ripple. Would the results of this trip be the same? At the Colored Convention was the affirmation he needed. But he needed action. Without it, all his talk to his congregation seemed nonsense to him. May the Lord forgive him his doubt. He was not strong in the faith and optimism he doled out to others. *What is it, Lord, that you ask of me?*

He wondered if Harriet had ever asked that question and decided she'd never had to. He admired her confidence. She never doubted. She only prayed for strength. He'd heard her: *Make me strong, Lord, so I'm able to fight.*

Once he'd met her at a convention in Philadelphia. So short in stature that she needed to stand on a platform, she seemed at first glance, vulnerable. Her bottom lip drooped in an attitude of perpetual sorrow, and her hands clasped before her gave her a humble demeanor. But once she spoke, her powerful voice reached every corner of the hall. She held the audience in a spell, carrying them with words as she had carried her people through danger. He was taken with her stern expression and how it changed; her eyes narrowed and widened with what she was saying, and her body swayed, leaned forward, and backed away as the stories developed. It was a dance she did. She had fire, and as she stirred it with her large work-worn hands, she drove her message and held her audience in the affirmation they so wanted to hear. At the end, she had no qualms about begging for money to supply clothing and passageway for runaways. Green was startled by the amount of money that poured in.

He would never have believed that such favor would be given to one so humble. Despite the plainness of her attire and coarse speech, or maybe because of it, people listened. Her stories were what he loved most about her. It was her ease and timing in delivery. She had a story for any lesson she wanted to make, just as good as some preachers and better than most. She knew a thirst for story was a basic human need, as strong as that for food and drink. Her stories were life itself, about everything tangible or intangible, imagined or real. The petite brown-clad, brown-skinned creature with her hair in a bun had a determined demeanor; her deep-set eyes held power. God was on her side. Her voice was proof.

Nodding in time with her words, she told about being struck by an iron weight as a child. *Yes.* Hit by a slave owner. With her fist in the air, she'd tell of the miracle of living through it for which her mother, Rit, praised God every day of her life. *Yes, praise Him!* Because of her injury, she often fell asleep in the midst of conversation, yet it was a good thing. While she slept, she received God's word. God spoke of her mission and warned her of danger. She was the vessel for His Word.

There was great applause when she finished. The abolitionists loved her. She was the living image of a great struggle. Where the preacher lived with a secret anger and fear, she did not. Was it merely bravado? Was she the true believer and only he crippled by doubt? Perhaps he was brave. He did what he could despite his fear.

Inspired, he traveled home with renewed hope. But when he came back to his fields, reality sank in once more. His apprehensions were affirmed by the news that Harriet's mother and father, Rit and Ben, were regulars on the patrollers' watch, as were the Quakers up near the mill. This was far from the haven Philadelphia had been.

One night, Harriet appeared at his cabin door. "I'm hidin' out," she said. "I'm waitin' on my sister, Rachel." He was not to worry about her whereabouts. She'd gotten most of her family to Canada. Except Rachel and her children.

"Time will come," Harriet said, "when Rachel'll have her chilren with her 'stead of bein' hired out. She not goin' to leave her chilren. I cain't stay with my mother and father, or even go near there and bring suspicion down on their heads, but I'm goin' to get them out, too, one of these days." The next morning she was gone.

For the next three months, she made her way through forest and field, darting, crisscrossing, and varying her path, appearing suddenly at his parishioners' cabins and staying for a time like an aunt come to visit. For days she disappeared from his sight altogether, and he worried about her only to find she'd been hiding in the marshes or off the path in the woods. That she wasn't identified by anyone in the white community amazed him. Surely, she *was* God's plan, just as she claimed.

By December, Harriet still had not been able to rescue Rachel and her scattered, enslaved children. Harriet needed money, and it was time to see Mr. Thomas Garrett in Wilmington to ask for funds. She needed to return to Canada and see about her family. Inspired by her persistence, the preacher saw the need for steadiness and prowess now more than ever. His heart eased. He consoled himself. His was not an exalted position in view of that larger world, but it was not *nothing*, and he was not helpless. He would keep his door open to the flow of his people, his sure and furtive resistance. But he wished he could do more.

All through winter and early spring he looked for her, especially on Saturday nights. When she stopped by his cabin, always in disguise, she'd warm herself by his fire and begin her stories.

She would put her elbows on her knees and lean forward. "Saw my old Master in town. I went right in there all bent over like I was some ol' woman just carryin' live chickens tied at the legs. Saw that devil Master and I put my head down. My bonnet covered up my face. I let go of the rope so the chickens was all a'squawkin' and in the excitement he didn't even know it was me passin' him right there on the street, that I stole myself and others, too!" When she laughed, her otherwise solemn face broke into deep creases.

So what if the stories were sprinkled with exaggeration? It was as if she was practicing them for the wealthy, who would be entertained by her plainspoken, colorful tales and who would loosen their purses. Oh, the paradox of Harriet's simplicity and complication. She'd become, in a sense, public, and what she offered went further than where her feet had carried her. With every story, she instilled hope.

To his relief, she returned one day in late spring. A white woman had given her a green silk dress the color of the deep pine woods, and after it had hung on a peg in the cabin for a few days and Kitty had admired it, Harriet carefully folded it and put it into a burlap sack. Under a new moon rising, she and a small group of runaways took off from the preacher's cabin. Weeks later, he learned of the uneasy trip. They had to go by a route that was far from her parents' cabin and the Quakers. Somewhere south of Wilmington, Harriet felt her heart going "flutter, flutter," and she knew God was warning her of danger. She changed her plans and cut across a stream she'd never traveled before. The water was deep and the men were afraid, but Harriet waded in until the water reached her shoulders, the burlap sack perched on her head. The men watched and saw that the water came no higher than her neck. When she climbed out on the opposite bank, they followed. She led them to another stream and then to a family who took them in for the night. Eventually, they made it to Philadelphia aided by people Harriet knew she could trust, people who provided money, food and clothing, and even shoes.

When she returned and told the latest story, he just shook his head. She was the Way. Her stories were bigger than she was and they fed his courage. He would go to see his son.

So after harvest and after the last hog was butchered and its bristles burned off, after the meat was cooled, quartered, pickled, smoked, and hung in the shed, after the wheat had been milled and the corn fodder for the cows stored, he and Kitty took off for Canada. He relished his freedom. He didn't have to run, praise the Lord, and wondered again as he had so many times in the past at the misfortunes of some and the luck of others, about who the Lord had chosen to serve in bondage and who He allowed to be free. And he questioned God's power over all. Why were some tested more than others? Yet those who propagated slavery were being tested, too. Which would they choose: to live out their lives in decency and justice, or demean and use their fellow man?

Within the parish, the Greens had been cautious about telling anyone but Elizabeth of their plans and only then because the mulatto boy, Edward, just twelve, had to be left in her care. However, once they were in Philadelphia, they traveled openly by train and watched the rolling scenery with fascination. They thrilled at the sight of mountains. They could see the villages in the valleys from a height they'd never experienced in the flat, placid terrain of home. The forests were taller, the trees of many different varieties, the train stations much more crowded, the strangers detached, the cold piercing, the farther north they traveled. Yet what Preacher Green had most worried about, the questioning of their papers, never happened. Was it part of God's plan for him? Part of the bargain he'd struck by promising to return to the heartland of the Shore and keep up the Lord's work?

Thin and gaunt, Sam Green, Jr. welcomed them to his cabin, which was meager against the Canada cold. Kitty worried. The community of runaways was strong, he assured them, and people looked out for one another. He made light of the sparse meals he served and the cough he'd acquired. Still, he was a happy man, working and looking forward to owning a scrap of land one day.

"Stay," he urged them. "We got friends here. Harriet help us with every trip, look out for us, and we help her, too, when we can. And nobody, not one, is afraid like we were. It feel like the Lord's heaven here on earth. I'm free. I'm truly free."

Satisfied, Sam and Kitty Green returned home, but tucked away the determination that they would join Sam Green, Jr. for good. They just didn't know when. And then, the preacher saw the advertisement in *The Cambridge Eagle* that brought the portent of change. The acreage he rented was for sale, and he hadn't known. He could never afford to buy the land on which he labored and that he wasn't told it was for sale affirmed the fact it would never be his.

In the still-dark morning, he sat by the fire, his open Bible in hand, his head bent over the pages. His finger pointed to a certain passage, but he deciphered nothing. He listened. Listening was part of any moment of day and night, more so now that the year drew to a close and masters reviewed assets and considered sales of their slaves to settle their accounts. Those chosen for sale might have an intuition, or hear a rumor, and they'd make their whispered plans. Night brought the sound of running feet and rustling leaves as they came to his cabin. He expected them. The air was eerie with restlessness. He walked to the window and looked out. It had begun to rain.

Behind him, Kitty slept. Her gray head just above the covers, face down, reminded him of a bird's nest. She was peaceful and the coming day probably would not be. The boy, Edward, lay on a pallet at her side. Green worried the "committee" might take the boy. Free or not. The pain of his children being taken never left him. Edward was orphaned, and the Orphan's Court could claim him at any time. He returned to his book, and although his eyes scanned the words, Green's worry wouldn't let him concentrate.

There. Rain had muffled the sound of leaves, but there was no mistaking the knock at the door, the half-whispered words, "It Harriet!" There she was, not much taller than Edward, with a shawl pulled over her head, her mouth puckered in determination, and an air of authority about her. The woman with her he recognized as Eliza. Her face was light-colored and broad as a melon. The smooth hair that strayed from under her shawl revealed her lineage. Although much younger than Harriet, she carried the weight of an older woman.

"More comin'," Harriet said. Muddy and shivering with cold, the women backed up to the fire. A short while later there was a second knock. As Green moved toward the door, the women scrambled up to the loft. Kitty, wide awake now, grabbed her frying pan and held it behind her. It was Peter, from Wright's Creek, which was farther north. They'd come south and were nowhere near where they should have been, but Green did not question Harriet. She must have had her reasons. Kitty reached into the trunk for dry clothes and hung a kettle of cornmeal and water over the fire.

"Josiah and his brother are comin'," said Harriet. "We met them this side of the Choptank. He went to my daddy's house up to Poplar Neck a while ago and left word he was ready to leave. He got a beatin'. Said it would be his last. He work for Hughlett, and Hughlett know his worth. Bought him for two thousand dollars and then he beat him so Josiah'd know who was owner and who was owned, he say. Didn't want the two thousand to go to the man's head. Josiah say, 'That the last time. Tell Harriet next time she come through, I'm goin'. And Bill, too.'"

Turning to the preacher, Harriet said, "I tol' 'em we gonna separate. We heard horses and I tol' 'em to meet up here. Only thing to do was to backtrack south from the way we come, away from the Choptank and close to East New Market. They never gonna think we be hangin' around in the county right under their noses."

When day broke, Josiah and his brother, Bill, had not yet appeared. Staying close to home, Green worked in the shed he'd built for the mule, oiling his tools and making a new handle for a hoe. He bent to his tasks as he listened. Once he heard the sound of horses close by, but they'd moved on, the dogs behind them yelping and barking. The gray sky held more rain and the earth lay soaked. He worried footprints would freeze and hold their shape long enough to be identified. Only another deluge of rain would erase them.

Josiah had once said despite his wife and three daughters, he'd run if he got the chance. "It do me no good to dwell on it," he said. "Cain't take 'em and I cain't stay. No woman can make me stay." He was tiptoeing around a truth and a lie, not knowing which way to go. "I cain't take no more," he'd say. "I be no good as a man if I stay." But his grief showed. Josiah was sorry. God, he was sorry.

Church tomorrow. Green would have to leave the fugitives in the cabin to wait for Josiah and Bill. He'd ride in to East New Market to see if rewards had been posted.

Underneath Josiah's name, the five hundred dollar reward was scratched out and one thousand written in. Under Bill, three hundred, and under Peter, eight hundred. Green and Kitty returned home. All through Sunday, they waited. Eliza grew restless, Peter paced, and Harriet slept intermittently. Once, Eliza went to gather eggs. "Hunch over," Harriet told her. "Don't let on you're young and fit iffen anyone come."

Monday, in the still dark of early morning, Josiah and Bill appeared. Josiah's fear exploded when he told of the night before.

"I hear the horses—two, three, I think—breathin' hard like we was, runnin' all night. We at the edge of the woods but close to the Morris farm. Heard them horses and I say to Bill, 'This it. This the shortest time bein' free any man ever had.' But Bill, he don't say nothin'. He just keep diggin' and diggin' where he knew Morris kept his potato hole. And I jump in. I don't even know where Bill at. He just cover me up with needles and leaves and then he run and I scared I ain't never gonna see him again. But he in the farm shed climbin' up the rafters, watchin' the horses go by. I hear 'em, but he say he seen 'em not two feet from the hole and they just go on by. I too scared to come out till he come get me."

The backtracking worked. The river would save them. That night, they would head once again for the Choptank through wilderness they knew well. They'd follow the river bank, cross narrow creeks by night, duck into inlets by day, even lie in the tall, hay-colored grasses in broad daylight and watch herons, geese, and eagles, and imagine themselves free. In his mind, Green plotted the escape every step of the way, and with every flight he thought of his son, and the courage it took to go. With the appearance of first star, they would run again and as the crowd of stars gathered overhead, they all would be reminded of that larger world, the one that stretched all the way to Canada. They would run east, then west, then north, and backtracking when necessary, southward and back again until they could no longer run. No matter if their stomachs groaned or their legs were numb with cold or the soles of their shoes were worn through. They would not believe that they would make it. But Harriet was sure. She would tell them again and again, "The Lord speaks to me, and He never led me wrong."

He knew Harriet carried a gun. At first, he thought it was for protection, but she let him know she intended to use it on anyone who would turn back, turn tail, or turn traitor; it was all the same to her. She would not allow such a paltry thing as anyone's fear to endanger them all. He smiled to himself. They would be all right, but he would pray anyway.

WHEELS OF CHANGE

———•——

*E*lizabeth watched Libby seated on the bench by the fire, warming her hands so she could work this evening. She had Addy's countenance. Calm pervaded the cabin whenever she was in it. But she took after her father, James, as well. Hers was a powerful presence. She was tall, broad shouldered, with huge hands, her mother's wide, round face, and her father's deep-set, serious eyes. She was handsome more than pretty with nothing that could be called delicate about her. She would bear children well. Eighteen this year, she worked close to home where she was sorely needed and she appeared at Miss Mari's each morning. The hogs were gone now and she mostly carded and spun wool and flax and tended to anything Miss Mari needed. She did not work for pay and asked for none but was allowed to take the yarns home to Elizabeth, who was pleased to keep Libby nearby. In the evenings and through the quiet winter nights, she'd taught Libby to weave on the old loom Perry had made, and sew. At first, she thought Libby wouldn't be satisfied with needlework. In truth, her preference was to be outdoors, but the lengths of wool and flax she brought home to Elizabeth were sturdy and well made. Although the wool and flax belonged to Miss Mari, she shared it with Elizabeth and paid her to do the weaving. Later, she and Libby made quilts, piecing and sewing with the smallest stitches all manner of cloth from old clothing or ticking Miss Mari had given them to the coarse muslin from flour sacks and the linen they'd woven themselves. Some quilts they stuffed with milkweed pod silk, some with tufts of raw cotton as it came off the steamboat. When finished, they brought the quilts to market. Once, Thomas Prouse bought one for each of the children, his own and those of his brothers, with a generosity that only came after harvest and before Christmas. But the coarsest clothing, the linen pants and muslin shirts, Miss Mari sold to landowners for their Negroes. Holding some of this clothing back, Elizabeth was pleased to have enough so that when runaways came through in rags, she could clothe them.

Libby worked with an energy Elizabeth no longer had, and she rested in the knowledge that Libby could carry on the work without her if need be. Soon Libby would be able to sew the blouses made of lace and fine white linen they called cambric, and fancy jackets out of silk and wool for those of means in town. What Elizabeth feared most for Libby was that because of her size, she would be made to do a man's labor, to slaughter pigs, haul logs, lay fencing, or dig ditches. Such a strong woman would be worth much on the auction block. She'd keep Libby home, telling James, Jr., Eziah, and Thomas, who made faces when they were hired out, that Libby's place was to take care of them all. She would cure ailments, feed them, keep them in line, tend the garden, weave and sew, help Miss Mari, and later, she would work the fields with them like always.

"Why, where you goin'?" Eziah asked Elizabeth.

"Nowhere. Just nowhere," said Elizabeth with her eyes cast down at her sewing. "Not if I can help it." The words were a whisper.

This morning, when Libby went out to start Miss Mari's fire, she found her sitting in her rocker by the fireplace, staring out the window. She didn't move when Libby entered with an armful of wood.

"Miss Mari? You all right?"

"Can't see this mornin', Libby. Scarin' me to death. I can tell where the window is but that's all." Her face was a map of lines running helter-skelter. She was older than Elizabeth, older than Perry when he died.

"I'm afraid I'm near my time, Libby," she said. "You come now, come every mealtime, and at night, help me to my bed. And tell Elizabeth to fetch the minister at the Methodist Church. No need to hurry, girl. Just come back and see if I'm all right, will you? Lord, your family has been good to me, I know."

Never had Miss Mari spoken so many words. Never before had she said "your family," having always referred to them as a "bunch of strays." But her tone softened now and she continued to stare at the window, her nose pinched and narrow, her thin lips set in a straight line, her troubled mind wanting to see more than her life and beyond her time.

Libby said, "Ma'am, I'll do it right away, even if I have to walk to town myself."

Miss Mari shook her head. Libby saw she'd be brave. She'd leave this world in her black dress with the ruffled collar and she'd be clean, her hair brushed. Libby would see to it. Libby was startled to hear Miss Mari say, "You take the spinning wheel."

Libby's heart jumped. "I'd be pleased to have it, Miss Mari."

"Consider it payment to do me right when I go. Say no more about it before I change my mind. I really ought to sell it, I suppose, but there's no more family, and I know you'll respect it."

When Libby brought the wheel home, Elizabeth said, "She must know she goin' to leave us. A woman who give up her wheel knows it's her time. Libby, you stay with her. Take the wheel with you and work there, and when the time come, you just bring it back. I'll send Eziah for the minister."

As she ran her fingers over the smoothed-down edge of the wheel, Elizabeth remembered the day August Woodson brought it by Miss Mari's, how his eyes had met hers in one brief instant before she looked down lest she be seen as disrespectful or inviting. She felt his eyes on her as she put a kettle on to boil. She halfway feared him. He kept staring until she faced him square on and was surprised at the faded blue eyes that met hers, their color so light they hardly had any color at all. He nodded and tipped his hat, shifting his weight from one foot to the other, waiting. She said the missus had gone to town and that she'd tell her he'd been by. She curtsied but still he waited and wiped his brow with his sleeve while she grew more anxious. With the sun streaming in, the wheel between them cast its shadow across his hands. Where she'd run her hand over the wheel rim as she did now, he had lain his rough hand on top of hers. She'd started, and he quickly withdrew it. Shyly, with his hat in his hand, he asked if he could touch her hair, her long straight black hair so unusual for a black woman. She dared not say no and kept her eyes downcast. He leaned across the wheel and ran his hand from her temple down along her braid, stopping in the middle of her back. Her hand, still on the wheel, steadied her. His hand, the wheel, the shadows, the smell of him, the dust floating in the sun stream—she was back in the moment when she dared not look at him, and she remembered that when she finally did raise her head to look at him, he was smiling.

"Well, I'll be. The only thing Negro on you is your skin," he said not unkindly and turned away. "I'll bet you're a conjure woman. I'll bet you know things no one else does."

"My grandmother come from the Nanticoke, from Chicone, belongin' to Algonquin," she said, an identity she'd never acknowledged before. Suddenly, it was a good thing to be. She did know things and try as she might the God of their church and the Jesus of their prayers had never been hers. The day was hers, though, the sunlight, this man touching her hand but going no further, her good fortune in this moment. But that was all. She had herself and it was enough. It was this, not her hair that set her apart. She was eighteen and would soon have a husband. Although Perry was owned, she would find a way to free him. Meanwhile, she felt a strange connection with this man and his sad eyes. Maybe it was her own power reflected there that she saw. He might even be a little afraid of her because of it.

She saw him many times after that, always from a distance and with respect in his demeanor, a tip of his hat, a regard. At first, it puzzled her and then she felt that he, too, was caught in the web of their time and wished it were other-wise. He had the look of someone unsure, someone seeking and not finding. *He had only to consider his beautiful wheels*, she thought. *Only that. They were the best of him.*

How infrequently, yet momentously, their paths had crossed and how often he was in her thoughts since he died. With her hand still on the wheel, she thought about Mr. Gaines, too, and Mr. John Prouse and Mr. Thomas Prouse. They were all gone, yet she was still here, carrying on in Perry's name. Most of what she'd accomplished was without the white man's permission. She was beholden to no one. She would visit Perry's grave this morning and tell him the land was in order, that the garden had come on, and a full crop of corn would come in this fall, that she'd go to the mill with a borrowed cart and return with cornmeal and enough money to buy wheat flour, and that the winter rye she'd planted was green now, ample for the mule and the cow. She would tell Addy how Libby was the daughter who would carry on, that Daniel was learning the iron and how she, Elizabeth, dreamed of their pairing, how the other boys were still with her, and how the family had withstood the tumult around them.

Libby stayed with Miss Mari and soon Miss Mari forgot to use the chamber pot and forgot to eat the corn cakes Libby made for her and then forgot to get out of bed altogether. She no longer moved anything on her right side, and her face lay twisted on the pillow. She forgot to look out the window, too, her eyes changing from frightened to blank, as if she didn't care. Libby saw how it was, how a body would not be frightened by advancing death and acceptance the only thing left. She knew that soon Miss Mari would forget to breathe. Meanwhile, the quiet hum of the spinning wheel kept them both company, and the steady pedaling of her foot marked time.

In a few weeks, Libby brought the spinning wheel home. Miss Mari had passed in the night. Elizabeth went with Libby to tend to things.

The creeks froze over. The boats on the river were encased in ice at their moorings. Ice-coated tree limbs cracked in the wind, the larger ones giving way with a blast that sounded like gunshot. It became impossible for farmers to break into their root cellars. Deep ridges in the roads from the mud of the month before made passage difficult for the horses and mules. Soon the snow swirled into huge drifts around anything that stood in the way, burying the dead sheep not to be found till spring. Trains and steamboats were stilled as well as the larger sailing vessels. Ties with cities were cut off. Prices on chickens and feed and everything else rose.

To Libby's dismay, the wood Eziah had piled near the door lay buried, as well as the maul. "You dig after it, boy. Don't you know better'n to leave it outdoors in the weather? That gone, you be lookin' for it till spring."

The boy hunched his shoulders. He hated a scolding, especially from Libby. He was the oldest of the boys now and thought of himself as protector of the family despite the fact that Libby was four years older. She was much taller than he, and with her hands on her hips she seemed like what he imagined a mountain to be, having never seen one. He admitted he was careless sometimes, but he had a lot to think about. This morning, he'd only come home to Elizabeth's to eat and split some wood and then he would set off again to Wallace's stables.

Wallace's favorite broodmare was colicky and bloated. Two of the stable boys told him to walk her. That he did, for hours on end, but when he returned her to the stall, she immediately lay down and would not rise again. Watching her misery, her twisting and turning in pain, he tried to get her to stand, worrying she would roll over and twist a bowel, but the mare stayed on her side. Eziah didn't know what to do. Wallace had taken off for a few days and had left him in charge of the mare. He was due back the next day.

Eziah did not leave the horse's side. He stayed all night worrying over her every breath and whinny. He lay down beside her, hoping the warmth of his body would comfort her and ease the pains. When he laid his ear on her flank, he couldn't hear anything, which meant she wasn't digesting food. Not a good sign. She was Eziah's favorite too, and seeing the honey chestnut of her hide and sleek movement in the field was his deepest pleasure. He knew if the horse died, he would pay with his own hide. Wallace was fond of horseracing and had often won the local purse. But he was also frugal. Instead of paying for a white overseer to manage the horses, he'd singled out a few boys to care for them and he very often forgot to pay, counting on the fact that most of them would be thrilled to work in the stables. In Eziah's case, he was right.

So this morning, after Eziah broke the ice on the water barrel, sloshed the bucket down, and hoisted it up again, he hurried back to Elizabeth's cabin. He knew he must not even stay for breakfast, but run back over the white fields to the stables and be at the horse's side. Lord, God. What if she died? What if she was already dead?

Blame was always on him. Yet, he'd been proud of his responsibilities as he swept the stables, pitched mountains of manure, and carried a million buckets of water and feed. His arms were the strongest of any boy his age for miles around. Longer, too. He never forgot his chores for Elizabeth and did them without complaint when he got home. He'd planted and hoed and reaped with the rest of them, but he lived for the hours he worked in the stables.

Wallace, on the other hand, was interested in Eziah beyond his work as stable boy. When he asked him on several occasions who his mother was, Eziah always said the same thing, "I belong to Elizabeth, sir," and his heart sank as he heard his own words. If anyone would sniff out the fact that he was not of Elizabeth and Perry's blood, it would be Wallace. As a lawyer, he knew everybody, and he knew how they were situated. He had access to courthouse records. He knew who owed taxes and who had other debts to pay, whose land could be had for a song. He knew who was legal, who belonged to whom, and who would turn a good profit. What the black population did or didn't do was no concern of his except if they wouldn't work, or couldn't. What was important was the money they'd bring in.

Eziah tried to stay clear of Wallace's severity, but he hoped he had become indispensable to him, caring for the horses with diligence, which is why he worked as silently and invisibly as possible under Wallace's critical and watchful gaze. Wallace did love his horses, and if there could be a common bond between him and Eziah, this was it. Eziah loved to watch the finely tuned muscular bodies of Mr. Wallace's horses, loved the horse smells and the glossy coats, which he'd brush for hours on end, loved the smell of hay and oiled leather, loved the way the horses nuzzled him and whinnied when he came in the morning. He tolerated any mistreatment directed toward him because of the horses. But he hated the questions about Elizabeth and their family, a topic Mr. Wallace never tired of.

"How many Elizabeth takin' care of now, boy?"

"You're the oldest, aren't you?"

"I saw a wagon go by your house yesterday. You had visitors?"

All of the questions were asked in a friendly, sly sort of way, a way that was going to pin trouble on a person no matter how that person answered. The questions were more insidious than the harsh words Wallace threw at him from time to time or the whip he used on him when something wasn't done to his satisfaction. Eziah'd learned to deal with punishment. He'd never told Elizabeth about the whippings until she asked what the marks were on his back when he stripped down one summer night. But he worried about his answers to Wallace's probing.

"You not goin' over there no more, Eziah. You free and he got no right to whip you. He got no right to ax questions either," Elizabeth said, with worry in her eyes. "And he ain't never paid you. It just like he own you." Unyielding, Eziah begged to go back to the horses.

And now, he rushed through his chores, thinking hard about what he could do before Wallace's return. He was sure the mare had gotten the colic from corn gone bad. He'd given it to her, so it was his fault. And he was sure he'd catch a beating for it. But, maybe not. Maybe things would turn out okay. He was fourteen and could shoulder misfortunes like a man.

Only a week before, Wallace had appeared at Elizabeth's door saying, "I'll take the boy in an apprenticeship. I can do it now or later through the Orphan's Court, seeing as how he doesn't belong to you or anybody else."

"You mean slavin' him, don't you?" she said quietly.

He squinted at her. "I mean teachin' him a good trade, indenture," he said.

"He already know a good trade. Mr. Wallace, sir, I don't mean no disrespect, but you not been payin' him. He been born free and he should be workin' for wages. Anybody indenturin' him, it'd be me. I need his help here." Which was an admission of sorts, she realized too late. He was not her son, and she'd just made it plain.

Under his broad hat, Wallace's stubbly beard wobbled. He could be patient for another minute or two. "I'll give you a hundred dollars for him, which is way more than that boy's worth."

To get rid of Wallace, she said, "I'll think on it," but she knew it was only a matter of time before he'd come by with the sheriff. Maybe she could help Eziah run. Maybe with the next runaways passing through. Unless he went to Preacher Green's. No one would challenge the preacher about a free black apprenticed for the church, would they? She hoped the others were safe—Libby, eighteen now, and James, Jr., just twelve. Thomas, being only seven, and Mary, six, were not in danger yet, although they already were good workers and had begun helping in the fields last year like all the others. She worried about Mary. The serious and desolate look on the child's face whenever she woke up in the morning haunted Elizabeth. It was as if she were saying, *so this is the world. This is how it is.* And Elizabeth would hold her, feel the child's soft breathing against her and be reminded how quickly everything changes, how the times to hold Mary and comfort her would be brief. The last baby. To be sent into the world one day, too. Elizabeth didn't want to think about it.

In a place where her people changed names all the time, why hadn't she told the census man they were all Burtons? No white man now alive would remember Addy wasn't her own child and she'd never said. She was the legal grandmother of the children. Her daughter was buried right out there next to her father. In Elizabeth's mind it was so. She'd never figured out how the white man's world worked or his God either.

As she watched Wallace mount his horse and leave, she suddenly felt time's weight pushing down. All the things she couldn't help swept into the cabin on a blizzard wind as she sat this morning, twining and braiding the fibers from last summer's Indian hemp. She'd been pleased to find it growing in a huge patch along the edge of her narrow cornfield. It would come back now, year after year. She'd told James, Jr. and Thomas to watch for it, and taught them how to extract the fibers from the reeds, how to make fishing line and cord so strong it could never be pulled apart. She told them as if she was giving a sermon, as if the cord could be extended in one long line into a future without her. She couldn't imagine the world without her, not out of grandiosity, but out of an inability to understand an eternal silence. Maybe she wouldn't realize death until she'd felt its coming. Maybe that's how the Great Change worked. Then, despite her preparations, denials, resistances, she would come to it stripped of all defenses. Her only comfort was what she'd taught the children, passing along those very preparations and skills. That and the land, the precious land. She knew she'd have a devil of a time letting go, the will in her so strong, the fight so constant. What lay ahead? The way things were going, so much anger in the world would all come to a boil. So many free, more of them every day, and so many made restless and brazen by the growing numbers, multiplying like the branches of a sycamore.

The worry over Eziah grew this morning. He'd said the broodmare was sick. He would catch hell over it. She'd said, "Eziah, I swear you be tradin' horse lovin' for Bible lovin' and whatever else Preacher Green ax you to do sooner than you think. I don't want to hear no more 'bout it. If anythin' happens, and here you workin' for free to begin with, I'm goin' to send you out of sight to the preacher. You may as well be puttin' good time in the church." But back to the stables Eziah went, running over the field in a beeline, his way made difficult by the deep snow.

When he entered the sun-striped stable where the mare lay, he realized she was dead. He stroked her great, bloated belly that still held a glimmer of heat. He sank down beside her long head, rubbed his hand over her soft nose as had been his habit, and looked deep into the brown globe of an eye as if searching for an answer. As if this were an ordinary day, he busied himself oiling and polishing the tack he'd used for her when she'd been hitched to the wagon for Wallace. Part of him listened for the sliding of the barn door that would signal Wallace's arrival, and despite all the strength he could muster, he began to sob.

He didn't know how long he'd waited. The inevitable came. Wallace strode in, looked at the mare, and came to a conclusion. Fault or no, someone was to blame, someone had to receive his anger. Breaths left him in great clouds of steam. He reached for the tack on the wall, looping the straps in his hand but allowing the bit to swing free. His aim was poor, but the iron hit Eziah often enough to leave welts all over his body. The blow that hit his head was the worst, and for a moment, Eziah felt as though there'd been an explosion and he was going down. Wallace said nothing. The silence contained misery and grief enough for the both of them. Then, Wallace screamed a high-pitched sound that cracked with intensity, shocking Eziah into consciousness. He ran. He felt his wounds swell and the sharp sting of cuts on his face and back and arms. He tasted blood on his lips. His feet churned in the snow, the words, "You damn nigger—I said to—damn fool nigger," following him. But, not far. Wallace's physical presence retreated as he went back to the barn, but Eziah knew his anger and blame would not.

Leaving the children with Libby, Elizabeth walked with Eziah along the deer path to Preacher Green's, a path no human foot had traversed. They stayed clear of the trails wide enough for horse and cart. In her sleeve, she held a knife and in her heart, determination to save Eziah from indenture. The man was lying. He would take Eziah and claim him. He'd deny the boy's age and probably keep him indefinitely. There would be many beatings that would stem from an anger that burned as long as day followed night. There would be no room for the man to see that what had happened was just that, a happening that couldn't be blamed away.

Today, the forest was a friend. She kept track of paths and thickets where the deer sheltered. She walked so quietly among them in summer and fall they were often startled by her closeness. "See, Eziah? You always walk a new path. They all come out to the creek and then we follow that, go west from there." He nodded although he could have told her the same thing. He would miss Libby and the children and Elizabeth. He would miss the horses. Would he always have to bend to the will of others? But with his bruises and the pain in his head, he thought it would be all right to go to Preacher Green. He might learn to read more words, books even. And he would find work in town like Daniel did, for which he would be paid like a man. He thought of the mare again, how they would chain her to the oxen and drag her over the same field where she'd run the summer before. They'd bury her beyond the fence and the powerful, beautiful flesh would disappear into the earth. They might have to wait till spring, though, or use the adze to break the frozen ground. The buzzards would come. He couldn't stand the thought.

He trudged behind Elizabeth's quick, sure steps and remembered the knife in her sleeve. It reassured him. "There's a way. There's always a way," she'd told him time and again until he believed it.

MATTIE, 2000

I see a young girl, 'bout twelve or thirteen or so, sittin' by the side of the road. She just sittin' there watchin' peoples go by. They hollerin' and singin' like it was Mardi Gras, but she not payin' no mind to the hullabaloo around her, just sittin' there with her elbows on her knees, lookin' like she waitin' for somebody she know to show up. I cain't do nothin' but watch. I go other places and see other things, but she come in my thinkin', time and again.

And then I see the swamp behind her and I think she in Florida or maybe New Orleans. I remember the swamp and how scared I was of it 'specially when the Sewanee River come up on a heavy rain. That water was black and full of snakes. Like it comin' to get you. I want to tell her to move quick if it rains, but I cain't. So I have to leave her sittin' there.

I cain't find Grandma Pattyroll. But whenever I see Elizabeth and Libby and the other chilren, I see a shadow. I cain't never make out who it is. Anyway, I'm seein' what happened around the time my grandma was born. I figure it was the same in Georgia as in Maryland. Maybe worse, because nearly everbody there was owned. Maryland was a mix. There was more free ones on the Eastern Shore than owned, and plenty of 'em to help the others.

But I get flashes. The same chile, younger, sweepin', scrubbin', left alone with a small baby. I never see her mama or papa around her. I guess they workin'. If it weren't for her size, I'd take her to be much older, her face so serious. I think it might be Grandma Pattyroll, but then she goes away from all thought like she still don't want you to know nothin'.

But when time rolls back, I see the chile again, clingin' to a woman, and then runnin' back to wrap herself around a man, like she not wantin' to leave her daddy, and sobbin'. And when I look at the man's face, I see James Spry. And I see her torn from him by the auctioneer and hear James Spry yell out her name, "Leola!" The chile is sold along with the woman who must be her mama. They both carryin' on somethin' awful.

Somethin' tells me it Grandma Pattyroll, and I know she and her mama are goin' down to New Orleans. The baby and then the girl I been seein' was our Leola, I'm pretty sure. Papa used to tease and say, "Here come Leola," and we kids would giggle and say, "That not Leola, that Grandma Pattyroll!"

So that's why the story begin with James Spry. That's why I been seein' 'im through the years in this here aftertime. It tells me this here Leola is James Spry's other daughter *and* Libby's half sister, same papa, different mama. And I'm part of Elizabeth's field in a way I never woulda guessed. I been studyin' it all those years, not knowin'.

There some kinda peace in that. Great day in the mornin'.

Feels like that last summer in Dorchester when the potatoes was ready and the harvester come through. Truckloads of potatoes went out to the processin' plant to make potato chips. I gathered my buckets and picked up what was left. There was plenty. I got right dusty truckin' 'cross that field barefoot. Got right down there to feel the earth. It was one of the pleasures and one of the things I miss now. My feets always hurt in shoes. I don't miss that.

It was early in the morning. Some of the mist from the irrigation tempted me, and I decided to shower. I kept a bar of soap under my old sink and went 'cross the road to Elizabeth's field where the corn was more than half growed. The pipes pointed south and traveled toward the house like a compass makin' giant circles 'round the field. Water rained down and I walked right in there and unbuttoned my shirt. I faced the sun, my back to the road in case anybody'd come by. There was a rainbow. I was slippery with soap and I was smooth all over when I thought again of my husband, Plato. Oh, yes. Bittersweet, that

Plato. I started to hum and then I started to laugh. If Webster had caught me, he'd a hadda fit 'bout soap in his corn. I spread my shirt wide like a sail behind me—doin' laundry at the same time. Like a baptism, it was. If I learned but one thing, it was about payin' attention to bein' satisfied and how it always come from simple things. Like bein' born again. Like this answer 'bout Grandma Pattyroll give to me in this here aftertime. It was the sunshine, the rainbow, the cool water, the clean runnin' over my body—all of it together.

I remember I wrapped the shirt around me, headed for the house for dry clothes, and put the wet ones on the wash line. I was ready for the day, ready for whoever'd come by. I waited under the peach tree with my thoughts bringin' tears. I don't know why, 'cept the world seemed so beautiful right then, and my life so precious, I had to spend a time 'preciatin' it. I thought maybe that's what dyin' was, just a different kind of surrenderin'.

Later that morning, traffic picked up. Webster went by in his pickup ninety miles an hour, with a wave of two fingers. He had a white shirt on, and a tie, so I knew he was goin' some place important. Then Fran, the mail girl, come by and yelled, "How are you, Miss Mattie?"

"Take some potatoes? I got a bucket for you."

She took 'em, and handed me the mail. The 'lectric bill. No gov'ment letter.

"Don't bother about it, Miss Mattie. I'll bring some crabs tomorrow. They're better than an old government check any day."

Her arms were two different colors. The one that stuck out of the window all the time deliverin' mail was brown as could be on a white person and the other arm was white as could be on a white person.

"Where Webster goin' all sweetened up?" I ax her.

"I hear he's goin' to court. Some kind of land dispute. He's claimin' rights to half those twenty-two acres over there," she say, noddin' her head in the direction of Elizabeth's field.

"How can he do that?" I ax her.

"Well, he's been tillin' it for awhile now, rentin' it, but then the law says over twenty years usin' it, you can claim adverse possession," she say.

"Well, I been tillin' this here garden for fifty year. Figure I can claim it?"

We both laugh. "I don't know nothin' about adverse possession," I say. "Sounds an awful lot like stealin' to me."

You'd think what was right was right no matter somebody's opinion, that there'd always be a higher law that had the final say. You could only hope justice would come 'round right. It depended on the side of them who could change the law or use it to suit themselves. What's dark inside a man—well, now—you don't ever know how that'll come down on you, even when there's a law, sometimes most 'specially then.

Which made me wonder where God was. Inside us or up in heaven? Did we only get to know who He was when we were in the middle of tryin' to decide what was right? It seem to me that struggle was more important than anythin' else and those with power sometime don't struggle enough. And now, in the aftertime, I see I was right about that. This ain't no heaven. But the souls of everbody tryin' hard in the worst of times—that must be where God is, right there on earth.

Some say they know God. Makes me think of the story my papa tol' 'bout a friend of his who worked around yards, weedin'. The white man he work for got him a harmonica. Give it to him for a Christmas present.

He learned to play that harmonica and said some white peoples axed him how he learn to play it because they couldn't play none. Papa's friend say, "It a gift from God. God told me. God showed me at night how to play the harmonica."

They say, "Don't see why God would want to do more for a Negro when he's a white God." Papa's friend say, "Well, whatever He is, He just showed me. I don't know if He colored or white, but I just knowed it was a gift from God."

I think peoples who say they know God have no idea just how big God is. And it seem like it okay to wonder 'bout it because it only when you ax questions that you begin to know things.

PREACHER GREEN AND THE
BORROWED BOOK, 1857

W inter was a harbinger of worsening poverty. Landowners were more anxious and hostile than ever, it seemed to Preacher Green. In town he'd heard men talk about a coming insurrection. During the long, bitter nights, patrollers continued their search.

Eziah was to stay until spring. When the snow turned the fields to mud, Green sent him with Edward to repair fences and care for the livestock, saving Green from going out in the severe cold. The boys split wood and spread guano for a neighbor while Green stayed within sight of them. At the fireside in the long evenings, he taught the boys how to read and write and often read to them until they'd grown sleepy and no longer listened.

He'd heard about *Uncle Tom's Cabin* from a Quaker friend and asked if he could borrow it. "There are two volumes, Preacher, and I'll deliver the second one when I'm finished with it. Tide's changing, my friend," the Quaker said as he placed the book in Green's hands. "The rest of the world is watching. If the church can't take a stand and decide against slavery then there'll be no place in heaven for those who participate. It's splitting the very church in two, just like the nation."

Judging by the condition of the book, it had been passed around many times. The brittle pages stayed stiffly fanned even when the book lay on the table. The story kept him company for the rest of the winter. He read far into the night, rereading parts of it and marking favorite passages to read out loud to the boys the next evening. He hoped his friend would soon finish the second volume.

From Harriet Beecher Stowe's pages, a hand reached out to him. What he'd experienced in his own life was boldly put down on paper for anyone to read. His heart was quieted by the story as it unfolded the truth of his existence and that of every black man he ever knew. He marveled at the bravery of the words, at the images of people so like those he knew, the exposure of events like those that had happened to him and his own where the law of the land was foe to his kind. The many-sided views of justice when it should be a pure and simple thing saddened him. How could justice enter into it when the enslaved had to depend on the character of the master for compassion? Did anyone really believe that slavery was made right if the master was kind? The enslaved needed anger enough to regain spirit and stake a claim for a rightful place. And the black man, free or enslaved, needed to own land and possess his freedom in that way. Nowhere was anything said about that. Yet without ownership, oppression was inevitable. He paused often and stared into space, his thoughts reeling and flying off into avenues he'd not seen so clearly before.

He read on, his small dictionary at his side. He missed nothing. He entered the world Stowe exposed, her thoughts, her perceptions, her sense of Christian charity, her views, and her prejudices, trying to understand while he exulted in her ability to get the whole of it down on paper. The characters were people he felt he knew intimately. He read slowly, savoring the words. It was a broad view, a vista that explored the contradictions of the black man's place in an otherwise free society. It would take supreme effort to change things. It would take years and several generations, but perhaps this book would begin it. As the stirrings of suspicion grew louder around him, he knew it was a dawn of sorts. In the wider world away from the fields outside his door, his people were not alone. *Praise God. He has not forgotten us.*

Tonight he stared into the dwindling fire, lost in thought. With a start, he realized that the time had come. The log had burned down to a few embers, and he judged by the length of its burning since sundown that it was time to go.

Neither the church nor his cabin could be the meeting place. Word had come by way of Daniel's watchful eyes and ears that tonight a few more runaways would come through, and Green had sent word to meet at the head of the nearby creek. He pulled on his coat, jammed a hat down over his head, and stepped into the night. He looked for the Big Dipper, followed its cup to the Little Dipper and then, at the end of its handle was the North Star. Its permanence reassured him of eternity and a planned destiny.

This time, nine of them were waiting in a huddle, their shoulders hunched. Henry, the apparent leader, reminded him of the tall and powerful James Spry. His jacket and overalls, torn and threadbare, were tight as though made for a much smaller man.

"Harriet say go to Otwell somewhere near the Delaware line. We goin' to pay the man eight dollars to get us up to Camden," Henry said.

"Hysh now," said Green. It was no good to say the entire route out loud should any one of them become too frightened to keep running and fail to keep the route a secret if they turned back. They were breathless, desperate, ragged, and determined. Seven men and two women. Three of them were armed and flashed knives for him to see, saying, "Don't worry none about us, Preacher."

He nodded. "We're goin' to Harriet's parents. It'll be just before sunup when we get there. You stay all day and then someone will take you on up the next night. Every place you go, somebody's goin' to take you the next piece." He said nothing more. The route changed its course from time to time along the varying patterns of deer paths, fox runs, horse trails and wagon roads to the shallow places off Hunting Creek, behind Linchester Mill and then on to Poplar Neck. He knew the way in every configuration.

Now, there was only his brief prayer before he led them, *Deliver us, oh Lord, into safe hands,* his thoughts focused on the run to Poplar Neck. They half-ran, half-walked, silently watching the stars hang brightly through the branches while the muddy places sucked at their feet. Behind him was Henry, dark as the night itself, a stout, muscular giant of a man whose master had wanted to sell him South. Then, a man called Denard, whiskered and bareheaded now that Henry had made him take off his white hat with the broad black band.

"Man on the run don't need no white hat to show where he's at," Henry had chided. And then came Thomas, so dark there was no difference between him and the sky, an intelligent young man who could have been the leader if Henry had let him. The two light-skinned women had been warned to keep their faces covered with a shawl. The others followed, indistinguishable bundles of tattered rags as he looked behind him. For the rest of the way, he prayed for them.

Somewhere near morning, they'd lost one of their number. A bad sign. He'd trusted them to follow and after he'd delivered the remaining eight to Ben Ross's cabin at Poplar Neck, he retreated. On the way back to his cabin, he looked for the ninth runaway not really expecting to find anyone. Whoever it was had had plenty of time to be long gone. A stiff wind stirred the trees and overran any sound a runner might make. He listened and watched as he walked, but could not still his uneasiness.

A breach in secrecy was likely now. He could understand the terror that might have caused the ninth person to run. He imagined him, whoever it was, returning to his owner and fairly heard the smack of the whip and the subsequent telling, for it was hard to imagine anyone of their own kind revealing anything without a good beating. He refused to believe anyone would betray them out of favor for themselves.

During the following weeks, he thought the story that came back to him was better than anything he'd read in *Uncle Tom's Cabin.* He admired the resourcefulness of the runaways in the fight for freedom. First came word of mouth and then in a few days, the newspaper article. The runaways were listed. The reward money was nearly three thousand dollars. Advertisements were posted in Delaware on the second day of the run. However, there was a betrayal other than the one he worried about that sickened him—a chain of lies for the reward money. The Negro, Otwell, the agent Harriet trusted and used several times before, had met the runaways a short distance from the Delaware border and had not only colluded with the white man named Hollis in order to split the reward, but let the sheriff in on the ruse. Otwell delivered the runaways to Hollis at the sheriff's home in Dover where the jail cells were on the second floor. Believing they were in a safe house, up the steps they went, with Hollis following, reassuring them they'd be warm and cared for during the night.

The story came to the preacher in brief details which he pieced together like the biblical passages he used for his sermons. He could see it all. He had prayed for two nights, and during the second night of his prayers, it was the one named Henry who had saved them. Green knew it would be him. The bright moonlight, too, had saved them as it shone through the jail cell window. It was a warning. Had God sent it? That bright patch on the floor interrupted by bars? So that when Henry stepped into the light and saw the shadows of the bars, his eyes flew to the window. He realized they'd been betrayed. And he reacted. "I don't like the looks of this," he said, and back-tracked. The sheriff, climbing the stairs with keys in his hand, intended to lock the runaways in the jail cell. Instead, he met them in the hallway as they scrambled out of the cell. It was the middle of the night, and even though he knew of their arrival, he'd neglected to grab his pistols. When he ran to his living quarters to retrieve them, the runaways were right behind him even as he entered the room where his wife and children slept. It was Henry who grabbed the shovel and Henry who dug into the burning coals in the fireplace and threw them into the room.

Lord, Lord. Green thought of the sheriff's wife and children waking to an uproar, with burning coals on the bed and floor and the sight of a huge black man who held a hot poker—who knew what he might have done with it?—and smashed the window open. They watched, screaming, he was sure, as the glass shattered and each of the runaways jumped to the ground and ran. Imagine their terror as Henry held their father, the sheriff, at bay with the hot poker, a threat which had perhaps already been carried out in their imagination a hundred times before and would now magnify their fear and loathing of Negroes. And well they might be panicked. There was no force as intense as a man whose freedom was at stake. Horrified, they must have watched Henry jump out of the window and scale the wall after the others.

No doubt the preacher's prayers had been answered. The sheriff, stunned and numb in the quickness of it all, finally got hold of his pistol and raised it to shoot Henry as he passed through the window, and glory be, *the pistol—praise God—the pistol had jammed!*

For the time being, the story had to end there, for the events that followed were confusing. The whereabouts of the runaways were not known for a while. Henry made it to Canada for all they knew, although Thomas Garrett, the Quaker in Wilmington who cared for and helped many who crossed his path, had knowledge only of Henry's companion. The others, it was said, managed to find their way back to Otwell with revenge burning in their hearts. Imagine the man pleading and begging for his life. Imagine the dilemma between desperation and mercy for those whom he had wronged. *Take us to Brinkley now. For real and for true, you bastard.* Which he did. And then disappeared. Or rather, he was allowed to disappear after he'd kept his promise and carried them to Brinkley, who used his horses to carry them to Wilmington. Eventually, every one of them made it to Canada except for the married couple. Their whereabouts remained a mystery. Although details drifted in for weeks, a comprehensive article written up in the newspapers from the white population's point of view called the group of runaways, "The Dover Eight." The name stuck. For the black population, it was a victory.

The news quickly spread to newspapers in the North. Those who were outraged at the loss of their property felt justified; the preacher's neighbors and the powerful in town blamed the abolitionists for all the trouble, and the free blacks, too, *damn them.* They were the ones who encouraged insurgency and gave the slaves their nerve. They were the ones who disrupted the happy scheme of things in a society that was well run and efficient. Who was to blame? What had caused this latest infraction? Who in the free black community was smart enough and leader enough to guide them?

From there, it wasn't long before talk was directed at him, the preacher farmer. He lived close to the road near the Delaware line. He had a sense of the outer world and had traveled to Philadelphia and Baltimore and had, no doubt, been in touch with abolitionists. He was considered clever and he could read. Hadn't he gone to Canada to stake out the place? Didn't he have a son there? Wasn't it because he'd been among the most trusted, educated Negroes that it was easy for him to take advantage of that trust? Hadn't he actually counted on that trust to do whatever he felt like?

He could feel the rising tension in snatches of conversation overheard on trips to town: *Run 'em all out of here. The blacks that are free tell those who are property that they don't have to be owned. Send 'em all to Africa. Don't give 'em a choice about it because the ones who'll leave will be the strong hard workers while the ones who'll be left will be the dumb and shiftless. Lynch 'em. Free and slave don't belong in the same country.*

Preacher Green's farm had not yet been sold. The landowner had never given him word that it was up for sale. He felt uneasy and wondered if the trip to Canada had anything to do with his present position. People who once were friendly kept their distance; neighbors with whom he'd had good rapport avoided him. He sensed he'd fallen from a respected place and there was no going back.

When they came for him, he was both expectant and disbelieving. They came in the dark of night on an April evening when the winds still had a chill in them and the time of planting was at hand. He'd spent the day plowing. When they entered his cabin, he realized he'd not be able to finish the planting, which meant his doom. They burst through the door, those "gentlemen" as the newspaper referred to the patrollers, and searched his cabin. They'd be disappointed; he harbored no evidence. They entered with the stomp of their boots on his floor and their minds full of suspicion. That was all, he told himself. There was proof of nothing. They took the letter from his son that he'd tucked in his Bible, the train schedules, a map of Canada, and the Stowe book he was reading. He was sorry he'd never received the second volume. With a start, he thought about the ninth runaway, the brief and detailed revelation of the trip to Poplar Neck and beyond, and began to worry not only about his own safety but also that of Harriet's mother and father who had hidden the fugitives on the previous Sunday.

Then, head down, with his hands tied behind his back, he walked behind Shadrack Morris's horse, praying. It was all he was able to do. The boys, Eziah and Edward, had been hired out only the week before to Mr. Eben Prouse or they would surely have been taken as well.

"Lean times," Elizabeth said to Libby, "hit those with better means the hardest, but we'll get by anyhow." She had no reason for such optimism with the destruction of the new crops by late frost and storms that caused water to rise so the earth gave way in places. Roads had flooded out, trees standing in water fell, hail pelted the cabin roof and tore at tender, budding plants. Then when Kitty came running across the fields, Elizabeth, with a curse on her lips, guessed that there would be more of the wrath of God. She waited by her furrow with a stick in her hand and paused in her task of replanting to watch Kitty's dark figure come toward her in the raw, gray day. But where the wrath that came down from the sky was dealt in equal share to white and black, Kitty's news of the preacher's arrest was not. And what about Kitty who lived on rented property with little chance of a crop this year?

"The sheriff come and Shadrack Morris and two others. They took him off, tied up, and walkin'. Lord, I seen bad days, Elizabeth, with my own chilren taken. But this! Ain't there no end to the sorrow?"

"He gonna be free, Kitty. You know they got nothin' on him, he bein' in good standin' and all," she said, but doubt choked her. It was like the uprooted trees, their undersides exposed in clots of tangled roots and mud as if the devil himself had pushed them up out of the ground to set himself loose.

Preacher Green had no previous cause to be in the newly built courtroom and had last seen the interior of the old courthouse on the day of Elizabeth's signing of her deed. Here the fine paneling, the brass door knobs, the judge on a pedestal seated before a stand handsomely carved, the high windows—all spoke of power and right, justice, respect for law and order. If your skin was white. Disorder if your skin was dark, a world gone mad with an order of disorder. A black man trembled in such a courtroom, which is what he did now, uncontrollably. He expected nothing in the way of justice. He had a court-appointed attorney, a Mr. Daniel Henry, who was a slave owner and not in sympathy with either the enslaved or the free blacks. In fact, he was a member of the infamous Slaveholders Convention, which subscribed to the belief that because of their abolitionist views, the Quakers had lost the respect of the white planters and had no choice but to consort with the Negroes. Yet, Mr. Henry seemed sincere enough in his desire to speak for him. Not a word was ever said about his involvement with runaways. There was no real evidence; they'd never caught him in the act. But he *was* guilty. Whatever they thought, he certainly was guilty of it. They'd find a way. Hadn't he always known the destiny that awaited him?

In the end, Judge Spence, Mr. Henry, and the prosecuting attorney, Mr. Griswold, told him to repudiate his request for a trial by jury. Maybe that was the right thing to do. Maybe one educated white man with a sense of fairness would offer a chance whereas twelve white opinions from the citizenry would surely spell disaster. No black man ever appeared on a jury since he was not considered a legal citizen. Even before the Dred Scott Decision, a black man could not testify against a white man, or even stand up for those of his own race, and certainly not after. So he expected nothing and put his mind on the grace of his God who he knew would stand with him. He no longer questioned. He'd already felt the Lord's strength pouring into him when they shackled him. He did not struggle or raise an angry eye. He did not have a body at all. He was beyond this earth and all its troubles as if he were somehow looking down on himself from some other place.

Lord, yes, he was guilty. Although he'd known for a long time this day would come, the knowledge had not deterred him from doing what he had to do. There were different kinds of moral right, and a man had to have his own sense of it in order to be a man. He looked through the high windows at the blue, clear sky, a fine day to be planting, working the mule and the plow, his feet scuffling through the brown earth.

His precious letter from Sam, Jr. and the map of Canada were shown as evidence. The point was made that the men mentioned in Sam, Jr.'s letter, Peter Jackson and Josiah Bailey, had indeed absconded. Then there were the train schedules. However, Mr. Henry explained, the purpose of the Act of 1841 was to prevent the possession of papers that would incite a desire for insurgency, and no such evidence was found. While words flung back and forth over the preacher's bowed head, his mind wandered, and when they were done speaking in their flat, self-confident, self-righteous way, the prosecuting lawyers and the sheriff took their seats while he, now standing before the judge, trembled and waited patiently. Was it patience when one could do nothing else? Was it bravery when one had no choice? He tried to look the judge in the eye. What kind of man was he? What was he thinking? Did he think with hatred walling him in? Did he feel God was on *his* side?

The voices went on. The evidence presented did not come under the jurisdiction of this law, repeated Mr. Henry. A map of Canada and a railroad schedule could not be construed as abolitionist or incendiary evidence. Still, the lawyers for the prosecution argued that the papers were evidence enough that Green was sympathetic to the runaways' plight. Hadn't he given information that would help slaves escape as evidenced by the train schedules and maps?

Judge Spence retired to his chambers. When he returned with his black robe flaring, and climbed the step to his pedestal, he banged his gavel and stated the Act of 1841 was not applicable to this case, that the object of Act 1841 (since it was a supplement put in place in the Act of 1831 after the Nat Turner uprising) was to prevent the possession of papers that might create discontent of an incendiary nature in the Negroes, and the case of Preacher Samuel Green did not come under its jurisdiction. He was to be acquitted.

He was stunned. He pulled back his shoulders. It was true that no one ever heard him conspiring with a runaway or caught him leading a slave through the woods or harboring anyone in his cabin or church. No. But did a tree that fell in the woods where no one heard make any noise? And what about the person who'd turned back? Who had he told about the harboring of runaways by Rit and Ben Ross? And had he identified him? Would that bit of evidence come to light later?

He was giddy with relief. He would walk out in the sun again, lift his face to the Lord in gratitude, greet spring, and finish his planting. But he had no time to relish those thoughts for long. There was something else, another matter from a corner he'd least suspected. It was not, to his surprise, the testimony of the ninth runaway that he'd worried so much about, but his having in his possession a copy of *Uncle Tom's Cabin*. Straining under the fiery reproaches of the citizenry, the attorney general, a Mr. James Wallace, and the prosecuting lawyer, Mr. Griswold, tried again. *Green's status as a freeman did not allow him to have abolitionist literature in his possession.*

Any white person could read *Uncle Tom's Cabin* without recrimination. The book had been passed around the county many times since its appearance. It was an overreach to say a person could be convicted for having a copy in his possession, but not for him, not for a black man in his position and circumstance with suspicion rampant and the desire for a scapegoat high. It was a narrow bend in the law that connected his reading the book to his alleged guilt. Judge Spence decided the book was abolitionist in nature, surely written to incite the Negroes' discontent and dissatisfaction toward God knows what acts of violence and theft, and its possession, therefore, was a clear violation of Act of 1841, Chapter 272. And that was that. The preacher was to remain in the county jail.

No one ever asked him if he'd read the book. If they'd asked, he could have told them he'd never finished it, that he'd never received the second volume and since he was in jail anyway, couldn't he read it to the end? But insolence and sarcasm were not part of his nature. He would remain silent, martyred, the only thing left to him.

Just before the second trial, sitting on the pallet in his jail cell and warming his feet in the patch of sunlight from the high window, he was surprised to hear the key turn in the lock. Alert to a possible lynching that lay foremost on his mind, he was much relieved to see Eben Prouse walk through the cell door.

"Aren't you afraid to come in here, Mr. Eben?" he asked.

"You've been a good friend. We've worked side by side all our lives. That's why I'm here. But I have to tell you, why don't you seek further counsel? Your lawyer, that Henry—you know what he is—a slave owner. He's friends with Judge Spence and the prosecuting attorney, that Griswold fellow. They're all in collusion."

He shook his head. "It's no use," he said, "I'm guilty."

"Guilty of what?"

He looked down at his bare feet, calloused and sinewy in the patch of sun. "I'm guilty, that's all."

"You don't even know what the charges are, do you? They're sayin' you're guilty for readin' a book, Preacher. It shouldn't matter what kind. It just ain't right."

He nodded. No matter what the charges were, he had helped runaways and they knew it. They'd get him one way or the other.

Prouse continued, "You know Judge Spence and Henry and Griswold hang together in the Slaveholders Convention. I don't trust any one of them. It's likely Henry was promised acquittal in exchange for conviction on the abolitionist literature business." Eben's face was red now and perspiration dripped off his chin. He wiped his face with his sleeve and glared out the window.

"No, no. I'm guilty." Green rubbed his eyes. The image of Eben Prouse was a blur, but he could still see the surprised look on his face as he said, "They take everythin', a man's children, his home, his work, his books, his church, his life. At least"—his voice shook—"at least let me own my guilt! The Lord will decide whether or not I acted in sin. The whole nation is readin' that book and respondin' with sympathy, from what I hear. Meantime, I say, let them do as they will, and maybe the outside world will read the papers and see what's happenin'. Maybe then they'll decide the right and wrong of it all, not just about me, but everythin' goin' on here. It's part of God's plan, I do believe. In the long view, it may do good. You know how the current in the river flows along and along and when it comes to shore, throws itself right up into a wave? Maybe we're seein' the wave come, you know, Mr. Eben? Washin' the land? Sometimes it takes a storm, but it'll happen."

Good would come from this even if it took a while. He looked up at the farmer he'd known all his life. The man had taken a day away from his planting to see him. He was touched.

Once more he stood before the new brick courthouse. With the acquittal, he had foolishly harbored a hope that it would bring justice. With his wrists in shackles, his disbelief that the book he was reading could cause a prison sentence returned to him. Having climbed the steps to the courthouse door, he stopped to read a poster nailed to the door:

For Sale
Will be sold at the Court House door
In the town of Cambridge on May 13, 1857
Negro woman
Aged about 23 years and her child aged about 5 years,

Slaves for life
We are authorized to sell said slaves without
Reservation and for no fault
Graham and Jenner, Attnys.

Words flashed through his mind: *We hold these truths to be self-evident—all men are created equal—the pursuit of happiness.* Across the street was the Episcopal Church, bulwark of the white and powerful, a stalwart presence in the heart of the city. *In God we trust.* The same God, surely. But God was above the church. Beyond it. Could not be confined to it. What was the church but men who believed in their own brand of righteousness? On the opposite corner stood the framed, two-storied Bradshaw Hotel where slave traders from the South gathered to bid at auctions and who, on this day in May, sat on the veranda watching the life of the city flow by, keeping an eye out for a sale. The slave pen stood close by. Ships waited at the dock. *The Georgia man. You be pickin' down in some cotton field 'fore you know it, without any of your family nearby. Half time, you walk most the way, chained to the one in front and the one behind.* Like James Spry. If he was guilty of anything, it was his reluctance to help James.

He was surprised at the number of people who'd gathered for his sentencing. Inside the hushed courtroom he faced once more the honey-brown paneling and judge's stand that had probably been honed to perfection by a black carpenter. The benches were filled with people. A few were from his own farming community but many were from the towns and large farms throughout the county who considered that what he'd done was aid in the theft of their property.

This time he was convicted. Indeed, despite its truthfulness and bravery, the book he'd read only part of could not change what was. Not yet. That the book had found its way into his hands was fate, he who read none other than the Bible. That he could read was an insult. That he could think for himself was a threat. That he could lead was cause for alarm. To those in power, these were the real travesties. He heard his full name read aloud, then, "*is* hereby sentenced to ten years in the state penitentiary by the Circuit Court of Dorchester County for having in his possession pamphlets..."

Behind him, he heard Kitty cry out. Ten years. If he'd been a younger man, it would have been worse. He was fifty-five with the best of his years behind him. He'd not wasted his time. He would probably die in prison, but he'd done what he could. God was the true judge, and he would not be afraid to stand before Him. *Thank you, Lord, for the strength you have given me.* He understood Harriet's confidence and power. There was no way to know it without suffering. It was through affliction and pain that God revealed himself. His prayers now were for Kitty, and Sarah—wherever she was—and Sam Jr., a long, long way from home.

"...or papers of inflammatory character and having a tendency to create discontent amongst or stir up to insurrection the people of color in this state, at the end of which time"—and here the judge looked down at him—"you will have to leave the state within sixty days or suffer the consequences."

That meant lynching. He did not need to be threatened. He would leave and join Sam, Jr. in Canada. He would tell Kitty to go without him and he would come later. Ten years later. Why hadn't he joined Sam, Jr. already? In his heart, he knew the answer.

Once outside, blinking in the brilliant May sun, he watched the crowd from the steps of the courthouse. Among them, a few friends, but he saw no one from his congregation. They would, of course, be staying clear of the trouble. The angry crowd ranted about his guilt with a wave of raised fists. His quiet, unassuming ways had not warranted such notoriety and he was sickened. He grew dizzy. They followed, shouting and cursing him down High Street as he walked by men carrying guns to the wharf. The grand old trees stood silent in contrast to the turmoil below. The windows of the big houses seemed to glare at him despite their lace curtains, despite the neat flower beds tended by the Negro men who did not turn around to look at him. Ahead was the steamboat that would take him to the state penitentiary in Baltimore.

The Lord sent tribulation a million different ways. But this, this was the hardest to bear. Yet deep down, he asked himself, hadn't he been born without freedom? Hadn't he had to buy himself? And did he not still own himself?

The black iron gates screeched and clanged in reverberation of his inner cries, and while the locks clicked smoothly behind him, he thought about how defining the present moment was in the history that would follow him. Although he was cut off from the world in this tumultuous year of 1857, he saw that he was also a part of something beyond himself and his tiny parish on the Eastern Shore. Forces gathered. The rains could never wash away the bloodshed that would come. The anger of the crowd had stunned him. Passions were high, and it wouldn't take much for there to be a riot.

He resolved not to waste time. He'd heard the Baltimore Quakers had established a library within prison walls and for this reason he was not dismayed when he faced a line of sixty cots in what was supposed to be the prison's hospital but was now the dormitory. He'd never stayed in a brick structure before. On the walls at man-height were carved the initials of those who'd been prisoners before him. He began to think about them and wonder if their stays were as unjust as his own. It was a revelation of sorts. There was a blurring of right and wrong despite what he might have said from the pulpit. And in the balance hung the actuality of a God who cared. Would God excuse such blasphemy? In anger and confusion, he muttered, *my very soul wavers.*

AFTERMATH, SPRING, 1857

———

*E*lizabeth held Mary in her lap and rocked her even though she was well beyond babyhood. She was six this year, but small for her age. Elizabeth had taught her to tear rags into strips, sew them together end to end into long strands, and roll them for rug making later. *You make three balls big as apples and then I'll show you how to braid.* The pile of rags included among other things, snatches of cloth from one of Daniel's shirts, a leg of Perry's pants, and a shift belonging to Addy. The sight brought her comfort. She began to hum. The child watched her face and as was her habit, reached up to hold her long braid. Soon Mary's eyes closed. They sat together for a sweet moment. Elizabeth studied the small round face so like Addy's, the unblemished baby skin, the curl of black eyelashes. The child slept soundly.

To feel a warm body pressed against hers happened seldom now. The best moments were always the ones that arrived without fanfare, never to be forgotten, never to be retrieved. Mary would awaken and wiggle away, but for now, the rocking was in tune with all the other rhythms she'd known, those of labor and worry, of loving and losing, rhythms that moved her forward whether or not she wanted to go. She recognized the deep, quiet place the child brought her to. It came from her own mother in her own long-ago beginning. The child would move through time in her own way, seeing things Elizabeth could never guess. She hoped Mary would recognize this peace when it returned to her through a child of her own or someone she'd love completely and unconditionally, a love leaning against her someday. *Pass it on, chile, pass it on.*

She did not know how long they rocked. The quilt she'd been working dropped to the floor, and her hand trembled as she reached for it to cover Mary. She kept humming. One of Addy's songs came to her:

> *Sit down, O sit down*
> *We gotta pray, sit down*
> *We gotta pray till we get blessed,*
> *We gotta lay our head down on the Savior's breast,*
> *Sit down, O sit down, and take your rest.*

Singing in church raised her up. The chorus of voices gave her gooseflesh but made her strong. Alone, her voice was nothing. Nothing at all. Preacher Green had bound them or the Lord had, or maybe it was trouble *and* Preacher *and* the Lord. It was the one aspect of church she could understand, how they all stood together. The rest she was never sure about. But the standing together was what she'd clung to over the years. Where would they be without Preacher? They'd wait like a band of lost sheep for a traveling preacher to round them up. She shook her head.

A lady in town hired Libby to do some sewing. Libby loved the excitement and smell of new fabrics, the way they arrived in paper bundles off the steamboat or were brought back in large trunks from trips to New York. But the missus who hired her would not allow her fine cambric to leave the house and be left to filth and ruin in some Negro cabin, so Libby sewed at the big house until the dress or coat was finished and then she went back home. A hoop sewn into each skirt was what Missus wanted this time, and she wanted to be the first in town to wear one despite the warnings about hoops attracting lightning.

It was too far to walk home each night, so Libby often stayed in the quarters in back of the big house. And it was on those occasions, she went to visit the smithy where Daniel worked.

They were almost the same age. Although Libby had grown tall very quickly, Daniel's growth was slow, and it was not until this year that he suddenly was taller than she. It happened within a few months' time, and when it did, she began to look at him with new eyes. On her last visit, she felt a strange shyness in his presence. It surprised her. She often watched him shovel coal into the furnace, his face glowing red as the fire. And when he turned to her, she watched for some small sign that he was pleased to see her, but he kept his head down of late and shuffled his feet. It made her impatient with him, wanting to tease him like she did when they were children, make him laugh, wrestle him to the ground, egg him on to throw stalks of mare's tail weeds as if they were spears and see who could throw the farthest. Who was this silent man in front of her?

This night she'd waited for him in the shed where he stayed behind the smithery. When he came, she stood before him with tears in her eyes.

"Libby?" he said. "What's wrong, girl?"

"They give Preacher Green ten years. Ten years! I don't know what we goin' do. What's Kitty goin' do?"

"I heard it. Man come in from Cambridge and tol' it. They say they would have lynched him if they could, so at least he alive."

That hadn't occurred to her. It wasn't like her to cry. She felt helpless, unsure. The world kept changing. She couldn't get her bearings. Suddenly, she realized how much she'd counted on Daniel. The teasing competition between them had grown into something else. She had no words for it. He was part of her life, her breathing, her childhood, and her home. Her new feelings were a puzzle, though. She loved all the family that was under Elizabeth's roof. How was this different? She wanted to breathe him in, wanted him to touch her. Nothing could be as good as the expectation of that or as painful should he refuse her. Suddenly self-conscious, she stepped back.

"I'll see you tomorrow. Maybe there be some good news, and I'll come tell you."

"Libby?"

She stopped and stared at him, at the smooth brown skin of his face with the slight whisper of a beard.

"Could you bring me one of Betsy's corn cakes? I ain't had one in a long time." He smiled at her, that foolish, devil grin of his kid days.

She laid her hand on his arm. "Yes. I'll do that. May not be tomorrow, but next time I go home."

He nodded. "You stay safe now. You don't belong on the streets this time of day without a note. Stay on the path between here and town, out of sight, you understand? Wouldn't want nothin' to happen to that corn cake."

She laughed. "Nobody knows I sneaked out. Besides I'm free as you."

He shook his head and changed his mind. "I'm walkin' you back."

She nodded and answered with her arm linked in his as he pulled her toward the path. For a brief second, he'd put his hand on her waist and then stepped in front of her. He turned to make sure she was still following, and each time he did, he was smiling. She vowed to get him corn cakes even if it meant an extra trip to town in the middle of the week to deliver them.

The next evening, she walked the four miles home. Without entering the cabin, she picked up a hoe and began to stir the earth, listening to the spring birds calling. Off in the distance, she spotted the boys, James, Jr. and Thomas, hoeing the new corn. She called to them and they began to chase one another across the field holding the hoes like lances. They'd be hungry. She would start the cakes if Elizabeth hadn't, and she wondered where Mary was. The trees had begun to bud out, especially the sugar maples. The wild roses and blackberry stems were faintly green and she hoped there'd be plenty of fruit this year despite the late start with a cold spring. Soon they would head to the mill stream to net herring and fish for shad.

As she'd entered the cabin with the boys running behind her, Elizabeth woke up. Mary stirred.

"You all right, Betsy?" she asked, for Betsy never slept during the day.

"Been dreamin' that all the troubles was fixed and we were makin' it easy. The chile does it to me. Such a sweet thing to hold a chile, you know?" She smiled at Mary and patted her on the behind.

"We out of cornmeal?" asked Libby.

"Low. Use up what's left for cakes and take some to Kitty. Poor lamb. She be havin' to sell everythin'. Got to get off the land soon. Hard as Preacher worked, he never could buy that piece."

"I was thinkin' to make some for Daniel, too."

"You see him?"

"Every evenin' when I finish with Missus."

"Mm hmm. I see how that goin' and where."

Libby turned the batter in the bowl and did not look up. "We ain't blood," she said, more as a question than a statement.

"No, you ain't. I can swear to that. And you know each other from little on up. And I know too, Libby, you be ready. Only one thing. If you go together with him and somethin' happen to me, you take the chilren, heah? You stay right here and keep the chilren. It'll be the last thing I ax you to do."

In a few weeks, an auction was held to sell some of the Greens' household goods and farm equipment. There wasn't much. Elizabeth saw the contents of the house scattered on the bare ground, the door to the cabin left open, the yawning blackness inside empty of sustenance and comfort. The latest hail-storm had ruined the garden Kitty had started, and the few who came walked around it as if it were sacred ground, a place that once held the promise of continuity and survival and now stood as the symbol of an end of everything, a strange contradiction for spring. Mostly colored came. They were people with nothing themselves, come to pick at the remains of a life and a way. They knew about endings, about things being scarce, and the threat of jail for those who couldn't pay. In jail six months and you'd be up for auction yourself. That's how it was.

The bidding didn't take any time at all: a bed, a table, and two chairs, the gig, the mule, and five hogs. Kitty gave the bag of extra clothes to Elizabeth to do with what she could. After the auction, Kitty would have a little money to live on. Things could be worse, she told herself. Preacher's life had been one of diligence. He'd had no debts. "Praise God," said Kitty. "You know I heard tell of a man in Carolina who bought his wife's freedom, and when he died, he had some debts so they took his wife and sold her to pay what he owed because she was his property. They said she was his *property*, you understand me?" and she shook her head. But because the preacher owed no one, Kitty kept her kettle, her cups and bowls, her spinning wheel and the Bible and lamp and went to live with a family in their congregation. The Lord opened a way as He always did for those who trusted in Him. She was "taken in," and she would wait for her husband. She would never leave for Canada without him.

Sorting through the contents of the bag Kitty had given her, Elizabeth made one pile of worn-out rags she would make into something else and one pile of usable clothes for the runaways: a pair of tow linen pants, two brown muslin shirts, a torn pair of Kentucky jeans, striped pantaloons, and dark ones, too. More runaways would come through, of that she was sure. She heard of a meeting in April where slave owners were more intent than ever in routing out those responsible for inciting slaves to escape. The anger had grown even worse with Preacher's conviction. She'd hold tight. Her cabin, so close to Federalsburg and the Delaware border, would take up the slack from the church and the Greens' cabin. With Preacher gone there was no one to reassure them, no one to turn to. To keep her cabin a safe house now was more important and dangerous than ever. Just before Preacher's arrest, two runaways left, then fifteen, then eighteen, then eight more. After his arrest, none left for a while, which was proof enough of his guilt, some said. Then five more left and the sheriff agreed with popular opinion that another way had been made open to the runaways. Then, while Preacher Green sat in the penitentiary, forty people ran in a period of two weeks.

After that, spring unfolded easily. The rye and wheat spread green over the fields between town and Elizabeth's cabin. Dogwood bloomed along the edge of the woods like lace trimming. Farmers complained the fruit trees were ruined with the late frost and bitter winds. The corn was off to a slow start, the plants small and intermittent. They would have to replant. Libby worried where the money for more seed would come from.

Meanwhile, the foraging Elizabeth had taught them saved them once more. With dandelion greens, tender milkweed shoots, mustard greens in the fallow field, tuckahoe along the creek, herring from the mill stream, and shad aplenty in the Marshhope, they would spend much time gathering. Libby explained to

Missus she was needed at home for a few weeks. Although she was sorry not to see Daniel, spring was in her bones, and she was glad of the sun's warmth on her back as she worked in the field, listening to the calls of finches and robins.

Then Daniel came. On Sunday, he'd borrowed a mule and a wagon. Mary saw him coming along the road and ran back to the cabin squealing, "Daniel here!" He wasted no time, and began to fix some of the roof shingles that had come loose, replaced the ax handle, and carried water, all the while grinning and teasing Libby, "What you doin', girl, actin' crazy, dancin' 'round like that, like you was 'witched?"

She laughed, couldn't stop laughing, and when he came off the roof, she put her arm on his shoulder. "You better watch out, girl, actin' foolish with me." Grinning. It was the not-so-serious Daniel. She chided him, "You come to see me, didn't you? Now you seein' me, what you gonna do 'bout it?" Words. Just silly words let loose into the air like dandelion seeds floating on the breeze. "This what I'm gonna do. You just watch." Words that made no sense but opened up a space, cut down briars, cleared away shyness. He grabbed her arm and pulled her along down the road.

Mary watched from the cabin door. "Can I come?" she said. But Libby never heard her.

Later, as he sat in the cabin with them over the evening meal, he told them the news. "Harriet's mother and father? Gone. She come back for 'em. Had nothin' but two wheels and the axle from an old chaise carriage for 'em to sit on and tied a board to it for their feet. Then she hitched up a horse and left. Maybe Ben's man helped 'em, I don't know. Tol' ol' Ben he'd be arrested knowin' what they knew about him helpin' the eight comin' through. Somebody tol' it. Maybe somebody who turned back. So Harriet come. She been plannin' it for a time. She come back right in the middle of all this mess with Preacher and got 'em out. They're gone," he said, and shook his head. "Word come through at the smithy yesterday and that's why I come," he said, stealing a look at Libby, who twisted her mouth to one side.

"Now you know that ain't exactly true," he said. He laughed then, a slow, easy ripple of sound that warmed the cabin. "I be goin' now."

Some changes come so easy, thought Libby. You go along and then a change comes like everything you ever hoped for and you wonder how the cups on the table and the bed where you lay your head could be the same. She was his now. They would always be family. She would become a Johnson, changed from Spry, but underneath, she would always be a Burton. The land named them. People would always say, "You know them what stay down to the Burton place?"

Soon enough, the new preacher came through. Elizabeth watched him that first Sunday with a wary eye. Dressed entirely in black with hands that showed no hard labor, he was not the farmer man Preacher had been. He rode the circuit and brought news of what the northern papers had said about Preacher Green's case, telling them not on Sunday morning, not from the pulpit, but individually, quietly. He said the northern newspapers saw Preacher Green's imprisonment as an outrage. Imagine a man imprisoned for reading a book. He told them that a few local farmers, school teachers, and merchants signed a petition and sent it to the governor on Preacher Green's behalf, despite the protest of local slaveholders, who propagated the idea that the Negroes were content with their lot. The new preacher fed their hope, telling them that like a wildfire spread by the wind, the desire for freedom's flame had caused many more to run.

The congregation took heart. They did not believe Preacher Green would serve the whole sentence. Meanwhile, as they gathered and prayed, their hearts sank at the flatness of the new preacher's voice, his spiritless delivery of the same words that had so inspired them when Preacher Green spoke. Like him, the new preacher could read and tell what the newspapers said, but he didn't know, of course, to tell Elizabeth when the land taxes were due, when her name would be among those still owing, and she forgot to ask.

This Sunday morning before church, she visited the graves of Perry and Addy. There were many changes, she told them. The last ship from Mr. Hughlett's shipyard was put in the water at the Jamaica Point. The white oak forest was nearly gone. The sawyers, caulkers, and carpenters were looking elsewhere for work. Everybody was afraid, more so since Preacher went to prison. No one trusted anyone. Land sold cheap; the crops had been poor. But she and the children were all right. She thought Libby and Daniel would marry one day soon. *We're carrying on*, she told them. Satisfied, she turned and walked back to the cabin and loaded Miss Mari's old wagon with the children and food for a church supper. Then, with Libby beside her, she started out. It was a clear, blue-sky day, so blue and cloudless she felt she could die on such a day and be happy. Proud of her family and thankful for food enough to share, she drove on to Mount Zion Church, which would always be Preacher Green's in her mind.

Delayed several times, the auction of John Prouse's estate finally took place. For Elizabeth, this was a special sorrow, one more bit of evidence that the world around her was changing forever. Or was it that she had grown old and had begun to pine for the way things used to be? The earth beneath her feet didn't stray from its rhythms, but the spirits the wind carried had become restless.

The auctioneer called out a stream of sounds that could not be understood until the last word, *Sold!* His assistant stood by. His thin, pale face hung over the ledger in which he recorded each purchase. Mr. Eben was there guiding his sister-in-law, Sophia, as she made her way among the scattered remains of her life. She gazed at her tin cups, saltcellar, and sugar dish that sat on the dining table in the yard along with her eleven remaining dinner plates and matching bowls, and wept. Their bed, the looking glass in which she'd grown old, the cradle all the babies had slept in, and her two spinning wheels—pieces of her life the neighboring families would take and she'd be left without so much as a cup to pass on to her children. John Prouse owed Thomas's widow, John Webb, Eddie Bromwell, Shadrack Morris, and Jefferson Wallace. And the list went on: John Webster and Loomis, the Fletcher brothers. Everything went, saddles, bridles, jars, the corn broom and carpet rags, combs, the rolling pin, frying pans, the spinning wheels and the loom, the grindstone and hogshead, ox yoke and sheep skins, barrels and kegs, all the beehives, the gum scantling and some maple, too, the root cutter, all the vegetables in the garden, scythes (four of them), and axes, nine hoes, the lot of oats (one hundred bushels), eleven stacks of top fodder and eleven of blade fodder, the wheat and oat straw, the lot of poultry, a cord of wood, and the remainders of the corn crop still on the ground. The total was

$648.58. All of it was owed. The farm would go back to the bank. Land, after all, was only borrowed.

Although she watched the auction to the end, Elizabeth bought nothing. She would have liked to get the pair of oxen and yoke to pull out the rest of the stumps where the roots finally had rotted, but Mr. Eben bought the pair for forty dollars. Maybe he'd let her borrow them sometime.

INSIDE THE WALLS, FALL, 1857

*A*s the oldest inmate, he was given the lightest tasks. He worked in the office sweeping, dusting, polishing, running errands, and washing the floor. Because he could read, he filed and sorted mail. Not that those tasks earned any money for the jail. Other men participated in smithery, coppering, and weaving so that the products of their labor could be sold for upkeep of the prison. He'd been assigned apart from them. It was just as well. In the office where he spent most of his time, he had access to newspapers. The news kept him from disintegrating. If he were to die in prison, which seemed likely, he would not do it in total isolation. There was, after all, some sympathy in the outside world for him.

This was affirmed when he had a visitor. The Quaker, Frances King, the same man who'd been responsible for setting up the prison library, approached him. His face was thickly wrinkled and flesh hung at his neck like a bulldog's, but his gray eyes were kindly and looked directly at Preacher Green as soon as he entered the office. Now those eyes almost disappeared as he said, "Sir!" and smiled, his abundant cheeks moving upward, causing him to squint. "The Reverend Samuel Green?"

He nodded. "They call me Preacher."

"Ah. You are aware, are you not, that Maryland will soon have a new governor?"

Of course, he knew. The governor used to be plain old Thomas Hicks, Registrar of Wills, born in East New Market, a neighbor and landowner, a man he'd known all his life. He nodded at King, but said nothing. He was afraid of hope for it most often delivered disappointment.

"He's a friend of mine. Perhaps, he will heed the petitions that have heretofore been ignored. If there is any way to assist you, I will find it."

The room had darkened. He did not know why this man would help him when his own church seemed to have abandoned his cause. The Methodists were in turmoil while the Quakers went on steadily about their business.

"You must not despair, Preacher," he said. "In the end, I do believe the Methodists will declare themselves. With petitions on your behalf, the accounts in the newspapers, and spirited talk in the North, Maryland may declare itself more Northern than Southern. It just may. And your case will bring it all to a head, seeing as you're one of the church's lay ministers."

Abruptly as the conversation began, it ended the same way. With a wave of his hand, the Quaker left. Green wondered if he would see Kitty soon again, or any of his congregation, particularly Elizabeth, or Libby, the second Elizabeth Burton. He could still hear her practicing the name she chose when she was twelve, every syllable distinctly pronounced. He smiled at the memory. He seldom allowed himself to think about home.

But he did think about the reason he was there and about injustice. Some days it was enough to consider he was there for a larger purpose, part of the gathering wave he'd told Mr. Eben about, but some days he wondered who God was and if He was a just God, or if He had merely set things in motion and stood back. For all his prayers, he wondered if God listened, or if He was so angry with men that He had decided to abandon them. If God was just, then what had the Negro done wrong?

And if the Negro hadn't done anything wrong, then surely justice would be served sometime. Was the task to wait for God to stop the injustices? Then the Negro's only recourse was merely to survive. Was the only path to God through suffering? At night, before retiring, the men talked. When they found out he was a minister, they looked to him for answers. For them, he persisted in the faith and told them to trust in God while asking for forgiveness, but when he said such things, his mouth grew dry and his voice wavered. He had to admit the idea that God was all powerful seemed absurd. If He couldn't stop the atrocities, then He was not powerful and neither was He just. And if He was neither, what good were prayers?

It pained him to think like this. He wanted his faith back. Living without it was the worst suffering.

Unless God suffered, too.

Then it occurred to him that believing in goodness might be enough. Maybe that was all one meant when one said one believed in God.

He withdrew. He did not want to talk to anyone about anything. He only wanted to keep his hands busy. Happiness as he once knew it was gone from his life. Now there was only distraction. When Kitty visited, he hadn't much to say. She brought him bread and peaches the missus in East New Market had given her and he received them from her warm hand with gratitude that brought tears to his eyes. She said she was well cared for, and she would come again when she could get enough for the steamboat fare. She looked older now, her gray hair drifting into white while sorrow lay in the shadows of her face despite her smile. His Kitty. Maybe God was there in his love for her. And if that was true, maybe He was also in Mount Zion Church where his people gathered. It was their spirit that drove him and what he needed now. They had created a God in their minds who was a participant in their daily life, an attitude he himself had propagated but lost to him now in this place of walls and bars.

Mr. King brought newspapers whenever he could. As the news spread, the whole country, it seemed, opined about his case. One, the *Easton Gazette*, claimed the Stowe woman deserved recrimination more than Preacher Green. She was interfering with the contentment of the local enslaved and their kindly masters. She spoke of cruelties that initiated thoughts unrelated to the benign situation of slaves on this gentle land. She was the cause of it all, as were the abolitionists who also should be run out of the country. What an abomination to write such a book.

Despite King's optimism, the new governor, Thomas Hicks, brought little hope. Even though he'd received a petition for pardon from one hundred fourteen ministers from the Black River Conference in New York, Hicks stated publicly that should he pardon Green, he would be "called an abolitionist and mobbed." Another paper, the church's own *Zion's Herald*, supported Green and spoke out against the Maryland faction of the church for their silence on the matter. Western and Northern reporters, clear about the foolishness of a ten year sentence for reading a book, delivered the facts, but the story was editorialized with sarcasm and humor. That his plight should receive national attention worried him. He did not wish to embarrass his following on the Eastern Shore or the ministers of the Methodist Episcopal Conference of which Dorchester was a part. Still, the story was not lost in the larger world and maybe events were developing just as they should. He returned to his prayers. In his doubt, prayer was the one habitual remnant he could not abandon.

ELIZABETH IN RAIN AND SNOW

*R*ain came in torrents for days on end. It gushed off the roof of Elizabeth's cabin in a wall of water, dug a trench in the sandy soil, thundered on the old boards and drove its way into every crack. She watched the dark trickles turn into rivulets on the walls and bade Mary to chink the logs with rags. The wind was high and screamed about them, visible only by the dark arms of the trees swaying, tossing the last of the leaves to the ground and into the watery ditches. It was difficult to see into the rolling darkness, but Elizabeth stared out the window, blissfully aware of the quiet safety of the cabin Perry had built. The children were sound asleep, all except Mary, who leaned against Elizabeth's arm as she sat watching the storm.

Beyond the rain was another sound like the complaint of a cat, and as she sat rocking and listening, trying to sort out the sounds that ran together, she thought the cry might not be a cat but that of a child. The fire was almost out. The cabin was growing cold. Elizabeth whispered to Mary, "Time for bed now."

"They's a little girl outside."

"No, there couldn't be, chile. All the chilren are in bed this late. Go on now."

She put out the pitch pine lamp and strained to see through the rainy dark. Branches tossed overhead; dead ones cracked and spun to the ground. Did she imagine shapes? Were they only the descending leaves and rush of the bushes? Then she was sure she saw someone crouching, running, bent against the rain, then the blurred shapes of many figures, some pulling children along. They could never be runaways. So many! They would never slip by unnoticed. The children would slow them down, cry out. But the runaways kept coming out of the woods. They watched her cabin, perhaps hoping to stop but knowing it was too much to ask with so many. A woman came toward the cabin, her head covered with her shawl, her arms curled around an infant. Surely not an infant. Surely not in the midst of a storm, not on the run, surely not. They'd never make it.

Elizabeth rushed to the door and flung it open. "Come on, then, come on. You'll be safe."

The woman hesitated. The others slowed, some hiding in the trees.

"Please," the woman begged. "You got somethin' to cover the baby?" Once inside, she peeled off the shawl with which she'd covered her head and the child. Elizabeth lit the lamp and nodded at her.

"I saw your light go out. Please keep it on. More's comin' and they be lookin' for the light to know they're goin' right. They ain't no stars to look for tonight." She spoke in a whisper as water dripped from her hair and down her face. She held out the baby.

"Is Harriet with you?" said Elizabeth as she laid the baby on the table and began peeling off wet clothes.

"No, but she told us how to go and where it be safe. She goin' to meet us."

"How many?"

"Was twenty-eight when we started out. Old man Pattison's goin' be surprised when he wake up in the mornin' and find everbody gone. Ever last one. He goin' to have to get his own breakfast." She laughed softly so as not to waken the baby, laughed despite the pouring rain, her sopping wet skirt that clung to her legs, and her shivering.

"We can't stay. We ain't far enough. Got to meet Harriet at the Quaker meetin' house up on the Federalsburg road. I only stopped because of the baby."

Mary, who had slipped out of bed to listen, crept back up the stairs to the loft and pulled her quilt off the pallet. She ran down the steps and held it out to the woman.

"I want to sleep with Granmom anyway," she said.

216

"Oh chile. You don't have to."

"The baby needs it," said Mary.

The woman smiled. "You be blessed," she said as she wrapped the quilt around the infant who still slept, the crease above his nose pronounced in the dim light. "You got your Granmom, your own house, and a heart full of kindness. We never goin' to forget you, though we never see you again. And I'm goin' tell 'im when he grown—if he makes it, if we all make it—how you give the quilt from your own bed for 'im. Thank you, heah?" And with that, she hugged the baby close and slipped out to join the others.

Hours later in the early morning dark, Shadrack Morris came through and pounded on Elizabeth's door. He pushed her aside and looked around the cabin. "Know anything about a bunch coming through here? Not that you'd say, I know. Not that you're not ready to do what every damn one of you will do to turn against us. But you be warned, Elizabeth Burton, to mind your own business."

When he left, she glanced around the yard. Layers of wet, scattered leaves covered the mud and whatever footprints there might have been. Mary hung behind her skirt. It was a miracle the man hadn't noticed the small smock hung to dry near the fireplace.

The rains diminished and one kind of gray led to another as the clouds lightened slightly and promised snow. Bringing Eziah and Edward to help with the pig slaughter, Mr. Eben came and shot the two pigs. Before he left, he took the singletree off the wagon and rigged it to the thickest branch so they could hoist one of the carcasses into the scalding vat. Year after year, Elizabeth hitched the vat to the mule and dragged it from Gaines's barn to the yard, careful to replace it when hog killing was over, as if Miss Mari were still a neighbor. When the fire was ready and the water brought up from the stream began to bubble, she and the boys used Mr. Eben's pulley to lift and lower the pigs into the vat. No one spoke. They took turns scraping the hair. One scraped, two tugged and pulled on the wet, slippery carcass to turn it. Finally, amidst a flurry of snowflakes, the pigs hung from the tree to be bled out. Elizabeth was satisfied. Every year hog killing was getting harder for her, but the boys took over more and more of the work. This year they helped with gutting and butchering. Both Edward and Eziah were experienced, but Thomas and James, Jr. had yet to learn. She showed them how to saw off the head and hooves, which she boiled for a time along with the liver, and then how to skim off the lard, take out the bones, and squeeze out the meat from the concoction in the kettle. When she pulled out the eyeballs, the two younger boys wanted to run off, but she said, "Stay here! You got to know how to do. You help me grind now." After that, it was a matter of mixing the ground-up meat in some of the water in which it boiled. When it jelled, they'd slice some off and eat it cold.

After saving the lard, the smaller cuts of meat she preserved in pickle jars and the salt barrel, saving the best part, the hams, to be sugar cured. She asked Libby to measure out a quart of salt, a quart of brown sugar, and a fourth of a pound of pepper, and then showed her how to use the mixture to rub down the hams. After the water was drawn out, she and Libby wrapped the meat in cloth and hung it in the smokehouse over coals Daniel had brought. Exhausted, she felt the bones in every part of her body speak to her. *Perry. Oh Perry. Remember hog killin' at Gaines's and everbody helpin' and all the plenty? And soon after, remember buyin' the land and the clearin' of it? What glory days those were! We looked forward then, not behind.*

For three days, she cut meat and tended the fire in the smoke house. She had some fine hams she'd sell at East New Market. It would be her last trip to town before winter set in. After that, she'd burrow in like the ground hogs. Pat-tyrollers came around often and were holding meetings again. There was talk about uniting against the freemen and the abolitionists, as if that wasn't what they'd always done. At Mount Zion they prayed for the runaways' safe journey, but it seemed to her the net was closing down on those who stayed, too.

Men hunted in the woods through the long shadows of late fall dusks and through the first flurries of snow before sunup on November mornings. Whether they were patrollers hunting for people or farmers hunting for deer and turkey, hunter and prey were in reprieve at midday when the woods were generally free of guns. The sun was high when Elizabeth thought about the chestnuts. Knowing exactly where a fine chestnut tree stood at the edge of the forest, she figured its harvest littered the ground along about now. After instructions to the boys to help Libby take the tobacco leaves down from the rack and bind them into bundles for stacking, she announced that she and Mary were going into the woods to gather chestnuts.

"I be helpin' you when I get back," she said.

She took Mary beyond their field and followed the county road for a while. The sky grew gray, but they were protected from the cold wind by the deep woods. Soon they were near the stream that still overflowed its banks from the rains. The thick branches of the chestnut reached over onto land Preacher Green had once tilled. They began filling the baskets. Mary recoiled from the sharp prick of a casing as she tried to extract a nut. Elizabeth called to her, "You get the ones layin' bare on the ground, and I'll get the ones in the husks. And watch yourself! Don't fall! It be like fallin' on a porcupine if you do, heah?"

Suddenly, far off in the distance, Elizabeth heard the shrill barks of hunting dogs like bursts of human screams, high-strung and agitated. She stood up, saying, "We got to go, chile."

Mary stopped for one more chestnut.

"No, chile. Run! Dogs comin' this way. Leave the basket. Mary, listen! We goin' home. Do like I say. Run on ahead. I'm comin', but you keep on all the way to the house. Don't look behind."

Mary set the basket down and took Elizabeth's hand.

"No," she said, freeing her hand and pushing Mary away. "Run as fast as you can!"

"You come, too!"

"I'm comin'. But don't look behind. Just get home." She saw doubt in the child's narrowed eyes, so she said it again. "Run, I tol' you. Run!" She swatted Mary's behind. Her hand, not used to striking a child, recoiled.

The barking was closer now, the clamor telling her there was a large pack— twenty, twenty-five dogs, maybe. They would tear through the trees, teeth bared, of a single mind. She could see them run out of the woods at the opposite edge of Preacher Green's abandoned field and speed toward her. The sound terrified her. She ran. The baskets spilled over, and she threw them down. She searched for sight of Mary's brown shift at the edge of the woods ahead. All, all was gray and brown and the child blended in, growing smaller and smaller until she disappeared altogether. The child must not be far from home now.

Suddenly, a pain in her heart stabbed her, and her back and arms suddenly grew achingly weak and useless. She gasped for breath and knew the dogs were almost to her when she stumbled and attempted to turn in another direction, to the left, toward town, hoping to steer the dogs away from Mary.

The rush and the yelping were almost upon her. She could feel the sinews in her neck tighten. Her flesh seemed frozen to the bone, without any strength or will; she was incapable of running and her breath was short. She did not hear her own screams or even feel the first wounds, her thoughts still focused on Mary, Mary reaching the steps, Mary opening the door and running inside. *Don't come back out, chile. Don't look behind and don't you come back out. Don't you dare.*

She covered her face. She knew if she fought the dogs, their frenzy would worsen. Not feeling anything now but the sharp pains in her chest, she dropped to her knees, her hands still covering her face, surprised there was no one, no posse, no pattyroller, no hunter, to call off the dogs, even now believing beyond hope that somehow there would be. Darkness came on her, her face in the leaves. That was the last thing.

Confused without reprimand or reward, the dogs circled Elizabeth's still body, nipping, whimpering. After a while, they scattered. Finally, at the sound of Shadrack Morris's whistle, they ran back to him. There was blood on the jaws of a few although he wasn't sure how many with the commotion they were in. He tracked them back to Elizabeth. Even before he saw her face, he knew who it was by the braid draped along her shoulder. Turning her over, he stared at the wounds on her face and neck and decided they were not enough to have killed her. Then he turned her over again, face down, remounted his horse and rode on. The dogs followed. He needn't tell anyone. There wasn't anything he could do anyhow. His sights were already turned to the future and the opportunity it held for a struggling farmer such as he, renting his land and feeding eight children. It was the land he thought of. The land.

Mary did not run to the cabin. Waving her arms and screaming, she ran to the shed where Libby and the boys were still binding tobacco leaves.

"Elizabeth say run to the house! Dogs is comin'!"

Alarmed, Libby dropped the ball of twine. "Now, Mary, I don't hear 'em," she said, denying the menacing possibilities that crossed her mind. Then she thought to add for Mary's sake, "If there was, somebody'd call 'em off. Where's Elizabeth?"

"She say, 'Don't look behind,' so I didn't."

Libby grabbed Mary's hand. "Show me," she said, fighting to keep her voice calm, but shaking Mary's hand as though that would make her answer quicker. "Show me where you been!"

They half-ran, half-walked the way Mary had come, with James Jr. and Thomas not far behind. It began to snow in heavy, wet clumps, bringing a deadening silence. There was no sound of the dogs.

"That way," said Mary, pointing. "No, I think it was this way," and she began to cry.

"Hysh! You goin' to get the dogs goin' again!"

Loblolly branches caught the snow and began to bend with the weight. Soon blades of dry grass, the sprawling shapes of the wild rose bushes, the bare honeysuckle vines that entangled the trees, the blackberry bushes and briars, each natural shape stood delicately outlined in white in a menacing beauty Libby would remember all her life.

And suddenly, there was Elizabeth, her long braid detailed by the snow, as were the folds of her shawl. They found her cold to the touch, blood already dried on the wounds, lying still as the woody growth around her. Libby strained to turn Elizabeth's body over and wiped the snow from her face.

Mary screamed.

"No use to scream," said Libby, holding her close. "No use to bring the dogs back. No use to get help. She gone," she said, mouthing anything, anything to help them all gulp it down. The snow would cover everything, them too, and in the spring there'd be nothing left. She'd always known it.

She managed to say, "We goin' to stay here, me and Mary. James, Jr., you and Thomas empty the wagon and hitch up the mule. Come along the road close as you can."

The whole world was white and black, the new snow frozen against the dark trees. The tobacco would have to be brought to market, the meat, too, and the children fed and cared for. She'd bring Mary with her to the missus and she'd teach her to sew. There was everything to do, everything up to her, but at the heart of it all, there was this new terrible stillness, an unbelievable dead quiet. A weight. She would not be afraid of death if that's all it was. But the vacancy that was once filled with love was unspeakable.

She wiped the snow off Elizabeth's shawl and hair, crying now, wishing that time could go backward, wishing for this morning all over again with Elizabeth in the cabin, cooking bacon and corn cakes, the way things used to be. Used to be. The words would mark her time on this earth—divided by the way it used to be when Elizabeth was alive and the way it would be ever after.

"Elizabeth!" She cried out, every syllable distinct, the way Preacher Green would have done.

It was but a week later, exactly three days after they buried Elizabeth alongside Perry, that Libby saw Mr. Wallace ride by in the early morning. She'd half-expected him. One quick glimpse of him out the window made her duck and whisper to the others, "Hysh! Mr. Wallace lookin' for us." She hadn't made a fire this morning, despite the snap of November cold because she planned to deliver the tobacco to Mr. Eben so he could sell the crop with his, and then she would go to market with the hams.

No one stirred. Soon the sound of horse hooves faded. Only then did she trust herself to rise and look out the window to see Wallace riding back across the field, his breath and the horse's made visible by the frosty air.

Leave the cabin or not? She decided they would go to Mr. Eben's and on to town anyway. Eben Prouse would know what to do. Besides, she'd told Daniel she'd come. After Elizabeth's burial, he'd promised, "When the new preacher come through again, we goin' to marry." They were the words she'd waited for in anticipating happiness, but now they were a necessity. She would not have to manage with the children alone. They would go on to town and she would stop by the missus and tell her she would begin sewing again in two days. She would ask if she could bring Mary.

James, Jr. was hitching up the mule when the sound of horses returned. Paralyzed, they were like statues in their own yard, James, Jr. with the reins in his hand and Thomas sitting on the steps of the cabin with his arms on his knees, staring at nothing, and Mary, hanging onto Libby's skirt. Through the trees, Libby could see who it was, already knew what awaited them. She saw with sickening certainty that she and the children would disappear from this land as quickly as snowflakes falling into a fire. Yet they had known what it was to be free. What if they'd never known?

The sheriff drew up into the yard. He wasted no time with niceties.

"How old are you, Libby Spry?"

"Just turned twenty-one, sir." She was not good at lying and began to rub her arms against the cold, against the intrusion, against the power and rule of white law. She was aware of James, Jr.'s bowed head and downcast acceptance, and of Thomas drawing closed the jacket that Elizabeth had made.

"No you ain't. You're nothin' but nineteen and you know it. And since you're the oldest, you and all the ones under you are wards of the state. Takin' you down to Orphan's Court now. You'll be indentured so that you can pay your way. Get in the wagon."

The words were spoken with curt finality. She patted Mary's head. It was too easy a step from indentured to enslaved. Numb, she watched the sheriff put the hams on the seat beside him. She knew he'd be back for the tobacco leaves as well as the mule.

Snow, like darts of ice, began in earnest as they were driven to town, to the law office of Mr. Jefferson Wallace, who waited for them. "No need to go to Cambridge," he said. "We can take care of everything right here." Libby was surprised to see Missus there also. Evidently, everyone knew of their fate before they did. Missus offered to keep her and Mary, too. She was to do all of the sewing without pay, plus other tasks as required to make up for her keep and Mary's. Mary could learn to fulfill household tasks as well as fieldwork until she was proficient. It was what indenture meant, that minors would be "trained in a skill" while earning their keep, Mr. Wallace explained.

She was grateful to have Mary with her, grateful at least to be near Daniel. They could still marry and she hoped it would be before she began to show. And then what? Would the baby be indentured as well? Until it was twenty-one? Or beyond?

Mr. Wallace would take the boys. He signed the papers with a flourish, looking up at them only once as they stood before him. Thomas began to cry. James, Jr. put his arm around him and pulled him close. Mr. Wallace had acquired them at last. She'd broken her promise to Elizabeth, but it couldn't be helped.

The land would wait for them, wouldn't it? As written up in Elizabeth's deed, the farm passed to Addy, and then to her heirs. She knew it had taken almost three years from the time of John Prouse's death to his farm's auction. In two years, she'd be twenty-one, of legal age. Later, when Mr. Eben came to see her, she asked him.

"Don't worry, Libby," he said. "I think you'll be all right."

But then, Mr. Eben didn't know everything. In fact, just after Christmas, she read an announcement in the *Cambridge Eagle*:

Trustees sale at Crotchers Ferry 10 Jan 1858—Land in District #2 where Elizabeth Burton, Negress, resided at the time of her death—22 acres—Jefferson Wallace, Trustee.

Elizabeth had been gone just six weeks. She hoped Perry's bones would rise up out of the ground and haunt the new owner.

"Will we get the money from the sale?" she asked Missus.

"I understand there'll be just enough to pay the taxes owed on it from a while back," Missus said quietly, never raising her eyes to meet Libby's to see that they were filled with tears. And for that she was grateful.

She was called to Cambridge to witness the signing of the deed by the Trustee, Mr. Jefferson, over to its new owner, Shadrack Morris, who bought the land for one hundred and fifty dollars. The date was January 13, 1858. "Last piece of land in these parts that'll ever belong to one o' *them*, I'll guarantee," said Mr. Morris after he'd signed the papers.

The next time the preacher came to Mount Zion Church, she and Daniel were married. They returned to their respective workplaces the next day, and the next and the next in endless procession. She had only to look at the burn scar on her right leg to remind her of the reality of Burton land and revel in the pride of having once held it. Therein lay the bones of those she'd loved who'd made the only home she'd ever known. And what if they hadn't? Each generation depended on the struggle of those who came before, but freedom to live your life was a relative thing, as skittish and elusive as the blackbirds. Unless they claimed it for themselves. Could they leave now? Head north? Steal her brothers?

"Wait," said Daniel. "They say war's comin'. We gonna keep on and see. Preacher Green always say a wave gonna crash over the land and wash it clean. So we'll wait, Libby. Heah?"

MATTIE, 2000

———————

I want to tell Gordy Elizabeth's field is in trouble again. But I guess he can see it for himself now. He was right 'bout what happen a long time ago. I seen Elizabeth's time come and I seen the law come into it. I seen where the chilren own that land for maybe five minutes. I know the names now: after Addy Wilson Spry come Elizabeth Spry, James Spry, Jr., Thomas Chambers, and Mary Chambers. Two different fathers tell that story. I wondered 'bout the part where I seen the man pay money for the land at auction and pass it on to his daughter, Miss Nettie. I don't have to wonder no more. I seen the chilren taken. But when I was still under the peach tree, I didn't know all of it. What I did know was because of Gordy, and I'm glad for the stories he tol'. How else would I know what to look for when I got here? How else could I come to find out I helped Elizabeth's field stay in one piece?

At the end of that last summer, when the field corn stood dry and rattled in the wind and the combines come by to gather it in, I sat watchin', rememberin' what work it used to be. Here it was the year 2000 and they could do a field in a couple hours, those big teeth combin' through the rows, liftin' the plants into the shredder, sortin' out the cobs, cleanin' off the kernels, and spittin' out them empty cobs and fodder onto the field. The dump truck sat at the edge of the field waitin' for the kernels—only the kernels. They poured into the truck like pieces of gold. Yellow dust scattered everwhere, and I couldn't help but breathe it in, my eyes waterin'.

I missed the corn plants then. The wide empty field always made the sky that much bigger. The wind made no sound now and there was nothin' to gather. I had the woman Elizabeth on my mind. It was true she was free and owned that old farm, just like Gordy say, only he made the story bigger than it was, I 'spect. But in the end, what mattered was a good story and a storyteller always exaggerated to make it more excitin'. You could say it was lyin', but there was always truth at the bottom of it. It was just a way of makin' a point.

What he say was, "Them twenty-two acres over there was good farmin' land, and they couldn't wait to get it out of black hands, 'specially a woman's. The pattyroller, Shadrack, wanted the land so bad, him rentin' a field up Vienna way with a house full of kids. Elizabeth was hardly cold in the grave when they put the land up for auction right there at Crotcher's Ferry, and he got it right cheap."

He tol' the story over and over. I could hardly bear to listen because Gordy didn't say she died, he say, "She was killed. Murdered. No tellin' of it in the papers. Nothing to stir up the blacks nor the whites neither, but the news went out like ripples on water. Folks around here knew about it because so many were helpin' runaways like she did along with Sam Green, and it was all meant to put the fear of God in 'em. They lived the same time as Harriet Tubman and you know how many *she* got out of Dorchester. A lot were runnin' at that time.

"And the preacher over to Mount Zion Church up there in East New Market, he'd been careful to keep his mouth shut about things he couldn't do nothin' about, but he was an agent. He was in danger all the time, feelin' so worried about it that when they come and find 'im and took that book from his house, he just say, 'It's true. I'm guilty.' But he wasn't talkin' 'bout the book. He didn't know that was against the law. He was thinkin' about the peoples he got out. But they never could get him for that. Oh, no. Only readin' the book.

"Sam Green, his name was." Here Gordy would sigh and shake his head. "He got a lotta 'tention all over the nation. Man in prison for readin' a book. The whites in the North turned themselves inside out over it." Then Gordy would smile and nod his head, satisfied. "It was in all the papers. My uncle told me that story, and the one 'bout Elizabeth, too."

"He say they 'spect she had a safe house. It was headin' toward winter time, when the man was huntin' and had his dogs with him. Elizabeth was in the woods next to her field. The only thing that woman feared was dogs. She must've heard 'em comin' and she froze. They came on her and she couldn't beat them off. And finally the man come and called off the dogs, but he never did stop to see if Elizabeth was hurt. Just went on and never paid her no mind. Same as murder in my book.

"She kept chilren and it was them what carried her back to the house. They cried like they was never goin' to stop. They ain't stopped yet, all the way up to heaven they still cryin', my uncle say. It didn't take long for that Wallace, from one farm over, to step in. Trustee. Makin' sure the young ones got taken to Orphan Court and the land put up for auction sale, that's what he could be trusted for."

That story is a little different from what I come to find out. It look to me like Elizabeth was dead before she hit the ground. Her heart, I guess. But you have to give ol' Gordy credit for a good enough story. Anyway, he was mostly right. They couldn't wait to get a holt of those twenty-two acres, more or less.

The day after my shower in the cornfield, Webster stopped by. He brought me a whole bushel of peas. A whole bushel. *What I'm goin' do with a whole bushel?* I thought, 'though it weren't like me to be ungrateful for anythin'.

He say, "Mattie, do you remember a hedgerow in the middle of that field over there?" He meant Elizabeth's field. I shrug my shoulders. I want to play dumb. I don't want to say nothin', but there was that bushel of peas standin' between me and him.

"Could you come to court and tell about that hedgerow?" he say. "You remember how I tilled all that land north of it all those years, don't you? And the other half, too?"

I had to say *yes*. I remember him tillin' all of it. *That don't make it yours, though,* I wanted to say, but I kept my mouth shut like Gordy woulda done.

He left, satisfied, without sayin' another word.

A few days later, Fran bring me the paper. She had to read it to me. They was callin' me to be a witness down to Cambridge courthouse 'bout that field.

Oh, Lord. *What I'm goin' do?* I thought. *Probly means another shower in the cornfield. And clean clothes, too.*

On the next day, Webster picked me up. I never rode in his truck before. Felt strange, and I kept lookin' out the window makin' talk 'bout what was growin' good in the fields, wonderin' if I was goin' to get a ride home after I said my piece.

I can't remember all they say. Some of it I didn't understand—all that lawyer talk—but I did understand Webster wanted that half a field, said it was his, said it was right close to his house and his granddaddy tol' him it were his, from where the hedgerow used to be on up.

But the owner had the deed. Still was twenty-two acres, more or less. Him payin' taxes on it.

"But you've been renting that land, right?" the lawyer say to Webster.

"No, sir, only half of it. The other half's mine 'cause I been tillin' it these past twenty years. Been tillin' all of it, but got rent for only half of it where it was marked by the hedgerow." It didn't hold. They got me up there and I had to say I never remember no hedgerow dividin' that field in half, even though I got me a bushel of peas for the right answer.

"What?" say the lawyer man. "He gave you a bushel of peas a few days ago? Wanting you to remember the hedgerow?"

I couldn't look at Webster. "Yes, sir, but I still don't remember no hedgerow. I been livin' 'cross the way fifty year. Far as I know," I say, "he tillin' all of it because he been rentin' the whole field since Miss Nettie's time." Gordy tol' me that, too.

Well, the story ends with them twenty-two acres, more or less, still sittin' there today in one whole field. Justice been done. And Elizabeth's and Perry's bones are in the ground somewheres, their spirits hangin' 'round no matter who owns it. And I had a small part in keepin' somethin' together.

I tol' the lawyer I didn't have no ride home. He understood my meanin'. He saw to it I got home all right.

DELIVERANCE, MARCH, 1862

————•————

*W*ith the election of a new governor, the preacher's hope was renewed. His faithful Quaker friend, Mr. King, visited regularly, bringing news.

"Governor Bradford, he is, my dear man," he announced. "There'll be new petitions now, and a listening ear, I know, despite his being a Methodist."

"So am I, Methodist," he heard himself say. "But there are different brands of Methodists."

On the next visit, there was substantial news. "The governor approached me twice about my opinion of your case. And he was much impressed that you were a Methodist minister. Evidently one of his first acts will be to grant you pardon."

When Kitty visited next, Green was elated. "You needn't make the trip again. I'll come to you soon," he promised. Although he'd had no assurances, he needed to hear the words spoken aloud and the hope they contained. Unwavering in her faith, she'd continued to wait, never once expressing any desire to leave for Canada without him.

On the 24th of March, a hearing was held. Petitions and letters of support were filed, as well as a letter from Judge Spence recommending he leave Maryland. Two days later, the pardon was granted. He was sixty years old, and he wouldn't die in prison as he'd feared. But as he waited for his release and it didn't happen the first week, or the next, or the next, he began to disbelieve the pardon.

Finally, in April, the same month he'd been taken from his land five years earlier, the warden came for him. It was the month of plowing furrows and planting seeds, and even though without land he could not accomplish what he always had, he would walk on open fields again.

Mr. King met him at the gate and clapped him on the back, almost sending him reeling. His friend extended a hand that held enough money for his passage to his home across the bay and guided him through the city to the steamer wharf.

"When you are ready to go north, let me know. We'll see you get to Philadelphia and if you're willing, perhaps you could speak about your case to audiences there."

In the end, he could say nothing to the man who'd kept his spirits up through the days of internment, but he held him in his eyes for a long moment and then wrapped his arms around his benefactor. Then he stood back and nodded.

He turned and walked up the ramp to the steamboat. It was his second birth of freedom, and he knew the relativity of it then, how it can be taken away and given by another, how you couldn't always take it or buy it or even trust in it lasting. But for now, he was a free man once again, going home to Kitty. He was not humble enough now to be thankful. This was his right. He was aware of the impermanence of things, of the prevailing winds that decided fate, and how his mere survival was a victory. *His right*—this walking out into the sun, breathing free air, and deciding what he'd do next. Deciding never to fear again.

The land passed before him in its long green chain, slowly widening where the pine forests stood and narrowing where the marshes lay. He took in everything as the boat steamed around the bend and up the Choptank where the masts of oyster boats spread like fence posts and the calling of the gulls mocked their passage. He'd be home by morning, and since it was Sunday, he'd go directly to Mount Zion Church and be reunited with Kitty. In the end, there wasn't time to let her know when he'd be coming.

He walked past the fishermen's cabins, where the oyster tongs and nets lay askew in yards along with buoys and eel traps and rotting skiffs. Fish smells filled the air; the washing on clotheslines billowed like sails in the Chesapeake wind. Shallow waves licked the shoreline where piles of oyster shells lay ready to cover the dirt roads. He turned inland.

Walking in open air was as complete a happiness as any man could hope to find. Except for the forests at the distant edge of the fields, the Dorchester sky was huge and the horizon uninterrupted. Along the road, a shape appeared out of the woods. At this distance, and with eyes that had grown dim, he strained to see what he hoped was someone he'd recognize from the community he knew so well. Slowly he realized it was a man who walked toward him. The swagger was vaguely familiar. As the man grew larger in his vision, he realized he'd hoped for too much. The man wore a hat jauntily placed on his head, a man he could not possibly know because the hat was a Union cap, an incongruity of enormous proportions in these parts. His vision came more from hope and homesickness than reality. He was hallucinating, drunk with his newly found freedom. But, no. The man who drew closer, he was sure now, was James Spry.

He stood in the middle of the road and waited. It had been a silence of nearly eighteen years. With each step James took toward him, he was reunited with the rich past he thought he'd lost. In it lay the redemption he thought he'd never know. James was alive.

"Hey!" He could not bring himself to say the name that haunted him for so long.

"Preacher?"

Playfully, he reached for James's hat and tucked it inside his own jacket, but said as any preacher, brother, friend would, "You're takin' your life in your hands wearin' that around here!"

"I come to find Addy."

There was much to tell James, but he'd spare certain details. It was the least he could do.

"She's gone, James."

"I thought she might be." James looked away, and it was some time before he said, "She always been frail."

"She died of heat stroke," was all he said. He told him Perry, too, had been gone for a long time now, and that he guessed it was cancer. Elizabeth, she kept the land and did well, extremely well for a woman alone, but with her death, the land was taken.

James nodded again, then shook his head. "They made it for a while, didn't they? And Libby and James, Jr.?"

"They're workin' close by. They'll probably be in church in the mornin', it bein' Sunday, so turn yourself around, James. You'll be safe there."

James nodded. He had to be reminded he was still a fugitive. There was good news, too, of Libby and Daniel's marriage and a child named Betsy, and of James, Jr. Would it be possible the enslaved father could claim a son born to a free mother?

They sat on the side of the road till dusk, reliving memories of people they both had loved.

"Tell me," he said, "how you've come," and waited as James hesitatingly spelled out the bitter years.

"I don't like to recount it," he said. "It best left in the past. But Addy, she always was number one, and if I'd stayed, I could've protected her." He said it as if the kidnapping had been his own fault.

"Maybe not, James. There was never much we could do to protect each other or ourselves." It was an apology of sorts. "So you ran?"

"I heard the North was takin' runaways to fight in the army. But then my master made us join up to support the Confederates—you know, make camp, cook, bring supplies—help build a battery. They were takin' even the old and unfit like me. That's when I run. They want us to support our own predicament." He shook his head. "Long ago, I walked south a hell of a long way. But headin' north, I run. Don't know why I didn't do it earlier 'ceptin' there was a woman and kids where I stayed. Wasn't any choice. When they gone—sold—I took off. Been headin' this way for a month. Man outside Richmond say he takin' recruits for the North. That's where I got the hat. I run again, but only to get home, see Addy. I'll join up when I leave here."

"Don't wear the hat now. It isn't safe."

"I know. I only put it on when I saw you was a black man like me."

"On the battlefield, you're free, you know. Paper said a new law was passed that says no Negro's goin' to be returned to his master if he's engaged in rebellion against the Confederates, whether he be military or not. There haven't been battles here, but public sentiment is not in our favor, not yet anyway."

No, the struggle here would remain at the edge of the fields in unnamed but deadly nuance. He knew from the newspapers he'd read in prison there'd be no decisive outcome for a long time. Maryland had yet to pass a resolution abolishing slavery as some of the other states had done, but it would have to decide at some point whether or not it was behind the Union. Nonetheless, amidst the strange contradiction in which they found themselves, here they were, he and James, just going down the road arm in arm on their way to see family like ordinary men and laughing in the manner of the free, the strain of hard years, for the moment, lifted.

MATTIE, 2000

ovember, and the last of the soybeans was in. They planted winter rye and it just begun to show. Come spring, there'd be waves of green, rollin' and answerin' the wind. But not now. The earth was brown and the peach tree was bare and plain, the air too chilly to sit outdoors. Fran drove by without stoppin', not knowin' that I sat in my kitchen wantin' company. Usually, she watched the house and if she didn't see any sign of life, she'd stop by to check up on me. I thought about the loneliness of winter, but that year I didn't have to get used to it all over again. That year was goin' be different. So would the next and the next. After fifty year on my place at the edge of Elizabeth's field, I was leavin', goin' down to Florida, down to Juanita. It be time.

It seemed right, after the fire that took the old barn 'cross the way one night. I saw the flames on my way to the outhouse. The barn burned like an explosion as if it was sayin' good-bye to the life I knowed, we all knowed, not that long ago. Smoke so thick it hid the moon. Then the wind took it high into the night like an upside-down twister. The flames stripped the sides of the barn where there was the last stores—bales of hay that showed the shape of the barn even though its frame was gone. A hundert year or more, that barn was. It stood in the middle of the field, the farmhouse long gone. I watched it goin' down. It went fast, but the sparks flew up a long time. There was nothing the fire company could do. They just stood around like they was—well, not enjoyin' it exactly—more like it was thrillin' to see something that big go so fast, something beautiful and powerful that you know wouldn't last long. All the way till dawn, I watched till there was just embers, red hot, like the stars in heaven had fell down.

It was a good time to leave. The old ways were gone, and I felt weak as a watermelon vine. So the next time I saw Fran, I axed her to help me get a train ticket. She say she was glad to do it.

The night before I left, I got up from my chair and stood where I could look into my three rooms. I was thinkin' 'bout what to take with me. I knew nobody else would live in the house after I was gone because there was no bathroom, no runnin' water, no stove. I loved my recliner chair but it was too big to take. I had a basket of the last of the tomatoes. I picked them green and they got a little pink. Bushel of potatoes, too. I thought I'd put everything outside the door with a sign that said *free.*

In my old trunk, there was a doll Grandma Pattyroll give me and two of the torn readers from the old school house in Blakely 'long with Papa's Bible and Mama's old quilt. I took those. I couldn't take the trunk but I could fit everthin' else in the suitcase Fran give me.

Leavin' was like losin' an arm or a leg. I wanted to remember all the creases, chips and scratches, the coffee pot on the hot plate, the table I'd covered with Christmas paper somebody give me, the bushel baskets piled up all grey from the weather, the green paint I did the walls with and ran out of and had to use white for the rest, the curtains I'd bought at the Dollar General. I looked at the socks I'd nailed to the doorframe to keep out the cold and said out loud, "I been warm. I not been hongry. I got friends both black and white, and I seen it all. I never axed nothin' from nobody, took care of myself and other peoples, too. I leave here satisfied."

There was the money Fran give me as a good-bye present, and the old picture album and my birth certificate, which I figured I wouldn't be needin' since I wasn't gonna be lookin' for work, and there was a Christmas card from January 3, 1999 from the lady I worked mostly for. It say, "Dear Mattie, Thank you for all you've done for us over the years. Merry Christmas and Happy Birthday. Here's something you can always use, money." Inside the card, the ten dollar bill was still there. I never spent it, savin' it for a day I'd need it.

I closed my eyes and made believe it was summer and I was sittin' under my peach tree cleanin' the silk off the corn, lookin' out over a field of pretty potato plants so green from the rain, the diesel quiet—how I loved quiet! And the hot sun on my skin. And the trucks passin' by, peoples wavin'. I had somethin' for ever one, corn, cantaloupes, potatoes, cucumbers, and beans after the harvester went through, cabbage from the garden and lettuce, too. And the tomatoes, the sweet juice on my tongue, the soft skin like a baby's, that I could give to them what didn't have a garden. Imagine that. No garden. No chickens cluckin' 'round either, layin' eggs everwhere. Nothin' to give away.

Life was so sweet in those moments that nothin' bad could change it. That's what made me long for life even as they were stickin' needles in me and I come to know this the end. It made me sad 'bout all the time behind me. The rest of it—well, it was just a story to put in the air with your breath. I wished Gordy was around to tell it to.

There was a knock on the door. Fran.

"Are you ready to go to the station, Mattie?" she axed, her hand holdin' closed the collar of her coat, her face kindly. "Is there anything you need help with?"

"No, Fran. But thank you. I don't need anythin' at all." And then I remembered somethin'. "There is one thing." I picked up my bag and got out my cash. "If I give you this, can you write a check for the telephone? I got no chance to get a money order."

"Of course, Mattie. Anything else?"

No. There be no loose ends. There be nothin' left to do. I was thinkin' of Mama now, like a circle drawn closed, and Mama and me together peaceful-like and knowin'. I'd been good like Mama tol' me. Well, most of the time.

When I went to Florida, I tol' the grandchilren and the great-grands what they needed to know 'bout their peoples, 'bout their great-great-grandmother bein' a slave, and I filled in the parts I didn't know like Gordy woulda done, how our peoples did and how they got free and how they survived, how the generations wouldn't be here if we hadn't struggled so, although no one could 'preciate it like them what traveled that road themselves. I had one thing to say to the young ones—"What you gonna do with your freedom? Think about it. Think about it hard."

That must have been all what that young girl—I'm callin' her by her name now, Leola—was thinkin' 'bout as she sat by the side of the road on Emancipation Day, wonderin' what she gonna do now, what would happen to her seein' as how both her mama and papa were gone from her and she hongry. Soon peoples took her in—she old enough to work by then—and she wound up in the orange and grapefruit groves in Florida, pickin' in the trees and packin' grapefruit and sometime puttin' string beans and strawberries in hampers like I did, earnin' her own money. I seen her with a young man, and in a little while, they goin' to Alabama to settle by the Chattahoochie River, on the other side of the bridge from where my family stayed in Georgia and she has a bundle in her arms. That's my mama, Emmie Elizabeth, just brand new. And then I knowed I must be in heaven.

Now I'm done lookin' back, I can look ahead. I see trees growin' on Elizabeth's field, their roots holdin' Elizabeth's and Perry's bones. Deer come and fox and hunderts of birds. Everthin' what went away comin' back, coverin' everthin' over with life. What's left is the story. Pass it along with yours. The tellin' keeps us understandin' things.

NOTES

---

*S*am Green was pardoned by the new governor, Augustus Bradford, in 1862, whereupon he and Kitty left for Canada. His case having received much national attention, he was asked to speak many times along the way. On one of those occasions, he met Harriet Beecher Stowe, who gave him a copy of *Uncle Tom's Cabin* so he could finish reading it. He returned to the Eastern Shore, but sometime in the mid 1870s, he moved to Baltimore where he is said to have died in 1877.

Emancipation occurred in Maryland on November 1, 1864. As late as 1867, there were 3,281 African American children held under indenture by local farmers. Under the guise of apprenticeship, this practice was seen as a way to perpetuate slavery and, therefore, was abolished by the Maryland State Assembly in that year.

Mattie's story is largely taken from an oral history dictated by Mary Taylor, and recorded in the Maryland State Historical Society Archives.

THE FAMILY TREE

Maryland Family

Elizabeth (free) m. Perry Burton (enslaved), childless

    Addy Wilson (free), raised by Elizabeth, m. James Spry (free/enslaved)

        Children: Libby Spry (free)

                    James Spry, Jr. (free)

    Addy Wilson Spry bears two more children with Levin Chambers (free):

                Thomas Chambers (free)

                Mary Chambers (free)

Georgia Family

James Spry (enslaved) and Sara (enslaved)

           Child: Leola Spry (Grandma Pattyroll) (enslaved/free) m. —

           Child: Emmie Elizabeth, m. John Henry Thomas

        Children: Willie Henry Thomas

                Elizabeth Mary Thomas

                Alace Ann Thomas

                Mattie Louise Thomas

                John James Thomas

Libby Spry and Leola Spry are half sisters.

70532485R00149

Made in the USA
Columbia, SC
10 May 2017